ROGUE SHOT

(A TROY STARK THRILLER—BOOK 5)

JACK MARS

Jack Mars

Jack Mars is the USA Today bestselling author of the LUKE STONE thriller series, which includes seven books. He is also the author of the new FORGING OF LUKE STONE prequel series, comprising six books; of the AGENT ZERO spy thriller series, comprising twelve books; of the TROY STARK thriller series, comprising seven books; of the SPY GAME thriller series, comprising nine books; and of the new JAKE MERCER thriller series, comprising five books (and counting).

Jack loves to hear from you, so please feel free to visit www.Jackmarsauthor.com to join the email list, receive a free book, receive free giveaways, connect on Facebook and Twitter, and stay in touch!

ISBN: 978-1-0943-8437-5

BOOKS BY JACK MARS

JAKE MERCER THRILLER SERIES
ABSOLUTE THREAT (Book #1)
ABSOLUTE DAMAGE (Book #2)
ABSOLUTE FORCE (Book #3)
ABSOLUTE PERIL (Book #4)
ABSOLUTE TREASON (Book #5)

THE SPY GAME
TARGET ONE (Book #1)
TARGET TWO (Book #2)
TARGET THREE (Book #3)
TARGET FOUR (Book #4)
TARGET FIVE (Book #5)
TARGET SIX (Book #6)
TARGET SEVEN (Book #7)
TARGET EIGHT (Book #8)

TROY STARK THRILLER SERIES
ROGUE FORCE (Book #1)
ROGUE COMMAND (Book #2)
ROGUE TARGET (Book #3)
ROGUE MISSION (Book #4)
ROGUE SHOT (Book #5)
ROGUE STRIKE (Book #6)
ROGUE ORDER (Book #7)

LUKE STONE THRILLER SERIES
ANY MEANS NECESSARY (Book #1)
OATH OF OFFICE (Book #2)
SITUATION ROOM (Book #3)
OPPOSE ANY FOE (Book #4)
PRESIDENT ELECT (Book #5)
OUR SACRED HONOR (Book #6)
HOUSE DIVIDED (Book #7)

FORGING OF LUKE STONE PREQUEL SERIES
PRIMARY TARGET (Book #1)

PRIMARY COMMAND (Book #2)
PRIMARY THREAT (Book #3)
PRIMARY GLORY (Book #4)
PRIMARY VALOR (Book #5)
PRIMARY DUTY (Book #6)

AN AGENT ZERO SPY THRILLER SERIES

AGENT ZERO (Book #1)
TARGET ZERO (Book #2)
HUNTING ZERO (Book #3)
TRAPPING ZERO (Book #4)
FILE ZERO (Book #5)
RECALL ZERO (Book #6)
ASSASSIN ZERO (Book #7)
DECOY ZERO (Book #8)
CHASING ZERO (Book #9)
VENGEANCE ZERO (Book #10)
ZERO ZERO (Book #11)
ABSOLUTE ZERO (Book #12)

CHAPTER ONE

January 18
9:05 pm Central European Standard Time
The skies above Engel Castle
Near Engeldorf-Pont
Luxembourg

A buzzer sounded. It sounded like the buzzer that would end a high school basketball game.

"Five minutes," Jan Bakker's voice said.

The voice was low, quiet, calm, and came through a speaker inside Troy Stark's helmet. Jan had recently pirated a Chinese communications app called *Fung Wah.* In Mandarin, the words meant "Magnificent Wind."

Jan had hacked the software, reverse-engineered it, and created a satellite and cellular-driven communications platform for their own use, anywhere on Earth, with end-to-end encryption. They could use it on almost any device, even crash helmet speakers.

It was the kind of thing Jan did in his spare time. He had told Troy he was becoming concerned that Chinese technology was racing out ahead of the West. He had stolen this app, not just to steal something from the Chinese, but because it was the best one he had ever seen.

"Be prepared to jump," he said now.

Troy nodded. "Roger that."

Then he realized that Jan, as brilliant as he was, was from the Netherlands. He might not grasp American military lingo. "Understood," he said instead.

Jan went on: "From the way they're deployed, I'd say they are not expecting an approach from the roof. I suspect you have the element of surprise."

Troy nodded again. "Yes. Right."

He felt a trickle of… something… in his stomach.

Butterflies. It was an unfamiliar feeling. Normally he went blank at moments like this, and felt nothing at all. But this time? It was a moment almost like no other. Except for Jan's voice, Troy was entirely alone. And yet, he wouldn't have it any other way. He wouldn't want to put another person at this kind of risk.

The old plane rattled and shook all around him. The sound of its engine was deafening, and the tiny rear cabin was shaking so violently that he wouldn't be surprised if the whole thing suddenly fell apart. The plane was not fully sealed, and an icy wind was leaking in from somewhere. The cold didn't concern Troy – he just noted it, then filed the information away.

Cold weather.

Troy checked the altimeter on his wrist. They were flying at about 8,000 feet. This was a good attitude. Outside the jump door's window, it was full-on dark. They were also flying without lights. Everything about this was to happen with no warning.

Troy breathed slowly, focusing on calm. Day jumps, night jumps, high altitude jumps, jumps in bad weather, jumps from bad airplanes like this one. He had jumped from just about every height and in every circumstance imaginable.

He had come into the country by car earlier in the day. He had taken off in this beater of a jump plane from a nothing airfield west of Luxembourg City, little more than a hard-packed patch of dirt tucked away between the trees. He hadn't met or even seen the pilot. This was also about deniability. He wasn't working with Jan on this mission, or anyone. There was no mission. No official resources were being used.

Dubois was not here. Gallo was not here. No one was here. They hadn't told Miquel anything.

"Weapons check," Jan said.

"Okay."

Troy was wearing a dark helmet, goggles, and a black jumpsuit. His parachute was dark. Everything about him was dark. He was black on black, a shadow.

"You have an MP5 submachine gun," Jan said. "Loaded with a 50-round, banana-type box magazine."

The gun was strapped to his back. Troy patted it. "Got it."

"You have five extra 30-round box magazines for it."

The smaller mags were stuffed in various pockets of Troy's jumpsuit.

"Yes."

"You have a Glock 26 semi-automatic pistol."

It was in a holster on his belt. The 26 was typically a concealed-carry gun, but his outfit didn't lend itself to that, and anyway, his opponents were going to know right away that he was armed. The holster was behind his back, for whatever element of surprise that might afford him.

"Yes," he said.

"You have a hunting knife with a serrated blade, inside a leather sheath, in case all else fails."

Troy nodded. "Taped to my calf."

He was strapped with weapons, just the way he liked it.

"You have two M84 stun grenades, very loud, and which will generate blinding flashes of light when they explode."

Troy patted the two cylinder-type grenades clipped to his chest.

"Flash-bangs, check."

"Good," Jan said. "The drones are hovering in place. I have your position and altitude monitored with a GPS tracker. Seconds before you land, I will drop the charges. They should blow a large hole in the roof and cause some shock. If you're quick about releasing your chute, you should be inside the house before anyone can respond."

"Where are they?" Troy said.

"I did a drone pass by fifteen minutes ago, checking for heat signatures. As far as I can tell, there are two people on the second floor. I believe one of them is the woman."

The woman.

Jan was a strange duck. He knew full well "the woman" in question was Aliz Willems, and that men had invaded her home and were holding her captive. Yet he kept the fact of her, and Troy's relationship with her, at arm's length. There were human feelings at play here, and Jan chose not to deal with them.

Maybe that was for the best. They were way out on a limb now. No law enforcement agency in the world would permit this operation. Troy was going rogue in an attempt to rescue his former girlfriend from kidnappers. If Troy and Jan still had jobs to lose, they would almost certainly lose them for this.

"There appear to be three men on the ground floor, and there is definitely one man outside in the courtyard, near the main gate. All of the men that I have monitored should be considered heavily armed and extremely dangerous. I would operate under the assumption that neither you, nor the woman, will receive any mercy from them."

"Understood," Troy said.

The buzzer sounded again.

"Okay," Jan said. "You're over the jump area. If you're going to go, now is the time."

"Thank you," Troy said.

"Be safe."

Troy went to the jump door and slid it open. It was spring-loaded and would close by itself after he was gone.

A burst of cold wind tore in. Everything – the wind, the engines, the rattle and clank of the plane – which had been loud a moment ago, suddenly became VERY LOUD.

He stood near the edge. The wind was in his face. He could just glimpse the underside of the wing, and open sky. Nothing else but darkness out there. Stepping out was a leap of faith. No more thinking.

Troy took a deep breath.

Just go.

He dove into the void.

The plane dropped away. Its shadow seemed to veer toward the stars.

He was falling fast.

There was blackness all around, and the sensation of plunging through space.

Adrenaline pumped through his body. A rush of pure speed came, the wind howling past his ears. He sensed his heart pounding in his chest.

He plummeted towards the endless woods below.

The wind whipped around him, making it hard to catch his breath. He spread his arms and legs, feeling the air against his body as he began to glide.

Now, his eyes caught on a circle of light far below. They were the lights of the castle, *her castle*, and all around it, the deep darkness of the forest. The castle was always lit up like that, she told him once, so that the local people could feel proud of it. At this moment he couldn't see it, but the house, her house, would be right next to, and below, and dwarfed by, the castle.

His mind flashed back to the photo of her the man in the streets of Madrid had shown him. She was bound with rope, tied up on a beat-up couch that made him think of a seedy motel or hideout somewhere. But Jan had done satellite and drone surveillance of her house and discovered they were holding her there.

Is it a trap? They're barely even hiding.

They told him if he contacted law enforcement, if they saw any evidence of police involvement, they would kill her. They said he was to await further instructions. But Troy wasn't the waiting type. So now this. No law enforcement, just Troy Stark making a surprise appearance and entering through the roof by himself.

He fell very fast. His own responses seemed slow by comparison. He checked the altimeter. 2,600 feet and dropping. Then 2,300.

The idea here was to deploy the chute as low as possible. His hand found the cord.

2,000 feet.

1,700.

1,500.

Pull. Now.

He waited one more second, then pulled.

He felt, rather than saw, the chute flying out above and behind him. With a sudden jolt, it jerked his upper body backward. He legs kicked. He glanced at his open chute, black against the black sky.

Now he was flying, in control.

The castle was close below him, and just to the left, lit up in the night. Its ancient stone walls reached towards the sky. Its turrets and towers stood silhouetted against the darkness behind it. Further to the left, he could see a narrow stone path winding its way towards the old medieval drawbridge. The castle was huge, a monster.

Aliz owns that.

The original guard house was built by the Romans, she had told him. Various dukes and princes and local potentates had added to the place over two millennia. The thing had been in her family for centuries.

Now he could see the outlines of the house, next to the castle. It was a big house, but seemed tiny compared to the fortress of stone it sat below. He steered toward it, coming in at an angle, scanning for window dormers and other obstacles that might be on its surface. Closer… closer… it was coming.

Between him and the house, he caught a glimpse of Jan's drones, one just a bit above the other. He fancied he could just see the grenades drop from the underside of the bottom drone.

He could! The first drone zoomed away, and the top drone moved into place, releasing its charges just a few seconds later.

He watched them fall in rapid succession.

Exciting!

The first two grenades hit the house.

Ba-BOOM

Bright explosions flashed on the roof, and then chunks of tile and wood and masonry, and a mist of light snow, flew through the air.

Troy watched as the second two grenades dropped through the cloud made by the first two. Somewhere inside the house, two more explosions ripped, these ones concussions of light and sound meant only to stun and not destroy.

Then the dark roof was there, just below him.

An instant later, Troy hit it. He landed hard, his feet making a THUMP on the slate shingled rooftop. Then he was on his butt, sliding across a thin crust of snow and ice, the pitch of the roof steeper than he imagined, his chute drifting down below him. He arrested his slide, stopped, and looked back as the chute settled on the roof.

"Oh, baby," he said. He could feel his heart racing just a bit.

There was no time.

He shrugged out of his harness.

Light snow swirled around him. Dark sky. Snow was falling, snow was still flying from the explosion, snow was everywhere. He slid toward the hole in the roof. It was ragged, torn up, and sharp along the edges. It was probably six feet across. He didn't look to see if anyone was there. He pulled a stun grenade from his chest, yanked the circular pin, yanked the secondary triangular pin and…

…dropped it in the hole.

He curled into a ball, eyes squeezed tight, face away from the hole. A second passed.

Behind him, he sensed the blinding flash, lighting up the space below him, and sending an echo of itself up into the night. Then, less than an instant later:

BOOM!

That got 'em. It nearly got me.

He turned over, slid all the way down the roof, pushed off hard with his hands, and dropped into the hole.

The fall was longer than he expected. There were high ceilings in this house, and he knew that. But these ceilings were very high.

He landed in a wide hallway, THUMP, the shock in his legs and up his back. He fell backward onto his butt. Then he rolled all the way over onto his knees.

A second later, he reached behind him and freed the MP5.

It was dark in the hall. Somewhere nearby, a woman was screaming. There were lights on in the room 50 feet away. Troy knew this hallway well. That room was Aliz's master bedroom.

A man stood in the wide doorway. He was wearing a dark hood and mask, like a ski mask. He came stumbling toward Troy, possibly dazed by the grenades that had gone off. He had a gun, a rifle. In the gloom, Troy couldn't get the make.

The guy lifted, sighted…

DUH-DUH-DUH-DUH-DUH.

Troy hit him chest-high with a burst from the MP5. The man fell straight down, as if a trap door had opened below him, the bullets piercing him where he stood.

The woman screamed again.

It was Aliz. She was alive.

Troy had a second of relief, but only a second. Heavy boots were pounding up the stairs behind him.

He glanced over the railing. Two men were at the bottom of the stairs. Their faces and heads were obscured by ski masks. They wore heavy ballistic vests over their clothes, jumpsuits and they carried rifles. Troy had no idea who they were or where they were from. It didn't matter. All he needed to know was they were bad guys.

One man sighted as he started running up the stairs, taking the steps two at a time.

Troy ducked back.

BANG! BANG! BANG!

The guy was firing randomly.

Troy ripped the other stun grenade from his chest, pulled the two rings in fast succession, and tossed it over the side. He dropped to the floor, rolled away and shut his eyes. Even so, he could see the bright light from behind his eyelids.

WHAM! The brain-rattling sound came a second later.

Troy lay on his back, MP5 out in front of him, facing where the stairs met the hall. One man came staggering over the threshold, waving his own rifle crazily.

DUH-DUH-DUH-DUH-DUH-DUH.

Troy shot the man and sent him back down the way he had come.

Two down.

Troy's ears were ringing. Bright afterimages, sort of reverse-negatives, appeared before his eyes. It was hard to see. He pulled himself to his feet, then moved along the railing, sighting down the stairs. The dead guy lay on his back, halfway down to the first floor. He was upside down, his arms splayed out below him, his legs above him, his blood pooling and running down the stairs. Other than him, the broad stairway was empty.

The second guy was gone.

Somewhere outside the house, an engine started.

Troy's balance was off. He had whacked himself pretty good with the stun grenades.

He turned and stepped carefully to one of the windows in the hall. He stood to one side and pulled back the tall white curtain. Out in the courtyard, a dark sports car had pulled out of the garage. A man ran out of the house, crashed into one side of the car, and fell down.

The passenger side door opened, and the man clambered into the car. The man had the confused movements of someone who had been exposed to a concussion grenade. He was worse off than Troy.

At the bottom of the short stone driveway, the gates were open.

The car peeled out in the thin sheen of snow and ice, slid sideways a bit as it passed through the gates, turned left on the roadway, and was gone.

Troy listened. Down the hall from him, Aliz was weeping now.

Everywhere else, it was silent.

"Jan?"

A tinny, faraway voice crackled through Troy's headset.

"Stark?"

"Yes."

"There was a lot of noise, a lot of interference. How is it…"

"Two down," Troy said. "Two just left in a car. Is that all?"

"I counted five men, six people in total."

"I'm missing one," Troy said. "The captive is in the next room."

"I wouldn't make any assumptions," Jan said. "I'd clear that whole house."

Troy nodded. "Got it."

He moved slowly and carefully toward Aliz's bedroom, MP5 up and ready. The feeling in the pit of his stomach was deeper than ever. These guys were animals. What might they have done to her?

He moved to the side of the doorway.

She was on the couch, more or less in the same position from the photo the man in Madrid had shown him. Troy understood it now. They had draped the sofa in Aliz's bedroom with some sort of old patchwork quilt, giving the impression that she was tied up on an old couch.

She wasn't gagged. Her arms were behind her back. Her ankles were tied together. She didn't seem injured. Her face was smeared with makeup, probably from all the crying. Her blonde hair was mussed. She was as beautiful as ever.

She looked up at him, eyes hard, but also wet.

"Is there anyone else in there?" Troy said.

"Who are you?" she said.

He pulled his helmet off, revealing his face.

Her shoulders slumped. She didn't smile. He couldn't say for sure, but she certainly didn't seem happy to see him.

"Troy," she said softly, as if reminding herself who he was. She shook her head, as if the very fact of Troy Stark, the mere thought of him, was a special kind of tragedy.

"Did you kill those men?"

Troy shrugged. He was dizzy, and he didn't care what she thought of him. "Two of them, so far. But at least two got away. How many are there? Are there any more in this room? Maybe in the closets? Are there any more in the house?"

She was still shaking her head. "They work for my brother. They weren't going to hurt me. It was all just a charade."

Her brother, Lucien Mebarak. The man behind the slaughterbot terrorist attacks, who had walked away and disappeared because of his wealth and power. Troy and Dubois had thwarted what would have been his most devastating attack. They had also killed a stack of Mebarak's men. And for icing on the cake, Troy had knocked him out that time.

Mebarak was angry at Troy. What he should be was dead.

"No," Troy said. "It wasn't charades. Men with guns, who tie people up, don't play games."

He went to her, kneeled down, removed the knife taped to his calf, and used it to cut away the bonds around her ankles. Then he turned her around and cut away the ropes tying her arms.

She smelled funky. Worse than funky, she smelled like a barn. Apparently, she had been sitting on this couch for a couple of days, with all the personal hygiene challenges that suggested.

She stood up. He offered her his arm, but she pushed it away. She walked on unsteady legs out of the room.

Troy figured she was going to find a change of clothes, freshen up a bit, maybe take a shower. She walked past the dead man slumped in the hallway.

Then she screamed again.

Troy came out to the hall. She was staring up at the shattered ceiling, the jagged hole blown through it, with chunks of rafter sticking out rudely like pointing fingers, and wisps of snow falling silently down from the sky.

"Oh my God, Troy! What did you do to my house?"

CHAPTER TWO

11:35 pm Central European Standard Time
A quiet side street
Luxembourg City
Luxembourg

"What are you going to do with her?" Troy said.

Alex was sitting in the driver's seat. His window was open because he was smoking a cigarette. The medieval street where they were parked was as narrow as an alley. Light snow drifted down, covering the cobblestones.

The city was a maze of streets like this, a tangle of history and modernity, with buildings that seemed to lean in towards each other, whispering secrets and stories of days long gone. The streets were lined with cafes and shops.

Troy knew the town a little bit from his time with Aliz. Around the corner from here was Saint Michael's Church, and just down the road was the Hollow Tooth Tower, a remnant of the city's ancient stone fortifications. Right now, in the middle of the night, the scent of fresh pastries wafted through the air – somewhere nearby, a bakery was getting ready for tomorrow morning's breakfast.

He supposed he wouldn't be hanging around this town much anymore. Aliz had broken up with him some days ago – at this moment, he couldn't remember exactly when. Too much had happened in the meantime. In any event, it looked like the breakup was going to stick. She didn't seem pleased to see him tonight, even though he only dropped in to rescue her.

They were from different worlds. Aliz had seen enough of Troy's world, and didn't like it. More than that, she didn't like Troy.

"We're going to disappear here for a little while," Alex said, blowing smoke out into the chilly night air. "Put her in a safe house in another country and sit on her."

Alex was dressed in a brown leather jacket and jeans. His dark hair was slicked back, and he had the scrubbly beginnings of a beard – more like a five o'clock shadow. Alex was small, thin and handsome. At times, he reminded Troy of a catalog model, or maybe an actor on an afternoon soap opera. The first time Troy met him, Alex had a full beard, was wearing a dark turban, and claimed he was a Sikh.

Troy smiled at the memory.

Alex, Troy had come to learn, was Troy's handler. Who or what Alex represented was not clear, but whatever it was, they both worked for it. Alex, and his unique skill set, had proved useful to Troy again and again. Troy wasn't even sure if Alex was really the guy's name.

In truth, it was very unlikely his name was Alex.

Tonight, Alex and three men dressed in maintenance uniforms had arrived at Aliz's mansion soon after Troy got there, and began right away to erase and eliminate any sign that something violent had happened.

"It's for her own good. She's insisting the gunmen worked for her brother and meant her no harm. But she has no evidence to prove that. She's got this strange relationship with her brother. The whole thing is like fantasyland."

Troy sighed. "I know all about it."

He still felt a bit sick. His ears were ringing just a little, and every time he blinked, there were tiny eruptions of light behind his eyes. The stun grenades had been Jan's idea. It was a good one, but you had to be careful with those things.

"She thinks this was all a trap set by him to get to you," Alex said. "But not even to hurt you. Just to capture you. She lives in a dream world."

Troy nodded. "It makes sense, except for the capturing part. He has reason to want to kill me. He was the one behind the swarming drone attacks, and in his mind, those attacks were supposed to make him a lot of money."

"Maybe he was," Alex said. "I doubt he made any money from it. And you did beat him up pretty good. That alone…"

He let the thought drift off.

"Or it could be the Albanians," Troy said. "Or it could be the Italians getting revenge for the Albanians."

Just saying these things made the sinking feeling he'd had earlier worse than ever. He and his team had just broken up a human trafficking ring in Albania and killed a bunch of its members. Troy had personally run through the leader of the clan with a sword.

"Anyway, we'll hide her out for the time being," Alex said. "She's obviously on the hit list."

“The kidnappers?” Troy said. “What about them?”

Alex shook his head. “If there were really five of them, one disappeared. We only found two dead guys in the house. Nothing so far on them. Looks like their identities have been scrubbed. Ghosts. But we’ll get a hit sooner or later. You can’t erase yourself completely.”

“Might want to call Interpol,” Troy said with a rueful smile.

Alex looked at him. He didn’t smile at all.

“We put drones and satellites on the two guys who made it out by car. They drove into the French countryside and ditched the car.”

“No interdiction?”

Alex shrugged. “No crime took place. Anyway, it’s better if they think they got away clean. We know where the car is. We’ll get in there and check it for prints and DNA.”

“The roof of the house?” Troy said.

He wasn’t asking the question that was plaguing him. But he was going to have to, and soon. Something needed to be done about it.

“Renovations are not my department,” Alex said. “You and your friend blew it up. But I’m sure someone else will fix it good as new.”

“What about my family?” Troy said.

This was the question. It was really the only important question.

Alex nodded. “Missing Persons wants me to talk about this with you. It’s important.”

Missing Persons was the one-eyed former Colonel Stuart Persons. For a time, Persons had been Troy’s commanding officer in the Navy SEALs. Now Persons was… what? Some kind of spy master, working out of a tiny office within the New York City Police Department headquarters, but his real allegiance was to an organization he declined to name.

Alex often came with messages from Missing Persons.

“So talk,” Troy said. “I’m listening.”

"He has people watching your mom's house and the houses of your brothers. But it's not foolproof. You know that. He thinks you should move your mother to one of your brothers' houses. That way, there's some consolidation. Possibly your brother Donnie's house, if you can convince her to do that. It's the most secluded, and the easiest to isolate."

“It’s hard to convince my mother of anything.”

Alex nodded. “I have a mother. I know how that goes.”

"She thinks I work for an international medical charity run by the federal government."

Now Alex did smile. "I doubt that very much."

CHAPTER THREE

January 19
4:05 pm Hong Kong Time (9:05 am Central European Time)
BCHB (The Beijing Chonqing Hong Kong Bank) Headquarters
Near Statue Square
City of Hong Kong
China

"The hidden and the visible," the driver said.

In fact, what he said, in Mandarin, was "you ming," which meant roughly the same thing.

That which can be seen, and that which cannot. The living and the dead. Men and ghosts. The light and the darkness.

The big yellow Hong Kong garbage truck was approaching the checkpoint at the driveway behind the towering BCHB building. Since the Occupy Hong Kong protests of a decade before, when hundreds of young people stormed and held the atrium of the building for weeks on end, security had become tight. There was no need for a police crackdown if the troublemakers couldn't get inside in the first place.

The man in the passenger seat called himself Li Gang, an instantly forgettable name that was not his real name. Li was perhaps the most common surname in mainland China. Gang meant "strength." There must be a million men and boys with this combination of names. The driver had been given some similar *nom de guerre.* The driver's name was so wonderfully forgettable that Li Gang had already forgotten it.

They had never met before today, and with luck, after five minutes from now, they would never see each other again. Not in this lifetime.

"Yin huan," said Li Gang.

He scanned the surroundings. The building rose many stories above them. The small guard house with the security arm down was just in front now. Before the guard house, and beyond it, was a maze of concrete barriers that created a sort of chute, forcing a truck like this to move at a crawl, and make repeated sharp turns.

The driver nodded and smiled. "Even better." The driver's face was squat and belied a sort of stupidity that Li Gang didn't like. But the man had a simple job to do, and perhaps that accounted for it. For a simple job, get a simple mind. On the other hand, the man enjoyed Li Gang's clever turn of phrase, so how dumb could he be?

In English, *yin huan* meant "a danger concealed within," or "misfortune not visible from the surface."

Li Gang had spent years in Canada and in the United States. He mused that a similar concept in English might be that of the Trojan horse.

The driver pulled up to the gatehouse. His window was already down. The guard wore a dark blue BCHB uniform. The driver handed the guard his photo ID – a very clever forgery – and a paper itinerary. If a problem was coming, it would come right now. Li Gang's breath seemed to catch in his lungs. He looked ahead through the windshield, as if he were bored.

Li Gang and the truck driver wore ridiculous orange jumpsuits with bright yellow reflective piping along the arms and legs, and across the chest. They wouldn't die in a traffic accident, not with these things on. Wearing these suits, it was impossible that they were anything other than hard-working garbage men. *Yin huan* indeed.

The guard scribbled something on the itinerary and handed it back. He ran the ID through a scanner, then handed that back. He barely glanced up the entire time.

The gate rose slowly.

Li Gang's breath returned, a rush of air passing out at first, then something more normal.

It was remarkable that an international corporation like BCHB, a colossus astride the global economy, would maintain such a low-tech method for vetting the garbage trucks as they came onto the grounds. The "security" was little more than a formality. But then, it happened exactly as it was explained to him it would happen.

He felt a tickle of fear at the bottom of his throat.

This was really going to work.

His life was over. For a moment, he considered the warm breeze coming in through the driver's side window. It was January. Hong Kong didn't have a winter to speak of. In Toronto, it would be cold and snowy now. Li Gang couldn't abide these climates near the equator. He preferred the distinct seasons of North America, and especially the cold and snow of deep winter. Which was something he would never experience again.

"Close your window," Li Gang said.

The driver looked at him.

"Close it."

The windows were bulletproof. Having them open defeated their purpose.

The driver touched the button, doing as he was told. Slowly, interminably slowly, the large truck wormed its way through the maze of concrete highway barriers toward the back of the skyscraper. In a few moments, they reached the building. A line of large green metal dumpsters faced them.

Beyond the dumpsters was a low entry to the parking garage beneath the building. The entryway was far too low to accept the height of the large truck.

What should happen now is the giant scoop above the driving cab should reach out, pick up the dumpsters one by one, and empty the contents into the back of the truck. The scoop was controlled from inside the cab. But that wasn't going to happen.

Instead:

"Back the truck into the garage entrance," Li Gang said.

"It won't fit under there," the driver said.

Li Gang shook his head. "It doesn't matter. Ram it."

"It will call attention."

"Yes," Li Gang said. "But it doesn't matter. There will still be time."

The driver hesitated. He was clearly wondering how he was supposed to escape if they called attention to themselves.

"Do it."

The driver shrugged, then made a sharp right turn, facing the back of the truck to the entrance of the garage. He put the truck in reverse.

"Hard. Fast!"

"Will it explode?" the driver said.

"No. Only the detonator will explode the bomb. An impact won't do it."

The driver shrugged again and stomped on the accelerator. A man going to his death shrugging about everything. Li Gang didn't know what to make of that.

The truck lurched backwards, gaining speed.

"Go! Go!"

The crash barely felt like anything. There was a crunch and an awful grinding sound. The heavy steel of the truck ripped and peeled back the sheet metal facade of the garage entry. The two men bounced around in their seats. Li Gang braced himself on the dashboard. The truck crunched a few meters into the garage and came to a halt, completely stuck.

Li Gang already had his pistol out. He had hidden it under his seat. He used the automated button to lock all the doors. He turned to the driver and pointed the gun.

"The Committee extends its deepest thanks to you for your service. And also its sincere apologies. They could not afford to be transparent with you."

The driver's eyes widened.

"You would have certainly been captured," Li Gang said, by way of explanation. "You would have been interrogated, and they would have broken you under torture."

"I don't know anything," the driver said. "I can't tell them anything."

Li Gang shook his head. "It's amazing what people sometimes know, and yet hide from themselves."

The driver reached for the door and put his shoulder to it.

BANG!

Li Gang shot him in the head. Blood sprayed against the glass behind the man. The driver slumped forward against the wheel.

Li Gang dropped the gun at his feet. He reached under the dashboard in front of him and pulled out a plastic panel. He tore it away and shoved it aside. There was very little left to do, but also very little time to do it.

He looked up. Already, men were running toward the truck. Three, four… five men.

One had a gun.

Then another had one.

THUMP. THUMP. THUMP. Bullets were hitting the outside of the truck.

The detonator was here, wired under the dashboard. It was a small, innocent-looking box. Its plastic exterior was dull and unremarkable, like an old clock radio gathering dust in an attic.

He pressed a button, activating it. A red digital readout came on. As soon as he activated it, a high-pitched beep began. It grew louder and higher in pitch. It was like a countdown, building in intensity until it reached some climactic state that only it understood.

Then it stopped entirely.

Li Gang gasped for breath.

The window next to his head cracked in thin, spiderweb-like cracks. They were trying to kill him. They were shooting the window, to no avail. But the glass wouldn't hold forever.

There were a few decisions left to make. The system was designed for a high-stress environment like this. Five minutes was a possible choice, depending on the circumstances he found himself in. Or two minutes. One minute. None of these seemed like good choices.

Thirty seconds was the smallest amount of time.

Li Gang pressed a red button, cycling through the options.

He landed on 30:00.

He pressed the green button just above the red one. Both both were bright enough for him to easily see. The first press of the green button was SET. The second press was START. He had practiced all this hundreds of times. He pressed the green button one more time.

Suddenly, the readout went to 29:99.

The countdown had begun. An instant later, it was 28:54.

The hundredths of a second flew by.

The only sounds were Li Gang's heavy breathing and the bullets striking all over the truck.

He looked through the cracked windows. There must be a dozen men in dark blue uniforms out there now, all holding guns, all firing at once.

Too late.

He glanced at the readout again.

23:11.

Twenty-three seconds to live.

He took a deep breath.

THUNK. THUNK. THUNK.

Heavier bullets hit now. The windshield cracked apart, but did not shatter.

He tried to think of something.

He tried to think of the jewel. The jewel in the heart of the lotus.

He glanced at the readout. 15:01. Going fast. No way to stop it now.

“All things,” he said quietly. “All things are one.”

The windshield caved in.

***

“If he’s angry that we escalated, he needs to look at himself.”

Megan Churchill walked the seventh floor catwalk inside the soaring glass atrium of the BCHB building in Hong Kong. Above her head, late afternoon sunlight filtered down from the roof many stories in the sky. Below her, tall bamboo plants reached toward the light. The escalators from the lobby on the ground floor to the reception area on the third floor were like twin metal snakes. On the fourth floor was the wide open food court, dense with foliage. It was a wonderful place to have her afternoon coffee, and she was headed there now.

She'd been here six months. She'd spent ten years in the New York office before that. She liked Hong Kong okay, and she loved to come to work in this building, but for her, this was all a step to bigger things. She had no family here, and had made few friends. She was career-oriented and a hard charger. She was on her way up, and everyone knew it.

Associate Director of Global Risk Assessment was a pit stop, and nothing more.

She had the volume up on her cellular, and the speaker phone feature engaged. She walked the deep carpeted hallway with the phone held away from her face.

"He's concerned that there was no warning before you went above his head."

Megan smiled. She shook her head. She wasn't even angry.

A guy named Glenn Faber in Legal at the London office had found himself in deep doo-doo, and was looking for someone to blame. A small subsidiary brand, a credit card issuer by the unfortunate name of *Presto!,* had been systematically harassing subprime borrowers who had fallen behind in their payments. Outrageous behavior like calls after 9pm and visits to the home were just a couple of the techniques they were using.

Some of these borrowers had apparently pushed back with cease and desist letters from their own lawyers. That didn't stop the harassment, so now there were lawsuits. One law firm had taken this on *pro bono* as a civil rights case. Suddenly, there were newspaper stories about it.

Glenn Faber had known about this situation since last June. In October, Megan's office had requested a full report on the matter. Now it was January, and Megan Churchill was still waiting for a report from some lackey named Glenn Faber.

Did she escalate? Yes, all the way to the top. BCHB had been an international bank since the 1830s. Now its good name was being dragged through the mud by the actions of a bunch of nitwits at something called *Presto!*

There was a slight tremble under Megan's feet. Somewhere, maybe from below ground, a rumble came, like thunder from a far-off storm.

"I asked for a full report from Glenn the first week of October," she said. "Is there anything more to be said? If Glenn is wondering why he finds himself in this position, tell him to look in the…"

The whole building shook.

Earthquake?

All around her, on the floors below, on the floors above, people began to scream. In the food court, people were pushing up from their tables.

Below them, at the bottom of the atrium, the very floor of the building seemed to erupt upward and outward. Megan saw it happen before she heard it. People on the ground floor flew through the air. The network of steel girders broke apart, and glass windows shattered.

The rumbling continued, shaking the building with relentless force. It felt as if the very foundation was being ripped apart.

Megan's heart pounded in her chest. She clung to the handrail, trying to maintain her balance as the floor beneath her heaved and cracked. The deafening sound of rending steel and shattering glass echoed through the air, mingling with the screams from below of those trapped inside the collapsing building. Across from her, the entire wall of the building began to cave in.

Glenn Faber needs to look in the mirror.

She had lost her phone.

Beneath her, the catwalk broke apart. For a second, there was a delay, as if the structure would defy the law of gravity.

Then she fell into the gaping maw that opened beneath her.

***

Michael Largent stood near the railing at the top of the outdoor lookout tower of Victoria Peak. He and his family had rode up here on the old tram, left over from British rule, that went nearly vertical up the hillside.

He was on a four-day stopover in Hong Kong with his wife and three small sons on his way to a new job in Singapore. He didn't love this city.

The crackdown on the city's autonomy over the past ten years by the Chinese authorities gave him a sickly feeling of complicity just being here. The crowds were too much – it was thought to be among the most crowded cities on Earth. The hotel was a thousand pounds a night. He was anxious to get into the new office and start work.

He'd be happy when they pushed on from here. But you couldn't pass through Hong Kong without at least stopping to see it, right?

Michael Jr., nine years old, was clowning around, attempting to climb up and sit on the railing. Behind and below him was a dizzying, panoramic view of the center of Hong Kong, with Victoria Harbour in the background, and the far shore further still.

"Mikey! Mike! What are you doing? Get down from there!"

"Daddy, it's not far down. There's another platform below us."

Yeah, there was another platform, and it was a good 15 or 20 feet below them. If Mike Jr. pitched over the railing and landed on his head, he'd be just as dead as if he fell hundreds of stories and landed in the middle of a downtown street.

"Honey, are you seeing this?"

No. His wife April was not seeing this. She was halfway down the platform, mixed in with the crowds of gawkers, with their cell phones, and their selfies.

Michael would have to pull the kid down himself. He took two steps toward him.

"Dad!"

From somewhere, an immense noise came. It was like a rumble of thunder, followed by a sound like the tearing of metal in a high-speed car crash. Only it was even worse.

All around him, people gasped. A woman shrieked, a sound that somehow almost as horrible as the first sound. It sends a bolt of electricity down Michael's spine. He looked to his right. A well-dressed East Asian woman was there, one hand covering her mouth, the other hand pointing outward at the city center.

Behind Mike, Jr., an explosion ripped through one of the high-rises in the bowl of skyscrapers at the foot of Victoria Peak. As Michael watched, an entire section of the facade shredded, and came down, first in seeming slow motion, and then with sudden force. The collapse threw a slow-rising dust cloud into the air.

Everywhere around them, people were screaming now.

"Oh my God!" someone shouted. "Oh no!"

Mike Jr. slid off the railing and began to turn.

Michael took two giant steps to his son. He grabbed the boy and turned him away from the view of the collapsing building. He put a big hand over the boy's eyes for good measure.

"Don't look at it," he said. "It's okay, honey. Everything's okay."

Now, the boy turned and was crying against him.

The sound of groaning and ripping metal continued to carry across the distance, as whatever was happening behind that giant dust cloud continue to happen.

Everywhere on the platform, people were weeping. A few were filming the disaster with their phones or digital cameras. A moment passed, then even more people were filming.

Michael glanced to his right. Down the line, April was holding the other two boys, their faces pressed against her stomach. She stared at the horrible, rising, spreading, brown and gray cloud that now blotted out half the horizon. The dust or smoke – smog from obliterated concrete and computer equipment and human beings – began to drift this way on the breeze coming off the harbour.

How many people? How many dead inside there?

They had to get back inside before that dust cloud reached here.

"It's okay," Michael whispered to his son. "But don't look."

CHAPTER FOUR

9:45 am Central European Time
Headquarters of the European Rapid Response Investigation Unit (ERRIU)
aka El Grupo Especial
Outskirts of Madrid
Spain

"You look like hell."

Troy nearly smiled. But didn't. He took a sip of his Rock Star Zero instead.

"Thank you. It's my best suit."

In fact, he was wearing a dark blue Brooks Brothers suit, with a red tie and black Italian leather shoes. He wore a silver and blue Breitling watch on his wrist – he had no idea what it cost, but it had been a gift from Aliz, so it was probably the most expensive thing on his body. He had even shaved before he came in. This was somewhat of a big day, his last day at Interpol, at El Grupo, and he wanted to look good. Apparently, he had failed in that regard.

Presentable, though. He figured he was presentable, at least.

"I didn't mean the suit," Agent Dubois said. "That looks nice. I mean the rest of you. Your face, mostly. You seem tired. Exhausted is a better word."

Troy shrugged. "I had a late night."

He was standing in the open doorway to what had been Dubois's office here at El Grupo headquarters. The whole thing had been disbanded, everyone was either suspended or reassigned, and Dubois was sitting at her desk, cleaning it out.

There were boxes around her on the floor. There was no laptop or phone visible – nothing that would give any indication she was here to do work.

She looked up at him. There was a question on her face. Her dark eyes flared, but she didn't ask the question. Troy noted that she was very beautiful in her own way, a way that was as different from Aliz as night was from day.

Dubois wore a dark bodysuit that hugged her curves – typical for her in the office. She had a wide blue belt around her waist and a matching sash that held her tall Afro in place. She sported big black combat boots on her feet. She had taken to wearing a small pistol in a holster strapped to her thigh. Maybe that was in recognition of how much combat she had seen in recent months. Or maybe it was an acknowledgment that after the mission in Albania, her life was in danger. Whatever else it was, that gun on her thigh was sexy.

He shook his head. "A friend of mine. Something I had to take care of."

"I heard," she said. "I was very sorry that happened."

"Thank you," Troy said. "So was I."

"Did you take care of it?"

He nodded. "I did. Me and some friends. It wasn't an el Grupo thing. Just a personal matter. It's not even something to talk about. But it's all better now, I'm happy to report."

He sighed.

Dubois sighed in return. "That's good.

A long, quiet moment spun out between them. Troy didn't want to hesitate like this. He wanted to really talk with her, get to the bottom of things. In a few minutes, he was going to get called in to a meeting with Miquel, and with some functionaries from Interpol. They had flown here from France – Miquel was convinced the reason they came to Madrid was to scope out El Grupo's headquarters and get a sense of what else it could be used for.

They also came to get rid of Troy Stark once and for all. They were going to chew Troy up and spit him out, in all likelihood. Interpol proper never wanted Troy on board, never wanted Miquel Castro-Ruiz to have his own agency, and never wanted the two men to team up. When Troy came out of that meeting, everything was going to be different. All of this was going to be over.

And knowing the elusive Agent Dubois, she probably wouldn't even be here anymore. God forbid that she and Troy should have even one serious, heartfelt conversation about what happened at the end of the last mission.

He had dropped into the ocean from a helicopter to save her after the yacht she'd been on exploded. They had shared a passionate kiss in dark, turbulent water. More than a kiss. And it had been coming for a long time. They both knew it.

Her perspective on it? It was a mistake, an accident, a thing that happened between two otherwise neutral people carried away by the emotions of the moment. That's what she claimed, anyway. Troy didn't believe a word of it.

"What are you going to do?" he said now.

Dubois shrugged. "I'm going to Paris to be with my mother. I'm worried for her safety. If they took a friend of yours…" She raised her hands as if to say DON'T SHOOT. "I'm not saying that's what happened. But if it did, or something like that, then they did it to target you."

Troy took another sip of his Rock Star. The can was warm. The drink was warm. That was okay. He liked the taste of it, and anyway, he didn't drink it for the flavor. He drank it for the jolt of caffeine. And whatever else they put in it – the energy it gave him didn't wear off like coffee normally did.

"I think that's true," he said.

"And if so, it means none of us are safe," Dubois said. "And no one close to us is safe. So, I'm taking a little time off – I have it coming to me because I was injured on the most recent assignment. I'm going to protect my mother. As I understand it, in two weeks from now I'll be assigned to the headquarters in Lyon. Hopefully, my mother will consider moving to Lyon with me, at least for a little while."

Troy took a deep breath. He had to carefully consider his words. This one tiny woman thought she was going to keep her mother safe from an international mafia. Dubois was a tough cookie, for sure. But if she thought she could fight off an entire…

It was like she could read his mind.

"I'm a stone killer now," she said, applying a funny American slang term to herself. "I won't let them hurt her."

He shook his head. He smiled ruefully. "You never killed anyone until you met me."

"He said with obvious pride."

"I'm not proud of that. But I am proud of some of the things we did together."

She pushed herself up from her chair. She came around the desk, stood on tiptoes, and kissed him on both cheeks, slowly, one at a time.

"Well, that's over now," she said. "And we're all on our own."

He was about to reach out and pull her into his arms, but he sensed a presence behind him. He turned, and Jan Bakker was standing there just outside the door, wearing brown slacks and a gray sweater. He was his normal imposing self – huge, broad, completely bald, with reading glasses perched on top of his head.

He didn't seem to have dressed any differently for this meeting than he would for a normal day at work – that was natural, because Jan wasn't on the chopping block. As Troy never got tired of being told, Jan Bakker was one of the best investigative data and systems analysts in Europe. If Interpol ever let him go, someone else would snap him up in minutes.

Jan didn't even look particularly tired, but then again, he hadn't flown to Luxembourg and back last night. He hadn't jumped out of an airplane, crashed through a roof, and killed a couple of guys. He had done his entire part from right here in Madrid. He had probably gotten to bed at a decent hour, sipping hot chocolate under the covers while reading a book.

Troy smiled at the image.

"Stark," Jan said. "They're ready to start the meeting now."

"Thank you."

A look passed between them. Jan had been instrumental in helping him save Aliz's life last night. He would probably never mention it. Troy wouldn't either. The truth was, Troy couldn't have done it without him.

"There was a terrorist bombing in Hong Kong not forty minutes ago," Jan said.

He had a funny way about him. He often presented information like this, matter-of-factly, without emotion attached, and without preamble. It seemed almost random. It could have been the score of a football match. He could have just as easily said, "I drink my coffee with cream and sugar."

Troy nodded. "I heard about it on the radio on my drive-in."

That was true, as far as it went. Troy's Spanish was much improved. But native Spanish radio announcers spoke fast enough that Troy picked up few details about the attack. The words tended to go by in a blur. He caught bits and pieces of it. A truck bomb had brought a large building down. Hundreds of people were trapped in the rubble. He knew that much.

It was horrible, but it was also not really his problem. Mass murder on the other side of the world was going to be a job for Chinese law enforcement and Chinese intelligence.

"Is that what this meeting is about?" Troy said.

Jan didn't smile. Jokes often didn't reach him.

"I think you know what this meeting is about."

***

"This hearing will be conducted in English."

A tall man with wispy, sandy hair was speaking. He called the meeting a "hearing," which surprised Troy. A hearing was like a trial. A trial about what?

There were nine people in the conference room, which was also a surprise. There were three people on Troy's team – Troy, Jan Bakker, and Miquel Castro-Ruiz, the Director or former Director of the European Rapid Response Investigative Unit. Everyone within the unit had come to think of as El Grupo Especial, or even just El Grupo.

The rest of the people, four men and two women, seemed to be from Interpol. The men were all middle-aged, as was one of the women. The other woman was young, with black hair tied in a ponytail. Troy took her to be a secretary, or maybe someone who did shorthand. She had positioned herself just to Troy's right. She placed a folder on the table in front of her.

One of them introduced the others, but Troy didn't catch all of it. A few names seemed familiar – Hans Jute, Second Global Director of something or other, Gregory Fawkes, something to do with Interpol Internal Affairs, and Max Davidoff, Director of Special Projects.

That last one was easy. If Troy wasn't mistaken, Max Davidoff was Miquel's direct boss. He was a broad guy with a perfectly bald head combined with a thick beard. He had a pronounced gut and wore an ill-fitting suit. His hands were large and thick, like he had spent half his career in a basement furnace room, opening and closing large metal valves with a giant wrench. He was staring down at the table as if he'd prefer to be anywhere else but here.

Troy knew how he felt.

"Miquel, if you need a simultaneous translation to Spanish, we have that capability," said a thin man, with another perfectly bald head, and wearing wire-rimmed glasses.

Miquel shook his head and snorted a bit of laughter. He wore an open-throated blue dress shirt and khaki pants. He was clean-shaven, and his hair was slicked and neat. But his eyes said he was tired. It wouldn't surprise Troy in the least if he decided to retire after all this.

"Hans, I understand English just fine. You know that."

There was an awkward pause.

“The hearing is being recorded. A full transcription of the proceedings will be provided to all parties involved. Dr. Anita Vilar of the Interpol legal department is here to represent the interests of Troy Stark. Mr. Stark, if you have any questions for…”

“I have a lawyer?” Troy said.

It wasn’t lost on Troy that the man addressed him as Mr. Stark, and not Agent Stark.

“Yes.”

“Why do I need a lawyer?”

“Mr. Stark, you have been accused of serious crimes by local jurisdictions while in the employ of Interpol, and while carrying out activities related to your work. It will be in your best interest to understand the nature of the accusations against you, and perhaps to refrain from admitting guilt. While we want to understand how these accusations came about, and take whatever disciplinary actions required, we also want to make sure your rights are protected. This is especially true if formal charges are brought against you in partner countries, and requests for extradition are made.”

Troy sensed a railroading coming on. He shook his head.

“This is the first I’m hearing of this. In America, we don’t usually walk into a trial and find out that we’re the one on trial.”

The man shook his head. “This isn’t America, and you’re not on trial. This is a disciplinary hearing. You were notified of it by email. We attempted to notify you by courier, but found no one at your address.”

“I must have been out,” Troy said. “Do you mind telling me what I’m accused of?”

The group of interlopers all looked at each other. The thin man in glasses nodded. Troy took note of him. He was small, and very well dressed. His gray suit look perfectly tailored. He reminded Troy of a guy who would wake up in the morning, make his bed, then go out and run ten miles before breakfast. He had probably done marathons before.

“Hans Jute,” the man said. “I’m Interpol’s Second Deputy for Global Intelligence.”

“That’s quite a title,” Troy said. “What does it mean?”

Miquel smiled. “It means I had to hold a gun to Hans’s head to stop him from interfering when you and the team took down the slaughterbot terrorists in New York.”

Troy looked at Jute with renewed interest. “You’re that guy?”

Jute’s blue eyes were hard. He nodded.

Now Troy smiled. He could finally relax, because he saw where this thing was headed. It was time to settle scores. Okay. That was fine.

This was probably over now. It had been fun, Troy supposed. They had done some good things. Maybe Missing Persons could find him something else to do. Or maybe he'd just return to New York and coach underprivileged kids in boxing or football. With a little luck, he could get off this continent before someone arrested him and extradited him to Albania.

"Hit me," he said.

Jute had paperwork in front of him. He moved a couple of the papers around without actually picking them up.

"You fit the description of one of two men who, some weeks ago, stole a helicopter at gunpoint from an alpine rescue station in Austria."

Troy shook his head. "Doesn't ring a bell. Lots of people fit descriptions of things."

"In London just a week ago, you are accused of being involved in the extrajudicial killings of individuals wanted in connection with…"

"If I killed anyone in London, it was in self-defense, during a request for an interview."

"You are accused of being involved. Along with another man who is unnamed."

"British intelligence," Miquel said. "Our team was inside the flat with assistance from British intelligence. We were investigating a ring of kidnappers and sex traffickers. But British government involvement is classified information."

Hans Jute seemed good at shrugging off information that he didn't like, or which didn't fit neatly into a story he was trying to tell himself.

His eyes never wavered from Troy. He didn't even acknowledge that Miquel had spoken.

"In that same incident, you are accused of denying basic rights to prisoners. Said prisoners, by the way, whom you were not empowered to detain. You are accused of extracting information through abuse bordering on torture. You are accused of employing verbal taunts and threats of summary execution to intimidate the aforementioned prisoners."

"I'm accused of taunting someone," Troy said. "Is that right?"

"The next day, and through to the next after that, in Albania, you are accused of multiple extrajudicial killings. This is the one most likely to stick. The Albanian government is irate that Interpol inserted a team into their country without prior agreement, and the team included not one, but two former CIA assassins."

Troy shook his head. "I've never been an assassin, not for the CIA, or anyone else."

"How many people have you killed while you've been working for Interpol?"

Troy shrugged. "I'm not a statistics guy. I don't keep track of things like that."

Jute turned over a page. "Before coming to Europe, you were a member of a highly-classified, CIA-sponsored irregular military unit known as Metal Shop, were you not? This unit carried out extortion and extrajudicial killings throughout Latin America, did it not?"

Troy smiled again. It was hard to believe the things they were bringing up. So far, no one in this hearing had bothered to mention that Troy, Dubois, and Carlo Gallo, the other former CIA assassin, had managed to save more than a dozen trafficked women, and had utterly destroyed an entire human trafficking gang.

"Do you watch a lot of television, Global Deputy Jute?"

Jute sighed. "Were you a member of Metal Shop before you joined Interpol?"

"There's no such thing as Metal Shop."

Miquel stood up. "Hans, this is ridiculous. The man should be given a commendation. The entire team should. They have risked their lives again and again to see that justice is served."

Everyone in the room was watching him. He raised a finger as if to say he was number 1.

"And, to be clear, no one in this agency acted without my knowledge and without authorization from me. Every decision that was made, and every action that was taken, happened under my direct orders. I was in communication with team members every step of the way."

Troy glanced at Jan Bakker. Jan was watching Miquel with interest, but not saying anything. There were times, multiple times, when the team was out beyond the reach of communication. There were actions that were taken because of split second decisions. Had Miquel put them in the position where these decisions needed to be made? Yes.

Had Miquel authorized the decisions beforehand?

Absolutely not.

Miquel was taking the fall here.

"Listen, can I say something?" Troy said.

The young woman sitting next to him put a hand on Troy's arm and leaned in close to him. "Let him speak," she whispered. "I advise you not to speak again during this hearing unless asked a direct question. Even then, it may be best to decline to answer."

"Who are you, please?" Troy said.

"I'm your legal representative."

Troy looked around the room. "My lawyer just graduated junior high school. I can't tell you how good I feel about that."

Jute was staring at Miquel now.

"Director Castro, are you admitting that the crimes your team members are accused of were the result of your direct orders?"

Miquel nodded. "Yes, I am. If such crimes were even committed."

"Did you knowingly hire former CIA assassins to carry out investigative-related work for Interpol?"

"There is a man working as a consultant for ERRIU who I know as a former CIA agent. But he left that agency more than a decade ago, and I do not believe he was ever an assassin. To my knowledge, Agent Stark has never worked for the CIA. He is a former United States Navy SEAL."

"Did you knowingly organize an alleged investigative unit within Interpol, that in reality operated more as a clandestine or black operations unit, which has carried out killings in England, Luxembourg, Switzerland, France, Austria, Albania and North Africa?"

Now Troy stood up.

"I've heard enough."

He looked at Miquel. "You don't have to take the fall for this."

Miquel shrugged. "Ultimately, the actions of El Grupo are my responsibility."

"Okay, but I don't have to sit here and watch it. If I'm not under arrest, I'll be going now."

He locked eyes with Hans Jute. Jute's eyes were calm and impassive behind his lenses.

"You're not under arrest," Jute said. "Not yet."

Troy nodded. He took one more glance around the room, but found nothing more of interest. He left without saying another word.

He went down the hall to Dubois's former office. The lights were out inside there. The door was open. Troy leaned in and flicked the wall switch. The desk was there with nothing on it. Her empty chair was tucked in under the desk. Her empty shelves were behind the desk and chair. Everything was gone, including Dubois.

CHAPTER FIVE

5:15 am Eastern Standard Time (11:15 am Central European Time)
A pedestrian walkway
The Brooklyn Bridge
New York City
USA

"It's much too cold to be out here."

The man's name was Richard Paul, and he was speaking to himself.

He had grown up in Australia, along the Gold Coast, the surfer's paradise, and now he was standing on a bridge over the empty space of the East River in New York City, in the middle of January. It was very early in the morning – the pitch dark before dawn. This was an uncomfortable time and place for him to be. He longed for hot, sunny days, and what he had right now was a frigid night. His breath escaped in a white plume.

Moments ago, he had climbed the urine-soaked steps on the Brooklyn side and walked out on the pedestrian ramp that led to this panoramic view of the city. The walkway was abandoned tonight. It was too cold. Few cars even passed on the roadway below – no one wanted to be out and about this time of day. Richard faced north and gazed out at the lights twinkling in the distance all the way up the East River.

The Manhattan side looked festive, millions of lights glowing on towering buildings, and some still decked out in the holiday spirit. The Empire State Building was lit up green and red. In contrast, Brooklyn and Queens were dark and low-slung, with a few lights blinking here and there in the wasteland. Far upriver, a helicopter moved from left to right across his field of vision. He followed its blinking lights until it was out over Queens somewhere.

Something to his left caught his attention. He looked down the walkway toward the Manhattan side. A man walked slowly toward him. The man was thin and tall, and he wore a long winter coat. There was something about the way he walked. He was partially hidden by the shadows, but he seemed to limp when he walked, and he seemed to be trying to conceal that fact.

The man was only about ten meters away now, still in darkness. He had his head down, obscured by the gloom. Then he stepped into the light of a lamppost and looked up.

The man wore a black wool cap on his head. His face was angular, with sharp edges. The most noticeable thing about him was the black eyepatch he wore, the band tight to the side of his head. Over the patch was a pair of glasses, the lenses reflecting the light from overhead.

Of course, the man limped. Richard Paul happened to know that this man had been injured in combat at least a half dozen times. Richard Paul knew more about this man than he cared to know. Every time he saw the man, he hoped it was the last time.

"Hi Dick," the man said. "How have you been?"

The man was the former Colonel Stuart Persons, retired. He had spent much of his career in the United States Army Special Forces. After that, he had been involved in black operations, ostensibly through the Pentagon's Joint Special Operations Command. But there was a lot more to it than that. Stuart Persons was a dark presence in the world.

Richard Paul guessed that Persons was in his early 50s. But he looked older than that. If someone told him that Persons was a thousand years old, Richard Paul would believe it.

"Colonel Persons. To what do I owe this…"

He gestured at their surroundings, the dark river, the biting wind, the towers of the bridge looming above them.

"...visit?"

"It's not a pleasure?" Persons said.

"No. I think you know that already."

Persons smiled. His hands appeared. A cigarette popped into his mouth. He lit a match and cupped it out of the wind, drawing on the smoke until a bright red ember appeared at the end of it. He inhaled deeply, then tossed the match away.

Persons gestured with the lit cigarette.

"This is a guilty pleasure."

Paul nodded. "Okay."

He waited for the point of this conversation. He had been lying in bed, fitfully awake, when he received a telephone call by a deep voice he thought he might recognize. The voice knew things about him that no one alive should know. Somehow, there were people out there who did know, and they were not good people. How they had found these things out was one of the great mysteries of his life. It was the curse of being Richard Paul.

In this case, the voice told him to leave his waterfront apartment in Brooklyn Heights, drive to the base of the Brooklyn Bridge, climb the stairs to this walkway, and wait.

It's a place where we can talk freely.

That meant it was a place where no one could listen in.

"I need a favor," Persons said now.

Paul shrugged. "I guess I figured out that much. But I'm not all-powerful, you know. I can't just clap my hands and make things happen for you."

Persons seemed to swallow a smile, possibly at the thought of Richard Paul being all-powerful. "You don't have a choice in the matter."

"I'll do what I can," Paul said.

Persons nodded. "Fair enough."

Already, Paul was growing irritated. It was an ugly thing to be owned, to be had like this. They would let him go. Years would pass, and it would seem as if the whole thing was in the past, that it was all over. Then suddenly, like tonight, one of them would reappear. And ask for a favor. But they weren't asking. They were telling.

"You'll be well compensated, believe me."

"What is it?" Paul said.

Persons shrugged. "How much pull do you have with Interpol headquarters in Lyon?"

"Do you answer a question with a question? Is that how this game is played? I'm Interpol's Special Liaison to the United Nations in New York City. I have that position because I wanted it. It didn't fall from the sky. It wasn't an accident. I felt like I could do good things in this position, and I felt like living in New York for a while, so the position became mine. That's how much pull I have. But you already know that."

Persons smiled again. "I suppose I do." His one eye watched Paul. That eye was supremely confident. It was the eye of a predator.

They stared at each other for a long moment.

"There was a terrorist attack in China a little over two hours ago."

Paul shook his head. "You don't say."

It was the biggest news on Earth, by a lot. It was already late afternoon in China. The BCHB building in Hong Kong had been destroyed by a truck bomb. At last count, more than 200 people were known to be dead, with many more trapped in the rubble. Paul had already fielded three calls about it in the dark hours of the night. He was anticipating a bad day today and was trying to get even a little bit of sleep when the call came from Persons.

"The Chinese want to believe that we did it."

Richard Paul shrugged again. Paul was powerful, in his way. He was large, he was influential, and people deferred to him. He could pull many, many strings behind the scenes, and often did. Yet he felt strangely ineffectual in front of Colonel Persons. It was normal, he supposed, to feel that way when in the presence of a blackmailer, someone who knew your worst secrets, the ones you'd do anything not to reveal.

"Maybe they have reason to believe that," Paul said.

Persons shook his head. "They like to believe that we instigate problems inside their country. Sometimes we do. They also like to believe that we do everything bad that happens anywhere. We don't. And they do a lot of bad things themselves. They're not blameless."

"Who did this bad thing?" Paul said.

"I don't know. There have been conflicting claims. My intelligence says the two guys in the truck were Chinese. But that doesn't necessarily mean anything, and their bodies were incinerated in the explosion. Nothing left, no bones, no teeth, nada, which means anyone can claim anything they like about them. There's nothing left of the truck, for that matter. Whatever hasn't melted down is under about a million pounds of rubble. Moreover, I've heard tell that one of the bombers shot and killed the other one right before the bomb went off. That suggests erasing evidence and covering their tracks was baked into the plan."

"You're getting a lot of information," Paul said.

Now Persons shrugged. "It's my job."

"What would you like me to do?"

"Now we're getting to the heart of the matter," Persons said. "The Chinese don't want our help investigating this. Relations are too tense. Worse than tense. But we need our fingers in that pie. We have interests to protect. We have to be close to the investigation."

A thought occurred to Paul. "You don't know if you did it or not, do you?"

"I know for a fact that I didn't do it," Persons said. "But there are a lot of cooks in this kitchen. If one of our own did this, and we find that out, we'll take care of it. But we need to know, and preferably before the whole world knows."

"What would you like me to do?" Paul said again.

"Interpol headquarters will send a representative to the investigation," Persons said. It wasn't a question.

Paul nodded. "As a courtesy, of course. Our help will in all likelihood be declined, considering the intelligence networks they have. But we will send someone as an observer at the very least. Call it a goodwill gesture. We're an international organization, and we work for everyone on the planet. China isn't our enemy."

"We need Interpol to send our guy," Persons said flatly.

"So inform the General Secretariat. I'm sure they'll get a good laugh."

Persons shook his head. It seemed like he wasn't going to say anything more.

"What's his name?" Paul said.

"Troy Stark. He works out of the Interpol office in Madrid, a tiny sub-agency called the European Rapid Response Investigative Unit."

"Never heard of it," Paul said.

"You wouldn't."

"Black operations?" Paul said. "Within Interpol?"

Persons took a drag on his cigarette. "Anyway, it seems they're dismantling it. And Stark's not on the best of terms with his employers right now. He's been accused of some things. But none of that has to matter. He's a good agent, sincere about doing the right thing, and we need him in Hong Kong. But we can't send him ourselves, for obvious reasons."

Richard Paul stared at Stuart Persons. If Persons wanted to send someone, the man must be a monster, right out of a nightmare.

Persons and his ilk had yanked Paul out of bed for this. They had him nailed for something he shouldn't have done and didn't like to think about. He was young when it happened. He had spent decades wrestling with the guilt of it. But that wasn't enough for these people.

The problem was that he came from a prominent family, with holdings in land, timber, mining and media. He had already begun his rise when the bad thing happened. Covering it up had brought him into contact with people like Stuart Persons. They knew exactly what they were doing when they helped him, and they played a very long game.

"It smells like a tall order," Paul said. "After all, the man has, as you say, been accused of some things. Pray tell, what things?"

"The usual," Persons said. "Murder. Torture. You might know a little something about those, eh? In his case, none of it is real. He was just doing his job, and they're looking for an excuse to hang someone. That's all."

Paul shrugged. "Troy Stark, huh?" It was an easy name to remember. He didn't even need to write it down. "Let me look into it. I'll see what I can do."

"Do better than that," Persons said. "Get him sent there."

"I thought you said it was fair if I do the best I can."

Persons took another drag on his smoke. "I didn't mean it."

"Nice to see you again," Paul said.

Persons shook his head. "No, it isn't. I don't like you, Dick. You know that. If you weren't useful, we would have buried you 20 years ago. But there's no rush. We can also do it tomorrow. We can wreck you any time we want. Keep that in front of you, always. And don't stop being useful."

Persons turned and walked off the way he had come. Paul watched him go, closely observing the slight limp.

When Persons was gone, Paul looked up at the cold stars and the wisps of cloud blowing across the sky. The wind was really whipping now.

Darkness seemed to gather all around him, and for a moment he thought it was a shadow from the other side. Perhaps it was THE shadow coming to take him for his sins. But when he shook his head to clear it, and he looked again, there was nothing except the night, the huge expanse of the city, and white steam blowing from a large nearby standpipe.

"Okay, I'll do it," Paul said to no one.

CHAPTER SIX

3:15 pm Central European Time
A flat
Neighborhood of La Latina
Madrid, Spain

The phone rang.

For the moment, Troy ignored it.

He was sitting in his little breakfast nook by the window, slowly sipping a cup of very good coffee. On the street below, people hurried along, bundled up against the cold. If things were really over, and they appeared to be, he was going to miss this place.

La Latina had turned out to be the perfect setting for someone as hard-bitten and cynical as Troy sometimes was – he was a man who had seen a lot of war. He had witnessed a lot of places that were destroyed and a lot of people that were destroyed as well.

Meanwhile, La Latina seemed to know nothing of that. It was a feast for the eyes. The narrow, winding streets were lined with colorful buildings that had intricate balconies and windows, each one unique from all the others. The vibrant colors of the buildings – bright greens, blues, yellows, and reds created an upbeat atmosphere. During the day, the streets were bustling with normal people going about their day. At night, the streets were filled with party types spilling out of the nearby bars.

Before the weather changed and grew colder, you could wander the streets and get hit with a barrage of different smells, most of them incredibly pleasant – freshly baked bread and churros, sizzling paella, spices Troy still couldn't identify, the occasional whiff of a flower stand, and the smell of freshly brewed coffee. Before he moved here, it hadn't occurred to Troy that coffee really smelled like anything. Coffee was a means to an end.

Now? He looked at the bright blue mug in his hand. Now it was something else. And it smelled really good.

He glanced around the apartment, taking it in. It was small, true enough.

Aliz had never said anything out loud about the apartment's size, but he sensed that she was uncomfortable with it.

For Troy, it seemed a perfect size. Sitting at this small round table, you could practically see the whole place. It was in an old building, like almost all the buildings in this neighborhood. There were high ceilings and hardwood floors that were polished to a bright and slick sheen. You could slide around in your socks if you wanted.

In the living room, there was an old fireplace that someone had bricked in during a long ago renovation. Troy figured the owners didn't want open fires inside the flats. All the same, he positioned the couch to face the fireplace, and sometimes lit a candle inside the alcove where the fireplace once had been.

To his left was the kitchen – indeed, the kitchen and this nook were part of the same room, more or less. The kitchen had a lot of counter space, an old double sink, and huge whitewashed cabinets that reached to the ceiling. The place wasn't gummed up with modern conveniences like a dishwasher and a microwave. Troy didn't want those things.

From here, he could look through the doorway into his bedroom. The bedroom had a larger bay window, just across from the bed. The early winter mornings here were cold, and before the heat kicked on, one of Troy's favorite things to do was stand in his underwear, sipping his first coffee, and looking down at streets and the lights of the sleeping neighborhood. The best mornings were when it snowed, and the winds blew the wisps of snow along the cobblestones.

He sighed.

"Man," he said. "I don't want to leave yet."

Almost certainly, Aliz had been kidnapped by her own half-brother, Lucien Mebarak. His men didn't even bother to take her out of her house. If it was Mebarak, then he had set a trap for Troy, a trap that failed rather spectacularly. But that didn't mean he would stop. And it didn't mean he would only target Troy.

Troy thought of his mother in the Bronx, in the small house where he and his brothers had grown up. Missing Persons supposedly had cops stationed outside the house, but how long could that last? And if the place got hit by terrorists or an assassin team, what could a couple of cops sitting and chatting in a squad car really do anyway?

The answer was clear as day. Troy needed to take out Mebarak. That was the only way to stop him. It meant Troy going after someone with the intention of killing him – premeditated murder. That wasn't really Troy's way. But Mebarak deserved it many times over.

This was something Troy needed to talk to Alex about. By now, Alex must have some sense of who the men were that died at Aliz's house, who the men were that ditched the car in France, and where they went afterwards.

Alex probably also knew where Lucien Mebarak was right this minute.

Troy imagined for a moment a world where the threat from Mebarak was eliminated, and where Troy kept this apartment a while longer, living here in Madrid, maybe taking cases that Persons gave him on a freelance basis.

Until the Albanians extradite you for murder.

He sighed again. He didn't want to leave. But it might be there was nothing here anymore. There was no El Grupo Especial. Dubois had already been reassigned. Jan Bakker was sure to be reassigned as well. Miquel had fallen on his sword and was probably going to be drummed out entirely. Gallo was gone and hadn't actually worked there in the first place. El Grupo headquarters would go back to being whatever it had been before. Or it would become nothing. It might even be torn down.

"Well, it was fun while it lasted."

Still, even if he was leaving, he owed it to his coworkers and their families to neutralize the threat from Mebarak. While Mebarak was out there, those people weren't safe either.

Kill Mebarak?

Troy had killed a lot of people. Few had deserved death as richly as Mebarak did.

But Troy had never murdered anyone in cold blood.

Troy's phone, which he had successfully ignored before, began to ring again. He glanced at the screen. It was the same person calling, a number he didn't recognize.

"Persistent, aren't we?"

He picked it up.

"Stark."

"Agent Stark, this is Maxim Davidoff, of the Interpol Special Projects."

It occurred to Troy that he might never have heard Davidoff's voice before. The man spoke with a pronounced accent, what Troy would think of as Russian or Eastern European.

Odd that he was calling Troy. As far as Troy was concerned, being addressed as Mr. Stark at that kangaroo court today told him everything he needed to know. He was a goner, just a guy on the street, no longer an agent, but a mister instead.

"Max, you are the Director of Special Projects at Interpol, are you not?"

"Yes," Davidoff said. "Director."

"What are the special projects?"

"This and that," Davidoff said. "Things that arise. They don't fit in other places. It doesn't matter what they are."

"Am I still employed at Interpol?"

"Of course. If you had not…" Davidoff paused, as if searching for a phrase. "...run away so soon, that would have been made clear to you. You report to me directly now. You are a… let's say... a one man band, at the moment."

"And Miquel Castro-Ruiz?"

Davidoff spoke slowly.

"No longer my employee, as far as I know. Possible that he retires. Possible he reports to Deputy Director Jute. People's careers take different turns. One day, you are up, one day, you are down. The next day, you are back up again. Not our concern in this conversation."

"What is our concern?"

"We need to meet. I have a possible assignment for you. A pressing issue. It has come down from on high. From God, you might say, or even higher than God."

Troy was intrigued. He had been sure they were going to get rid of him, or already had. Now, they were giving him a new boss and a new assignment.

"Are you still in Madrid?" Troy said.

"Yes. Of course."

"When do you want to meet?"

Mebarak. Taking down Mebarak. Would that qualify as a special project?

"Now," Davidoff said. "This evening. Will that work for you?"

***

This is where he wants to meet?

The tapas bar was small and crowded. The place was dimly lit, with only a few flickering candles on the tables. The walls were adorned with colorful tiles and posters, and the space was cramped with tables positioned close together, and groups of people talking and laughing.

Glasses and silverware clinked, and there was some music playing in the background that Troy could barely get – he felt the bass from it through his body more than he heard the music itself.

He found Davidoff at a table near the door to the kitchen. The man was sitting with his back to the wall, watching the door, as if he were some mafioso expecting his murderers to show up at any moment. He was dressed better than he had been this morning – in a dark blue suit jacket with a light pink dress shirt open at the collar, and a gold chain around his thick neck. The guy could be at a nightclub in Moscow. A long wool coat hung on a peg at the side of his table.

In contrast, Troy was dressed down in jeans, boots, and a leather jacket. It was cold out, but the walk here was not long, and Troy still had one foot out the door from Interpol.

Davidoff nodded and smiled as Troy approached.

"Stark. Welcome."

The place was five blocks from Troy's flat, but Davidoff was welcoming him.

He gestured at the seat opposite him. "Please sit."

Troy's noticed Davidoff's big, thick hands again. He also noticed that Davidoff had rings on several fingers. His style was anything but the bland gray g-man persona a lot of Interpol guys liked to affect. He seemed to be going for "aging mobster" instead.

Troy slid into the seat. The two men shook hands.

"Is this a good place to talk?" Troy said. The words from his mouth seemed to disappear into the wall of noise that surrounded them.

Davidoff nodded. "Very good. No one will overhear us. No one will think we are anything but two simple guys."

Troy nodded. "Okay."

Davidoff gestured at the table. "I ordered us two beers. Do you want to eat?"

There were indeed two bottles of beer on the small square table. They were both open. Davidoff's was half-empty. There was a small glass near Davidoff's right hand with an amber liquid in it. Davidoff didn't mention the glass, and Troy didn't ask.

Troy gave the beer bottle a long look.

"It's all right," Davidoff said. "We are colleagues. I didn't drug the beer."

"And if we weren't colleagues?" Troy said.

Davidoff smiled, a big goofy grin that seemed nothing like the man it was attached to.

"You would wake up in a warehouse, tied to a chair."

"I like you already," Troy said. He picked up the beer and took a long gulp of it. He might as well find out who he was dealing with right from the start.

"Food?" Davidoff said.

Troy shook his head. "No. Just business, if you don't mind."

Davidoff nodded, but the smile disappeared. He seemed almost sad, as if the real tragedy here wasn't that Miquel had been railroaded for taking risks and saving lives, but that he and Troy Stark weren't good enough friends already to enjoy a meal together.

"Okay," he said. "It's fair to want that."

"Yes."

"You've seen the Hong Kong disaster," Davidoff said, without any more preamble. It was a statement and not a question.

The truth was Troy knew it had happened, but didn't have any details. He had barely looked at it. He suspected that all over the world, people were probably glued to their TV screens. But his life in the past several hours had been consumed with thoughts of El Grupo breaking up, with the vulnerabilities of its various members and their families, including his own, and with ways of putting a stop to the threat from Lucien Mebarak.

He was irritated that he hadn't heard anything from Alex. That irritation was like an itch inside his mind, one that he couldn't scratch, and which was growing larger and more distracting all the time. Alex turned up when he turned up – often with perfect timing. But when he didn't turn up, he was impossible to reach.

"Yeah," Troy said. "I've seen it."

"More than 300 confirmed dead," Davidoff said. "Unknown number still under the rubble. Lucky that thousands were not killed. There have been many rescues from the upper floors. The building was shredded, but did not come all the way down. They say it was a fertilizer bomb, like the one used in Oklahoma City decades ago, only larger. Simple to make, simple to acquire materials, hard to detect. Simple to detonate. The Chinese say this suggests Americans were involved."

Troy shook his head. "Anybody can make a bomb like that. You don't have to be American. The IRA once blew the London financial district to smithereens with one."

Davidoff raised both hands, palms upward.

"The Chinese say what they say. The Americans say what they say. Of course, both are liars."

Troy said nothing to that.

"Discover the truth by comparing the lies," Davidoff said.

Troy nodded. "Okay."

"Politics is war by other means."

Troy nearly laughed. It must be Empty Platitude Night here at the tapas bar.

"The Chinese have rejected American assistance. They have issued a statement blaming America for fomenting unrest in Hong Kong, and for encouraging trouble between Taiwan and China. If the Americans did not build the bomb, or lend assistance to those who did, certainly they created the conditions for a bomb to be made. So goes their theory."

He had Troy's attention. The last thing anyone needed was a war between the US and China, if that's where these statements were leading. The last thing anyone needed to find out was that the US had its fingerprints on this bombing. Troy couldn't imagine anyone in American intelligence would be so stupid.

Well… he could imagine it.

"The Chinese will accept an emissary or… let's say an envoy… from Interpol. This is good. China is a member nation of Interpol, but has distanced itself in recent years."

Davidoff shook his head.

"What they will not accept is an agent. Nor an investigator."

He lifted the glass with the amber liquid at his elbow and took a long sip from it.

"An observer. That's what they will accept."

He took another sip, watching Troy over the rim of the glass.

"You."

Troy sipped his beer and smiled. He tapped his own chest.

"Me?"

Davidoff nodded. "Yes."

"It doesn't make sense," Troy said.

Davidoff raised his bushy eyebrows, but didn't respond.

"Do you know how much Mandarin I have?" Troy said, indicating the first of China's two major languages. *"Ni hao."*

"*Hello*," Davidoff said. "That's good for a start."

"Ni hway shuo yingyu ma?" Troy said

Davidoff laughed out loud. "*Does anyone here speak English?* Oh, that's very good. I predict you will make many lifetime friends over there. My confidence in your visit would be sky high, except that so few people in Hong Kong actually speak Mandarin."

Troy shook his head ruefully.

"You know how much Cantonese I have?" he said, indicating the second language of China, spoken through most of the south and by the locals in Hong Kong.

Davidoff waved in his own direction with one meaty hand. "Give it to me."

Troy shook his head. "None."

"It's a long flight," Davidoff said. "There is time to learn."

"I don't get it," Troy said. "Don't you guys have any China hands around? You know, somebody who was a diplomat in China, maybe speaks the languages a bit, knows the culture."

Davidoff stared into Troy's eyes. "Of course they do. But it doesn't matter who they have. They want you."

"Who does?"

"The General Secretariat of Interpol."

He said it matter-of-factly, as though it was self-evident.

"Why?"

Davidoff shrugged. "I don't know why. Many reasons, I can imagine. Simple reasons. Maybe the Americans put pressure to have you sent. That way they have somebody there, instead of nobody. They like you and trust you, and think you are a reliable instrument of their imperialist foreign policy. Your previous combat record suggests that you are. Also, maybe Interpol would like to get rid of you and send you to the other side of the world. Maybe they are tired of your American cowboy act. It works too well. It makes them look bad. Maybe they want to give you an assignment where you cannot succeed, where you will be ineffective. You see, it will not work to just murder your way through China, demanding answers from your victims before you..."

Davidoff waved a hand.

"Expire them. Execute them. Whatever you do to people whom you don't like. The Chinese will not allow it. Relationships are more complicated there. The Chinese will put you in a re-education camp. They will bury you under the camp. You will have to be patient and negotiate instead. Communicate."

The man was teasing him. Davidoff might be the first person with a sense of humor that Troy had met at Interpol. He must be Russian.

"In a language I don't speak or understand," Troy said.

Davidoff's boyish grin from before returned.

"I'm certain they will give you a good English speaker. But yes. Let's pretend the Americans want you there. And let's pretend Interpol wants to get rid of you. Let's even pretend they want to punish you. Of course, it's a punishment. The Chinese do not want you. You will be radioactive. Even if you could help them, they would not want your help. So off you go. Bye bye, little birdy."

Davidoff made a pantomime with his thick hands that indicated the two wings of a bird flying away. There was something oddly graceful about it.

"This is the assignment?" Troy said.

Davidoff sipped his drink again. He seemed to be enjoying himself.

"This is it."

"Are there any other possible assignments?"

Davidoff shrugged. "None that they told me about. I think it's this or leave the organization. I suspect they would prefer if you did leave."

Troy had to at least tell Davidoff what was on his mind.

"There is a man named Lucien Mebarak," he said.

"I read your files," Davidoff said. "I can tell you Mebarak is not the priority. He has connections to organized crime, but his whereabouts are unknown. There is an open case file. He will make a mistake one day. He will turn up somewhere, and there will be enough evidence to arrest him. Until then..."

Davidoff shrugged his big shoulders.

"So this is it," Troy said.

"Yes."

"When do you need to know?"

Davidoff looked surprised. "Know what?"

"Whether I'm going or not," Troy said.

"Now," Davidoff said. He frowned, almost comically, like a circus clown might. "Now would be good. Naturally. It's a pressing matter. Why delay?"

Troy sat and stared at Davidoff for a long moment. The sounds of the crowd in the bar seemed to press in on Troy again.

Why delay? It was a good question.

Because he had been hoping they would send him after Mebarak. Failing that, he was thinking about going after Mebarak himself.

Also, he wanted to speak with Alex before he did anything. Troy was worried about his family in New York. He was worried about Dubois and her mother. He wanted to help Miquel keep his job, if that was at all possible. The Albanian mafias were lurking in the back of his mind as well.

I killed Mateos Baruti. I helped destroy the Baruti Clan.

It gave him a sick feeling. Almost certainly, whatever was left of the Barutis, or their friends, were not behind Aliz's kidnapping. It was too soon. They hadn't begun to take their revenge yet. They were still licking their wounds. But they were going to come for him, and possibly all of El Grupo, at some point.

Troy had to call Missing Persons. Maybe going to China would keep him in Persons's good graces. Maybe American intelligence really did want him over there. Persons would know something like that.

But Troy had to guarantee his family's safety before he did anything. It was a troubling thought. He could spend the rest of his life trying to protect his mom and his brothers, and their wives, and their kids, from an attack that was unpredictable and might never happen.

"Treat it as a working holiday," Davidoff said.

"I'll go," Troy said.

Davidoff nodded. "Good."

He handed a business card across the table to Troy. "Call me sometimes and let me know what is happening. I am your boss, after all. I will need to make a report."

CHAPTER SEVEN

7:30 pm Eastern European Time (6:30 pm Central European Time)
Foinikion, Island of Carpathos
The Greek Islands
The Aegean Sea

"The project was a complete disaster."

Lucien Mebarak spoke slowly and carefully, trying to mask the full extent of his frustration. In fact, he was so frustrated that a person might say he was enraged.

The man in the mask nodded slowly. "I agree. I lost two good men. Two of my best. The plan was flawed from the beginning."

Lucien took a sip of his drink, a lovely cloudy white mix of ouzo and water. On the table in front of him was the bottle of ouzo, along with a large plate of very nice Greek *mezes*, including grilled octopus, cheeses, garlic bread and olives, not that his guest was going to sample any of it.

Two of Lucien's armed bodyguards stood nearby, close to the wide sliding glass doors of the house. One of the bodyguards in particular, Teodor, was a favorite – a man Lucien had trusted with many important tasks.

Lucien gazed out at the darkness. In the day, this patio overlooked the pale blue waters of the Aegean, though everything was black now, with just a few lights in the distance. The house was built on a rocky outcropping high above the water. It was designed to capture a sweeping southern exposure, facing down the coastline, but also out to sea, and to the west, as far as the eye could see.

From this spot, there was a wide staircase down to the pool deck. The pool was an infinity pool, by the light of day, made to trick the eye into thinking it was an extension of the sea itself. At night, the pool was lit from underneath by bright blue lights. The house, the setting, the cliffs, the ocean, all of it was beautiful.

Here at the top, Lucien had set a roaring and crackling fire in the large stone fire pit along the cliff's edge. It was a chilly night, but the fire gave off a lot of heat.

Lucien regarded his guest again.

The man called himself The Bishop, and he had come highly recommended as someone who could get things done. In this case, the thing Lucien needed was the creation of a decoy that would lead Troy Stark to his doom. In fact, the end result that Lucien needed was Troy Stark dead on the floor, with multiple holes in his head and body.

Not only had the operation failed spectacularly, it had backfired, and Luc's dear sister Aliz had been disappeared into some sort of shadowy American protection program. She was gone completely, taken by agents who had arrived on the scene soon after Stark had killed half of the men the Bishop had assigned to the job. No one seemed to have any idea where she was.

The mask The Bishop was wearing was more of a hood that covered his entire head and zipped down the back of his neck. The mask was white, and it depicted The Bishop as the grimacing face in a stage play. It had eye holes and a mouth hole cut out of it. The eye holes were dark.

The Bishop also wore a black jumpsuit with sleeves that came to his wrists. He wore black gloves on his hands. He wore heavy black boots on his feet.

The last time the Bishop was here, just a week ago, he had declined a drink. He had declined the offer of food. He had declined to shake hands. He declined any offer of hospitality or welcome from Lucien. This time around, Lucien didn't bother to offer anything, not even a handshake. He simply sipped his own ouzo and ate his own food.

The Bishop's act, which had seemed disturbing and even a little frightening the last time he was here, had worn thin. He was thought to be a very dangerous man, and he was obviously a paranoid one. But his performance – or better put – the performance of his men, had been abysmal. If this was the caliber of the people he had working for him, perhaps the Bishop was not someone worth worrying about. Stark had fallen from the sky and routed four men all by himself, even though the men were supposedly waiting for Stark to turn up.

"The plan was fine," Lucien said. "The execution of it was poor."

The Bishop's eyes flashed anger.

"The prisoner could not be harmed," he said. "That left the men with their hands tied. When the subject arrived, they had no leverage."

“The prisoner was my sister,” Lucien said simply.

The Bishop nodded. “Half-sister. Who you have resented your entire life. I know the story, and when first we talked, it seemed like you were willing to allow harm to come to her, if need be. Then you backed away from that idea, leaving the men exposed.”

The Bishop wasn’t doing himself any favors. Reminding Lucien Mebarak how much he knew about him was a dangerous activity. Arguing with Lucien Mebarak was equally dangerous. This was especially true after the Bishop had been revealed as less formidable than Lucien once supposed. The glow had come off the Bishop.

Lucien shook his head. “I love my sister, in my own way.”

“You should have decided that before the operation began.”

Lucien said nothing.

“Or picked another option,” the Bishop said.

“I don’t remember any other attractive options being presented.”

“His mother.”

“I told you before we began. I have a soft spot for mothers. My own mother was the light of my life for many years.”

Lucien sighed. He was going to have to find another way to get to Troy Stark, but probably without the help of the Bishop, or any outside organization. It was better to keep these sorts of activities within a closer network. Going forward, if he was to get Stark, he would have to do it with his own resources.

“I can tell that we do not see eye to eye,” the Bishop said.

Lucien nodded. "That's true. On this one thing, I think we can agree."

The Bishop shrugged. It looked somewhat odd for this wraith, this nightmare vision of a man, to make normal human gestures. The Bishop presented himself as a sort of demon. He would be better off if he acted like one.

“In that case, if you can pay me the remainder of my fee, I will be on my way. And I will hope we can find some way to work together again in the future.”

Lucien gave a small head shake.

“It was half up front, and half after the project was completed. The project wasn’t completed.”

“The project was completed,” the Bishop said. “The woman was taken prisoner. She was the perfect bait, and the subject came to rescue her, as predicted. He came in an unexpected way, and your stipulations made it impossible for the men to…”

"The project was not completed," Lucien said again.

How would it look if Lucien Mebarak paid the full amount for half-completed jobs?

The Bishop's voice began to rise.

"You caused the death of two of my men."

"Talk to Troy Stark about that," Lucien said.

He glanced at Teodor, but said nothing, and made no other sign. Instead, he reached out, and took a piece of cheese, a small slice of garlic bread, and an olive off the plate of mezes.

All the same, the Bishop caught the glance, turned and looked directly at Teodor. Teodor was not a tall man, and not physically imposing. If anything, the Bishop was much larger.

Teodor stood there, staring impassively, in a windbreaker jacket, jeans, and white sneakers. He made no movement that would cause anyone alarm.

The Bishop turned back to Lucien.

"I'm afraid I must insist."

Lucien was chewing the food. He shrugged and waved a hand as if dismissing the entire issue.

"Okay," he said. "Whatever you like. I see no reason to…"

The Bishop's entire body seemed to relax as soon as he knew he would be paid.

In the same instant, Teodor took three quick steps across the patio from where he had been standing. As if by magic, a pistol with a long silencer attached appeared in his hand. He stepped up to the Bishop.

The Bishop saw the movement from the corner of his eye. He turned to face Teodor, began to push himself out of the chair, and…

CLACK!

Teodor shot him in the middle of the forehead. A mist of blood sprayed out the back of the Bishop's head. The silencer made it sound like someone hit a single key on a typewriter.

Without another annoying word, the Bishop slumped back into his chair. His head dropped sideways and rested on his shoulder. You would almost say that he had fallen asleep in the chair. From beneath the bloodied mask, his half-open, heavily-lidded eyes seemed to stare across the table at Lucien.

Teodor stared down at the Bishop's lifeless form.

"What shall we do with him?"

"Take him out in the boat. Weight him down with chains and cement blocks, and drop him to the bottom of the sea."

Teodor nodded. "Of course."

"Thank you," Lucien said.

So that had settled everything. The Bishop was gone. There would be no more working with outsiders on this problem. Lucien and his people would take care of Troy Stark on their own. It would require some thought, but Lucien was good at thought.

Stark was vulnerable. There was no man in the world who didn't have his weak spots. For example, he seemed to have tender feelings for his partner, the French-African woman named Dubois. Lucien wouldn't put it past Stark if the man was playing with the hearts and bodies of both Aliz and Dubois at the same time.

And unlike Aliz, Dubois could be harmed. Lucien's men could harm her as much as they liked. She would amply deserve it for the things she had done to Lucien.

As Lucien watched, Teodor and the second guard gripped the Bishop under the arms and dragged him toward the stairs down to the water. They didn't bother to remove his mask. That was good. Who really cared who he was or what he looked like?

There was a puddle of blood on the stone patio where the Bishop had died.

Teodor was a good man. Lucien knew that when he was done with the body, he would make sure someone cleaned up the mess.

Lucien took a sip of his ouzo. It was making a warm fire in his belly, which he enjoyed. He reached out to the plate to take another finger sandwich.

To his left, Teodor and the other bodyguard brought the Bishop to the lip of the steep staircase, and pushed him over the edge. The Bishop's body disappeared on its way down to the pool level. Lucien caught a last flop of the Bishop's arm before he was gone.

Lucien approved of this method. It was easier and quicker to roll the Bishop down the stairs than it was to carry him. And it showed him less respect. This was all very good.

As long as someone cleaned up afterwards.

CHAPTER EIGHT

7:45 pm Central European Time (1:45 pm Eastern Standard Time)
A flat
Neighborhood of La Latina
Madrid, Spain

"China," Missing Persons said.

There was something surreal about talking to him on the phone. It was like Troy had been adrift at sea without a lifeline, and now here it was. Alex was still nowhere to be found, but Persons was better. In a sense, when Alex talked, he was just the mouthpiece for Persons. It might as well go right to the heart of the matter.

It was somewhat surprising that Persons even took this call.

"Yeah," Troy said. "I just found out a little while ago."

Troy was sitting on the edge of his bed. His half-packed bag was at his feet. He was going to the other side of the world. He didn't know for how long. He was still debating what to bring. Weapons weren't going to happen. They were bringing him over as an observer, not as a special operator or even law enforcement.

So far, his luggage consisted of a couple of suits, jeans, dress shirts, a pair of nice shoes, and a pair of sneakers. The rest he could probably pick up as he went along.

"It's good," Persons said. "We can use someone like you over there. Friends of ours aren't getting anything from the Chinese. The Chinese are keeping us in the dark, and deliberately so."

"Do we know anything?"

"Only what we read in the Chinese newspapers. And that's what they want us to read. It's a blackout. They're talking about expelling our diplomatic corps. The Secretary of State is over there right now for a grand opening of the newest tallest building on Earth, slated a few days from now. No one's even sure the Chinese are going to let him stay for it, or if that ribbon cutting is even going to happen now. They're talking a good game, that they won't bow down to terrorism, but it wouldn't surprise me if the thing gets canceled."

“What is it?” Troy said. “The tallest building?”

“Yes,” Persons said. “The tallest building in the world just sprouted up in Hong Kong. The Golden Dragon Peace Tower. You know these East Asian and Gulf Arab countries. They’re always trying to open the newest tallest building in the world, as if that makes a statement, or means something.”

“Didn’t we used to do that?” Troy said. “The Empire State Building, the World Trade Center.”

“We did,” Persons said. “But in those days, it really did mean something.”

“And they’re going to cancel the opening?”

“I don’t know,” Persons said. “It’s probably beside the point. There’s been a terror attack. That’s the issue. Now the Chinese are making runs at Taipei with fully-armed supersonic fighter planes, then pulling back at the last second. The Taiwanese are in a constant state of high alert. The chances of a miscalculation by someone are growing all the time.”

“Any word through backdoor channels?” Troy said. He was playing along, as if Persons would divulge anything to him about backdoor intelligence channels.

“Did you hear me?” Persons said. “I said Lloyd Garelli, the Secretary of State of the United States, is in China at this moment. He went for the building dedication, but no one there is talking to him. If anything, they’re ignoring him. A paranoid type might suspect this whole thing took place to kill off the good diplomatic vibes that were starting to unfold.”

Troy thought of the cheesy, grinning, gland-handing lightweight that currently occupied the office of the Secretary of State. The guy had been governor somewhere. He was the heir to a mustard fortune. He’d been in a secret society at Yale, maybe at the same time as the president.

Troy was surprised at himself, and at how much he knew about Lloyd Garelli. Usually, he knew next to nothing about politicians.

It was the ads on TV. They were clever. They became stuck in your head. And they lodged the man firmly in your mind.

Garelli’s Spicy Hot Mustard! Now that’s what I call a HOT DOG!

They probably sold a lot of mustard, too. And it was good mustard. Troy could admit that. The best thing about Lloyd Garelli was the mustard recipe his great-grandfather had invented.

“I don’t think Garelli was the kind of backdoor channel I was thinking about,” Troy said. “I’m sure you know that.”

To Troy’s mind, American military intelligence and Chinese military intelligence must be in conversation all the time. An End of Days style war was always a possibility when the major players were involved. Anything could start it, a small misunderstanding of intentions, and the best way to forestall something like that was by talking.

“Nothing,” Persons said. “Communications are closed. Maybe you can crack that nut open a little bit.”

Troy shook his head. “I doubt it. But I’ll try.”

“Try to sound a little more confident. That might help.”

“It’s been a long week,” Troy said. “There’s been a lot of heavy lifting on this end. Now I’m going to Hong Kong. I don’t speak the lingo and know next to nothing about the culture.”

“That never stopped you before,” Persons said.

“Thanks.”

Troy said it flat, trying to give Persons a sense of what this really felt like. A few days ago, he had been in Albania in mortal combat with a human trafficking gang. Then Aliz was taken hostage. Then Troy dropped out of the sky to rescue her, and she was mad at him instead of at the kidnappers. Meanwhile, El Grupo had been disbanded and scattered to the winds, Dubois was gone, and Troy had no idea what kind of danger was brewing.

Now, he was off to China in a few hours.

“When’s your flight?” Persons said.

“Midnight,” Troy said. “12:05 am.”

“Direct?”

"Yeah. Fourteen hours in the air. By the time I get there…" Troy wasn't even sure, with the long flight and the time change, when he would arrive.

"It'll be nine o'clock tomorrow night, their time," Persons said, doing the math for him. "That's okay. They won't have solved this by then. World War Three probably won't have started yet. They'll give you some kind of minder or escort to take you around. Here's what you need to know. In China, the names are reversed. The first name is actually the last name or surname, and vice versa."

Troy shook his head. He already knew that much.

He gazed up at the ceiling. He had decided. Whatever happened with El Grupo, or with Interpol, he was going to keep this apartment and live here in Madrid. The world could go ahead and…

"So if they give you a handler named Troy Stark, he will present it as Stark Troy."

"I know," Troy said.

"Yeah, but listen. The names have meaning. Troy Stark doesn't really mean anything, but Stark Troy will mean something. Both names will mean something individually, and they will often add up to something together."

"Is that going to help me?"

"It'll endear you to the guy. Ask him what his name means."

Troy was silent.

"Also, if he is Stark Troy, call him Mr. Stark. Don't call him Troy. That's disrespectful, unless he invites you to do that. You don't just call someone you don't know by their given name. And definitely don't call him Stark. It's Mr. Stark. Also, if someone hands you their business card, treat it like it's made out of glass. With inscriptions etched in gold. Hold it in both hands and stare at it for a while. It's the person's job, practically their whole life, and they're proud of it. This is a big thing there. Don't just take the card and stick it in your pocket. That's insulting."

There was a pause over the line.

"You should write this stuff down," Persons said. "You're liable to forget it."

Troy didn't move from the bed. He made no effort to get a pen or a piece of paper.

"Okay."

Persons waited a beat. "Ready?"

"Yeah."

Persons plunged on. "Avoid direct eye contact when you can. Don't stare at people. It's intimidating. It's taken as a challenge, and you're likely to have it blow back at you."

"Like with a dog," Troy said.

Persons ignored that. "The oldest person in any group usually has the seniority, and therefore the authority. That person gets more respect. Deference, even. It's probably a man. Let him make any necessary introductions. Careful when you shake hands with him, though, and really with anyone. They give the dead fish handshake over there. They barely grip at all. So be mindful of that. I've noticed you tend to crush people's hands when you meet them. This isn't a contest of who has the strongest hand."

Troy shook his head. He looked up at the ceiling again. But there were no answers on the ceiling.

"Loss of face is a major problem. Respect and honor are everything. It could take you months to grasp all the ins and outs of that. So I'll just leave it at this: try not to offend anyone. You're a big, strong guy. That's enough. More than enough. Don't throw your weight around. Don't talk too much. In fact, say and do as little as possible. You're there to observe and pick up whatever information you can."

Troy said nothing. How did Persons know what Troy was there to do?

Easy answer: he didn't.

"Stark?"

"Can you imagine?" Troy said. "They're sending me, and these are the 11th hour cultural lessons I'm getting, not even from Interpol, but from you. It would be funny if I wasn't the one doing it."

"Okay, but think for a minute why Interpol might be sending you."

Why? Because I'm the best man for the job?

Not likely.

"Think for a minute..." Troy said.

Persons cut him off. "I don't mean think about it now. You've got all this time coming up in the airport and on the plane. If you think about things a little, it should become clear to you. But we're not going to talk about it, not now, probably not ever. So don't bother to bring it up."

Troy held the phone away from his face and stared at it.

What is he saying?

Persons was so accustomed to speaking in riddles, that not only would someone eavesdropping not understand him, the person he was talking to didn't understand him either.

"I got real problems, Colonel," Troy said, changing the subject. China was already wearing thin. He wanted to talk about the more important thing.

"I got this guy I have to deal with. He's hanging around out there, and he's trouble."

"I know about your problem," Persons said. "For the time being, you let me worry about it. Your family will be okay. I promise you that. It isn't always visible, but there's always someone watching. I called in markers to make this happen."

Troy breathed deeply. It felt good to hear him say it.

"What about my partners over here?"

"We're doing what we can. Our reach is a little more limited over there."

"And his reach is longer, and better," Troy said.

An image came to him of Dubois, a big gun in her tiny hand, holed up in a one-bedroom Paris apartment with her mother.

Stay away from the windows.

"Hang tough," Persons said. "Go do this, and do a good job. Put the other thing out of your mind. We're looking for the man in question. When we find him, you'll be the first to know. Then we can take care of everything. We'll put it to bed. I also promise that."

Was he talking about assassinating Mebarak? Arresting him? That wasn't clear. But knowing Missing Persons…

"Good," Troy said. "Because I don't like loose ends like this. Alex was supposed to…"

"Alex got called away abruptly," Persons said, instantly cutting off any talk about Alex.

"Where did he go?" Troy said.

"See if you can guess."

There was another long silence over the phone. Troy could hear Persons breathing.

"Look Stark, I have to run. Meetings, you know how it is."

"I know. You probably have the President waiting in the narrow hallway outside your door. Behind some of those boxes."

Persons laughed.

"That's the spirit, kid. Keep your chin up."

And just like that, the line went dead.

***

"Where did you say you're going?"

Troy shook his head and checked his watch. It was getting late. He had to leave for the airport soon. Talking to his mom was always like this.

"Hong Kong," he said slowly.

"Why are you going there? They just had an explosion there."

"I know. That's why I'm going. Because they had an explosion."

"But why you? Because you know about bombs?"

That would be a good tack to take, maybe. But Troy decided to stay with the whole international medical organization story he'd been trying to convince her of for months.

"People were hurt, Ma. People were killed. I work for the federal government. It's foreign medical aid. So they're sending me to…"

"I thought you were becoming some kind of policeman. You were in the Navy for years, and that was fine. I don't really get why you left. Then you worked for the police for like a week. I don't know what happened to that, either. You know, I saw you on the TV the other day at the hearing you went to in Washington, and they were accusing you of all kinds of horrible things. It was on C-SPAN."

"I know, Ma. I was there."

"I know you were there. I just said you were there. Your denials were…"

Troy sighed. "Anyway, I'm going to Hong Kong."

"Hard to believe, let's say. Does our government really do these things? Assassinations in Mexico? Drug dealing? Robberies of drug lords?"

Troy shook his head. He wished this was a perfect world, and it wasn't one, not by a long shot. Failing that, he would prefer his mother not have to think about black operations units sending murder and kidnapping squads to Latin America. And he'd really prefer if his mother didn't have to think that her son played some part in that.

I didn't. I got tangled up with Enrico that one time.

Explain that to her, though.

"I don't know, Ma. I don't work for that section of the government."

"No one at the hearing said a word about you working for the federal government at all. They didn't seem to know what you're doing now."

"Mom, it doesn't really matter what they said. It was a kangaroo court, and they were making things up for the TV cameras. I just went there because…"

"You know, because I worry," she said.

Here it comes again.

He didn't know why he played along with this. But he did. It was like a raging whitewater river; he got caught in it, and then he got swept along over the rocks.

It was afternoon in New York. He pictured her sitting in her living room chair, the TV silently playing a news station across from her. Or maybe even re-running his Senate testimony. He pictured cops sent by Colonel Persons sitting in a car somewhere nearby, watching the house. They'd better be there. God help them all if they weren't.

"Everything is fine," he said. "What are you worried about?"

"You," she said. "Remember when you got the job with the police department? Why didn't you just keep that job? Your brothers work for the police. It's a good job. You get a pension at the end of it. At your age, you could retire in your early 50s. That's not bad."

"I told you, Mom. Something better came along."

"But I don't understand what that is. You never explain it to me."

"No, I've actually explained it to you again and again. I work for the federal government. It's a charitable arm of the government."

As soon as he said *charitable,* he knew it was wrong. That always seemed to set off alarm bells in her mind. It made her think he was doing volunteer work.

"We do medical…" Troy began.

"But what are you doing for money?" she said. "That's my question."

"They pay me money, Ma. A lot of money. The money I'm making now… I've never made this much money before in my life."

He reflected on the truth of that statement. He was getting paid by Interpol, and by Missing Persons's bogus international charity. Persons had even given him a bonus, over and above everything else.

Aliz had also given him cash from time to time. That would stop now, which was probably for the best. But Troy was working hard. And for the first time in his life, the money was piling up. He was beginning to understand now how, sometimes, spies got rich.

"You just said it's a charity."

Troy rolled his eyes. "I misspoke. It's the government. They do medical work on behalf of other countries. Call it foreign aid. It's not really a charity."

"But why send you? You're not even a doctor."

"Mom, I have to run. I'll be on the plane for about 14 hours. I'm not sure how long I'll be over there. It could be a while. I'll call you when I can."

"You're not a doctor, though."

She was doubling down on the doctor's idea. Maybe she could trap him with that.

"I'm going there to assess the situation, not to treat the wounded. The Chinese have plenty of doctors."

“I’m surprised they even have electricity. They’re supposed to be behind us. It wasn’t that long ago, we thought of China as a backwater, didn’t we?”

“Anyway,” Troy said.

“Anyway, I’m proud of you, Troy. I’m proud that they’re sending you.”

She was capable of that, too. It wasn’t often, but she could suddenly surprise you with something endearing, even touching.

“Thanks, mom.”

“You’re my youngest son, my baby, and I love you whatever you decide to do.”

“Even if you don’t know what it is,” he said, and smiled.

“That’s right.”

“Okay, Ma. I’ll talk to you soon.”

“Have a safe trip,” she said. “Wherever you’re going.”

CHAPTER NINE

January 20
9:15 pm Hong Kong Time
Hong Kong / Chek Lap Kok International Airport
Hong Kong Special Administrative Region
China

"Checked baggage, sir?"

Troy shook his head. The baggage claim area was closed. People with checked bags had to retrieve them by the side of the plane. Troy had a garment bag over one shoulder and a small leather overnight bag hanging from the other shoulder. This was all he had brought.

"Enjoy your stay."

Troy was wearing a leather jacket over a t-shirt, jeans, and boots. When he stepped across the threshold from the giant Cathay Pacific Boeing 777 airplane into the closed environment of the passenger ramp, he got a momentary sense of the warm air outside.

It had been cold in Madrid. It was cold on the plane. It wasn't cold here.

Fourteen hours in the air was mercilessly long. He felt like he'd been bludgeoned. Three full meals had been served. Ten full beers had been drunk. There were dozens and dozens of movies available on the screen in front of him, but not much to his liking. He wasn't a movie watcher. He would start a movie, watch it for 20 minutes, then start a different one. This went on for hours.

He had no team now. He had no information available to him. He had simply flown here on the orders of someone he'd barely met before. No Bakker, no Dubois, no Miquel. He was entirely unprepared. Even Carlo Gallo brought something to the table - a capacity for violence that was almost the match of Troy's, and an arch sense of humor, at least. Troy was here, on his own, with no one to work with and no one to back him up.

It was a dreary state of affairs.

He stepped along the tunnel, his head feeling like it wasn't quite attached to the rest of his body. His legs were far away, doing their own thing, carrying him along, but if they suddenly decided to do something else, he wasn't sure he'd be able to stop them.

At the top of the ramp, near the closed check-in desk, a group of five men in dark suits were waiting. One of the men held up a handwritten sign in red block letters. MR. STARK.

There was almost no one else around.

There had hardly been anyone on the plane. It was somewhat surprising they had flown the behemoth at all. He'd asked his British flight attendant about it. She told him Hong Kong was in lockdown. It was a restricted zone now. The only people allowed in were necessary personnel and people who lived there. No one was allowed out. For the time being, everyone was a suspect. There was no telling when this period would be over.

Apparently, the Chinese government wanted to get to the bottom of things, and the way to do that was to keep everyone who was in town when the attack occurred right where they were. You can't escape if you can't leave. People were trapped in the city. A dozen nations had already lodged formal complaints with the United Nations.

"Well, they can't arrest everyone," Troy had said.

The flight attendant offered a pained smile, but no response.

He reflected that if they were letting him in, he must qualify as necessary personnel. That was a nice feeling. He was one of the good guys, flying in to help out. He couldn't really be a suspect because he was somewhere else when the attack took place.

Everyone is a suspect. The United States is a suspect.

"But not me," he said under his breath.

One of the men stepped up to Troy. He was the smallest of them, and they were not a tall group to begin with. Troy stood a full head taller than the man who approached. The man appeared to be the oldest. He had hair spotted with gray, and crow's feet wrinkles around his eyes. If what Missing Persons had said held true, that should indicate he was on the one in charge.

"Mr. Stark?"

Troy nodded. "Yes."

The man held out his hand. Troy took it, but didn't squeeze. The two hands limply touched, as if neither one had bones or muscles or cartilage in them, as if they were simply hanging bags of meat.

"I am Mr. Wei."

"Nice to meet you," Troy said.

"Step this way, please," Mr. Wei said. He gestured with his arm.

Perhaps it was not nice to meet Troy Stark. Troy glanced at the other men in dark suits. To Troy, their faces were nearly identical – stone-faced and expressionless. There were no guns in evidence, but Troy guessed the men were carrying them. They were cops, right?

It occurred to Troy that he didn't know what they were. He was flying so blind, he didn't even know who was supposed to meet him here. Whoever they were, they didn't bother speaking to him. They didn't ask him how his flight was. They didn't offer him a glass of iced tea. They made zero effort at hospitality.

The group walked down the wide concourse, the men flanking Troy on either side, Mr. Wei in the lead. The terminal was brightly lit, super modern, gleaming and new, with steel arches like an abstract work of art soaring high into the cavernous space, glass walls three stories tall giving nearly 360-degree views of the runways surrounding them. The runways were visible, flanked by red lights, but mostly the airplanes were parked in rows at the terminal gates.

The place was deserted, like a ghost town. Neon signs advertised various shops and restaurants, all empty or nearly so, and digital overhead boards displayed arrival and departure information. Troy glanced up at one of the departure boards. All of the flights were marked CANCELED.

No one was getting out.

Troy hadn't been to Hong Kong in a long time. If nothing else, it was a beautiful airport. The group passed under a string of lights two stories above them, sort of like a chandelier, and sort of like a crystal waterfall hanging down.

There was a constant underlying hum - of electricity maybe, or perhaps machinery - that he couldn't place. The emptiness made the sound apparent, when normally the buzz of conversation and rolling suitcases, and clicking heels on the polished floor would cover it up.

A calm, robotic female voice made an announcement in several languages, the voice echoing up and down the terminal. Troy didn't listen to the English version.

The men walked him to a narrow hallway off the main concourse. The group passed along the hall, the ceiling just above their heads now. Just a group of guys – outside of Mr. Wei, no one had been introduced. At the end of the hall was a door. One of the men flashed a white card at a black panel mounted by the side of it, a light flashed green, and he opened it.

The entire group passed through, Troy at its center.

The door to the room shut and clicked, seeming to lock automatically behind them. It was just a nondescript, empty room with a long wooden bench hanging from one wall. There was a table made of green metal along another wall. The room was outdated and barren compared to the magical, modern airport on the other side of that door.

"Please disrobe," Mr. Wei said.

Troy turned to him.

The man nodded, but did not look directly into Troy's eyes. "Yes."

Troy placed his bags on the floor. One of the men immediately picked them both up and carried them over to the green table. Another man joined him, and they unceremoniously opened the bags and began to remove their contents. Troy wasn't surprised by this, so he barely glanced at them. The *please disrobe* part, though. He hadn't been expecting that.

"Come again?" he said.

Mr. Wei gestured with his head toward the bench.

"Your clothes. Please remove to the underwear."

"Is this part of Customs?" Troy said.

A different man spoke up, in perfect English.

"There won't be Customs or passport control. You are our honored guest, so you are being moved on a fast track. But we must verify that you are carrying no weapons on your person, and have no listening devices or other equipment that might suggest…"

The man trailed off.

"Spying?" Troy said, trying to be helpful.

The man shrugged. "If you like."

"So I'm an honored guest, who you don't trust at all."

"You are an unknown quantity," the man said. "How can we trust you? We declined American participation. So the Europeans send an American."

"Highly suspect," Troy said.

The man smiled, a thin slice of a smile. "It is said that Europe is only an arm of America."

Troy looked across at the group of them, facing him in a line now.

"You guys want to show me your business cards?" he said. "Maybe that will get us off on the right foot. You know, break the ice a little. Trust is earned, I get that. I'll hold the cards with both hands while I look at them."

No one responded. The three men, the ones who weren't quietly and methodically and systematically going through his bags, simply stood and stared and waited for him to take off his clothes.

"This is an auspicious beginning to what I hope will be a fruitful relationship," Troy said as he took his jacket off. He looked back at the men again.

Dead silence now. Eyes staring at his legs. No smiles, or hints of any.

Maybe they just didn't get sarcasm. It was hard to catch things like that in a language that wasn't your mother tongue. Nuance. Nuance was tough. Troy knew that already, but sometimes he allowed himself to forget it.

Don't talk too much. Say and do as little as possible.

That's what Persons had told him. Maybe it was good advice.

Troy sat down on the bench and removed his shoes. Then he unbuttoned his dress shirt and took that off. He took everything off, right down to his boxer briefs. He was wearing a pair of ridiculous green Christmas-themed briefs that were covered in candy canes and snowmen and reindeer. He'd been busy recently and didn't have a lot of clean laundry.

As he undressed, he handed the articles of clothing to the men, each one pawing through his pockets, feeling the linings of his leather jacket and his jeans, looking for hidden compartments in his shoes. They found nothing, of course – no weapons, no wires, no nada.

He stood and held his arms out wide. He wasn't going to let this go much further. The culture was supposed to be about respect, but they weren't respecting Troy. In another minute, he was probably going to find himself right back on the next plane to Madrid. That seemed fine. What could he possibly do here? He was a stranger, an interloper, possibly even the enemy. They didn't want him in Hong Kong.

There are no planes back to Madrid.

Troy sighed.

"Socks, please," Mr. Wei said.

Troy looked down at the black ankle socks on his large feet. Across the toes of each one was a white, leaping jungle cat.

"They're small socks," Troy said.

The man nodded. "Please. As you must understand, we all have our orders. Even you, I assume. You have your orders."

"My orders are to cooperate with your investigation and your requests."

Mr. Wei nodded again. “Please, in that case.”

A moment later, Troy stood barefoot in the middle of the room, his toes on the cold floor, the men standing around him. They eyed his tall, muscular body, riddled with scars, and in a few cases, bullet holes. A few of the holes were very fresh, red and raw.

Their faces remained expressionless, only a flicker in their eyes here and there betraying that they had any thoughts about him.

“You guys want to do a cavity search?” Troy said.

One of the men smiled at that. “As we understand, you are a policeman. You work for Interpol. Surely not an investigator? Surely not… a desk jockey?”

The man seemed to wrestle with the term. But when he said it, the rest of the men laughed.

Troy had no idea what they really knew about him or didn’t know. Maybe they were just being coy. Maybe they had seen all of his files, including the classified stuff. Or maybe all they’d seen was his top sheet – name, title and department, nationality, date of birth.

“I was a soldier before I joined the police.”

“Ah. The Americans fight many wars. The Chinese are friends to all nations.”

Troy shrugged. “I guess that’s why someone blew up your building. That’s what friends are for.”

Stop. Just stop talking.

Mr. Wei gestured at Troy’s clothes draped on the bench. “Please get dressed,” he said, and the group of men all stepped out of the room in unison, almost as though a secret signal had just been given.

Troy looked at the table. His bags were closed up tight again, as if they had never been opened. Maybe they had put everything back the way they’d found it. Or maybe they had stuffed it all in willy-nilly. Maybe they had even pocketed a few things. Troy was very tired, hadn’t been watching them closely, and wouldn’t put it past them. But he was so tired that he didn’t really care.

Slowly, he put his clothes back on. He ran his fingers through his hair as a final touch, but there was no mirror in this room to check his look.

***

“Where to now?” Troy said.

The five men solemnly escorted him through the airport to the exit.

There was almost no one in the terminal. Troy's plane had a capacity for something like 400 passengers. If 40 people had gotten off that plane, he'd be surprised. Those passengers all seemed to be gone now, swallowed by this enormous empty airport.

A sleek black car waited at the curb. A man stood in front of it. He wore a dark blue suit like the men with Troy, but his tie was pale blue, creating a nice contrast. He was a put-together dude with a chiseled face, broad shoulders, and he was taller than the others. His suit was tailored closely to his body. He looked as if he might have played a contact sport at one time. He was handsome, almost like a TV or movie actor. It was hard to put an age on him. His hair was dark, his face was unlined, and he looked like he had never shaved before. But his eyes showed the confidence that comes with experience.

Troy guessed he was in his late 30s.

"Mr. Troy Stark," Mr. Wei said. "This is Mr. Zhao Fu, with the Ministry of State Security. This organization is like your American FBI."

Troy nodded. "I know what it is."

The Ministry of State Security was kind of like the FBI. But it was also like the CIA and the KGB and the dystopian novel *1984* all rolled into one. If you were a person who found yourself disappeared for an extended period of time, and then you suddenly reappeared and began making abject public apologies for your behavior, chances were good you had been in the loving hands of the Ministry of State Security.

"Mr. Zhao will be your host during your time here. If you have any questions about the situation in Hong Kong, or the crime that was committed, he will be your source of information."

"Welcome," Zhao said. He held out a hand for a shake.

Like the others, he didn't smile. His eyes were flat and expressionless. He didn't seem hostile, exactly, but he didn't seem like something other than hostile, either. Then again, he was the first person who had offered a welcome.

Troy extended the dead fish hand for the man to barely make contact with. The man gripped it firmly and squeezed it hard, like an American might do. It happened before Troy was ready, and he had no time to squeeze it back.

It's not a contest of who has the strongest hand.

"Thank you, Mr…"

Troy had a bad moment. He hesitated. He almost said Mr. Fu.

The exhaustion was setting in. He had just gotten off the plane. It had been a long week. The guy's last name, which came first in China, was…

"Mr. Zhao," the man.

Troy grinned. "Mr. Zhao. Thank you."

He turned to thank the other men, but their backs were to him, and they were already going inside the airport without another word.

"Who are those guys?" Troy said.

"Airport security team," Zhao said. "Not terminal guards. Top level security. Threat assessment. Planning."

Troy turned back to Zhao. The man had opened the car door and popped the trunk. He gestured at the open trunk and then at the passenger seat.

"Shall we go?"

Troy nodded. "Gladly."

He put his bags in the trunk, slammed it, then slid into the passenger seat. Zhao had already gone around to the driver's seat. The steering wheel was on the right-hand side. The city was a British colony through the dawn of automobiles all the way up until 1997. People here drove on the left side of the road, like they did in England.

Zhao pulled out into the roadway and headed for the airport exit. There was no traffic. Troy sank back into the seat and leaned his head against the headrest. He breathed deeply. He could go to sleep right here.

Zhao patted the dashboard.

"Fully electric vehicle," he said. "Chinese design and manufacture. Very advanced technology. It's a beautiful car. They put the prototype on the streets of Hong Kong for testing. We're fortunate to have one."

Troy didn't care about the car. Electric vehicles were a dime a dozen as far as he was concerned. The point was supposedly to save the environment by running cars on electricity. If so, the whole idea fell apart when most of the electricity was generated by coal, like it was in China. But that was an argument for another time. He had just met this man. They might as well try to get off to a better start than he had with the airport squad.

"What does it mean?" Troy said.

Zhao was watching the roadway. He made a face that said he was puzzled. His English seemed exceptional. But maybe something had been lost in translation.

"What does what mean? Electric vehicle?"

Troy shook his head slowly. "No. Your name. Zhao Fu. What does it mean?"

"What does your name mean?" Zhao said.

"Nothing," Troy said. "Our names don't mean anything. But Chinese names mean things. So I'm asking you, out of curiosity, what your name means."

Troy watched as outside the windshield, the car approached a gate. Zhao slowed the car, paused, and the gate went up, allowing them through. They were out of the airport. A moment later, he was accelerating and merging onto an empty highway.

Troy had to admit the car had pretty good zip. He supposed that was the deal nowadays. Electric cars were getting better and better.

"I want to tell you something," Zhao said.

"Tell away."

"We are not friends. I didn't choose this task of shepherding you around Hong Kong. It was handed to me, and I had no choice but to accept it. No one expects this relationship, or this fact-finding mission of yours, to bear fruit. For me, it's more of a punishment than an honor."

Yeah, but Persons said the name thing would...

Troy nodded. "Same. I didn't ask for this. You think I wanted to fly to the other side of the world to hang around with people who don't want me here? Guess again. They sent me here to get rid of me."

Troy paused. Maybe he was saying too much again. But it felt good to let this guy know he didn't have the market cornered on being annoyed. At least Zhao hadn't spent three hours in an airport and 14 hours on a plane.

"Do you want to go straight to your hotel?" Zhao said. "Or would you prefer to go to a bar for a couple of drinks?"

"Are those the options they told you to give me?"

Zhao nodded. He still didn't take his eyes off the road. "Yes."

"Is that how we're supposed to build a relationship?" Troy said. "By drinking?"

"It's been done that way before. We can tell stories of the punishments that brought us to this shared fate."

Troy stared at the roadway. The car was zooming along through a sort of concrete canyon. There were massive sound barriers on either side of the 10-lane highway. A handful of other cars were out here with Zhao's exciting prototype.

“I’d prefer to go to the site of the disaster,” Troy said. “I want to see it with my own eyes. Can we do that? Can we go to the bombing site?”

Zhao shrugged. "There's no reason why we can't. I have the right credentials to enter the area. I've been there twice so far. I have to warn you, though. It is horrifying to look upon. If I take you there, don’t blame me for the negative feelings you will experience.”

Troy didn't answer for a moment. Did the man think Troy was going to fly all this way and NOT go to the bombing site?

“I don’t mind a little carnage,” Troy said. “I’ve seen similar things before.”

Zhao shook his head. “Not like this.”

Troy played along. He might be getting somewhere with Zhao. Maybe they were kindred spirits, and that’s how they ended up in this boat together. He wasn’t sure, but now was no time to ruin it by arguing.

“That may be. But I still want to see it.”

Zhao nodded. “Okay. We’ll go. Very good. Commendable commitment to duty. But we can only look. I must insist that you take no photographs or video. Images of the scene are tightly controlled. It’s too devastating to be viewed widely at this moment.”

Troy was okay with that. “Understood.”

They drove on in silence for a long while. The airport was well outside of the city center.

“What did you do?” Troy said. “That they punished you like this, and stuck you with me?”

Zhao frowned. “It isn’t what I did exactly. It’s more who I am, or what I am.”

“What are you?”

“In the opinion of my superiors, I’m too individualistic,” Zhao said. “I think for myself too much. Too many times, I have acted without consulting those around me. I don’t always follow the proper protocols. I don’t always ask for permission, though I am trying to get better about this. In the past, I have valued results over respect for seniority or hierarchy. This can be bad for a younger officer."

“I doubt being with me is going to help you fix these problems,” Troy said.

Zhao shook his head. “I doubt it, too. The truth is, I am being given an American to witness how not to behave.”

Troy nearly laughed.

Zhao smiled. It was there and then gone a second later. But it was there.

"What did you do?" Zhao said. "To be punished in this way?"

Troy looked out the side window at the passing roadway.

"Oh," he said. "I killed a bunch of guys."

Zhao looked at him. His eyes widened.

"Don't worry," Troy said. "They were Albanians."

CHAPTER TEN

10:35 pm Hong Kong Time
BCHB (The Beijing Chonqing Hong Kong Bank) Headquarters
Near Statue Square
City of Hong Kong
China

"Brutal," Troy said.

Troy and Zhao stood on a concrete plaza overlooking the ruins of the bank building. They wore N95 masks and welding goggles over their eyes. The mask made it hard to breathe. The goggles kept fogging up, making it hard to see.

Troy was trying to absorb the enormity of the disaster. It was all around him, a total sensory immersion.

This wasn't a crime. This was an act of war.

Below, and rising into the sky directly across from them, was the destroyed skyscraper. It stood as a hollowed-out shell. The center of the building, where the truck bomb must have been parked, was reduced to a giant pile of rubble, with jagged edges and pieces of masonry and twisted metal beams jutting out at odd angles.

The remaining structure continued to stand, charred and blackened to 20 stories high, the windows blown out, the interior shredded like paper, and the steel frame like a skeleton holding it up on either side. Above 20 stories, the upper floors and the roof were sagging, apparently ready to collapse and drive downward. Troy could picture the momentum, acceleration, and sheer force it would create when it finally dropped.

Beyond the wreckage was the skyline of downtown Hong Kong and, beyond that, the sweep of the waterfront. But the immediacy of what was in front of Troy made the rest of the city seem to fade into insignificance.

The air was thick with the acrid smell of smoke and burning debris. The stench somehow penetrated Troy's mask and filled his nostrils. The taste of ash and smoke seemed to coat his tongue. The heat from fires still burning beneath the rubble radiated off of the ruins, making the humid night feel ever thicker and heavier.

Giant bright klieg lamps cast a harsh glare on the ravaged building, exposing every cracked and crumbling wall, every piece of debris scattered on the ground. They bathed the scene in an unnatural brightness, making everything appear stark and surreal. The intensity of the light also caused a slight burning sensation in Troy's eyes.

Beneath the glare of the lamps, rescue workers clad in heavy gear and masks dug slowly through the piles of rubble and debris, their flashlights casting small beams in the dark crevices. The workers were covered in gray dust, their orange vests standing in contrast against the landscape of destruction.

The glow from the fires beneath the rubble radiated an eerie red-orange light that flickered through the haze of smoke and debris. It gave an otherworldly feel to the hellish scene.

Suddenly, the building made creaking and groaning noises, as if it was still alive and in pain. An alarm sounded, like an air raid signal, and then the men in their heavy gear were stumbling down the mountain of rubble and running away from the building. A landslide of falling debris broke the eerie silence, tumbling down from the upper floors. There was a crash and a clatter of metal and stone, and a cloud of smoke rose, obscuring the entire site.

"There's so much rage in my country now," Zhao said. "So much rage because of this."

Helicopters loomed in the sky above their heads, the sleek metal bodies a stark contrast against the gray and white smoke that billowed beneath them. The light from the fires beneath the rubble, and the lights illuminating the destruction, glinted off the metallic bodies of the choppers, making them look like dark insects against the sprawling cityscape. Troy could hear the THUMP of their rotors, and he imagined that he could almost feel it from the ground.

If he were someone people here knew and trusted, he would tell them to move those choppers a mile away. The beating of their rotors alone, the vibration of it, could cause a building in this weakened condition to collapse. But no one was going to listen to him.

"Have you ever seen anything like this?" Zhao said.

For a moment, Troy was transported to another place, and another time, years before.

"Stark," someone behind him whispered fiercely.

"Yeah." His own voice was calm.

"Do you see the building across the street?"

Troy scanned the street to his left. Much of it was completely destroyed, one pile of rubble after the next. There was a ruined building still standing maybe fifty meters across the way. It looked like it had been about eight stories, the whole facade of it sheared off and dropped into the street. He could tell that it had a lobby on the ground floor once upon a time - the front doors were blown out. The entire building, what remained of it, was dark.

He nodded. "Yeah. I see it."

"That's the fallback position."

"Okay."

"Once you fire, that's where you go."

"Roger that."

There was fighting very close. Troy could hear the sound of cannon fire and the heavy WHUMP as the missiles found their targets. The ground trembled from the force of the explosions.

Up the ruined block from here was a helicopter on its back. Its rotors were broken and scattered over the street. Its spine was broken, its tail rotor snapped off. It was an American helicopter downed in the battle zone.

Inside it were two corpses, the pilots, still strapped to their seats and hanging upside down. How it had come down was anyone's guess, but it was mostly intact, and that meant someone, likely ISIS fighters, were going to come and try to loot the technology on board. ISIS couldn't do anything with high-tech gear themselves, but maybe they could sell it to an interested party. Just because ISIS and Iran were mortal enemies didn't mean they wouldn't do business.

In fact, ISIS were already on their way now. The fighters were moving up the street, running, doorway to doorway.

Soon, a group of them gathered around the helicopter. Troy counted them… eight, nine, ten… maybe as many as a dozen.

They climbed inside the helicopter and inspected the bodies of the pilots. The ones on the outside scanned the surrounding buildings. They seemed to take their time. None of them were in a hurry to head back to the war.

"Stark? Ready?"

"Yeah."

Troy went about his business, relaxed, almost as if he were just practicing. He hefted the rocket launcher, and unfolded the stock. He placed his left hand along the length of the barrel, lightly, lightly. You didn't want your grip too firm, too soon. The index finger of his right hand caressed the trigger mechanism. His knees bent slightly, his back was ever-so-slightly arched.

He took another deep breath.

"Steady…" the stern voice said. "Steady."

Troy became rigid under the weight of the heavy gun. He put his right eye to the sight. The men around the helicopter appeared large, like he could reach out and touch them. His finger tightened on the trigger.

"Anytime you're ready," he said.

"Fire."

Troy fully depressed the trigger. The missile left the tube with a WHOOSH, the force of it rocking Troy's strong body. He watched it go. It seemed to fly away in slow motion, and he almost imagined that he could see it spinning.

He watched the missile's tail signature zoom across the space between here the helicopter. There was a blinding flash of light, then a long, rolling BOOOOOOM.

Troy ducked into a squat as flaming shards of metal and shredded chunks of instant human corpses flew in every direction. Some flew right past him. What was only recently a helicopter was now a flaming ball, lighting up the darkness in the middle of the avenue. Toy could hear the crackling of the flames.

He dropped the spent rocket launcher and ran low across open territory toward the wrecked building. Other men followed him, outright sprinting.

Troy could hear his own breathing, gasps in his own ears.

He passed through the blasted entryway of the lobby. He threw himself to the ground and rolled into a ball. He lay in the dust and darkness for a long moment.

Already, other men were kneeling around him, preparing their weapons. There was no time for celebration. If anyone had survived that explosion, the fighting would begin again any second.

A man named darted across the threshold, alive. He crouched in the corner across from Troy. Something moved behind him.

The man turned, and three small children appeared, still as statues, at the bottom of a crumbling staircase.

The man waved at them. "Go away! Get out of here!"

The children stared at him with dirty faces and big dark eyes. They didn't look afraid. They didn't look like anything. Just blank.

They've seen the horror of war. Again and again, they've seen it. You just showed it to them one more time.

"Have you?" Zhao said, breaking Troy out of his reverie. "Have you ever seen anything like this?"

Troy shook his head. "I don't know. I can't remember now. Maybe not."

Behind them on the wide plaza was a makeshift command center. The rows of tents were stark against the backdrop of the climbing hillside, the bright white and grey fabric providing a sharp contrast to the smoldering rubble below them. The tents were each a few feet apart, evenly spaced and organized, creating a sense of order in the chaos.

Hundreds of people were here, even now, working into the night. There was a constant buzz of muffled conversations and the hum of generators powering the computer and communications systems from the parking lot to the far right. Over there were dozens of military trucks and police vehicles, in some cases with lights flashing red and blue. Thick colored-coded wires ran between the tents, connecting screens and devices that flickered with information.

To the far left was the wide tent where the bodies were being collected. A large air conditioning system pumped cold air into it. One flap of the tent was open at the moment, and Troy caught a glimpse of the inside.

There were rows of folding tables, the tables draped with white cloth, now stained with blood and grime from the bodies lying on top. Full bodies, limbs and torsos were placed onto a table, some possibly still identifiable and others just piles of flesh and bone. Many of the bodies were blackened and charred, almost unrecognizable as human forms

Black body bags were piled around the tables, most of them formless and empty, but some already full and zipped tightly shut.

"When did this happen?" Troy said. Between the long flight, the jet lag, and the lack of sleep, he had lost all sense of time.

"A little over 30 hours ago," Zhao said.

"They've done a good job setting up here."

Zhao shrugged. "Of course."

"What is this place normally?"

"It's usually a public park. There is a stone staircase that comes up here from behind the bank building. Workers would eat their lunches up here on nice days."

Troy turned back to the view of the inferno. The thick gray cloud from the debris slide was beginning to dissipate. Already some of the rescue workers were filing back onto the rockpile, probing the dark cracks and fissures with their flashlights.

"When was the last time they took someone out alive?"

Zhao looked at his watch as if the answer was there.

"Three hours after the explosion."

That hurt. There were men down there risking their lives, who could be buried at any moment in an avalanche or a total collapse. As the hours passed, the odds of them finding another survivor grew long and longer. And yet, Troy knew, unless someone told them to stop, they would dig into that pile for weeks to come, latching on to any glimmer of hope.

"How many dead?"

Zhao shook his head. "No one knows yet. There were more than three thousand people inside at the time of the attack. Most of the bank workers on the upper floors survived. Two staircases near the front of the building were still intact after the bombing, and people were able to work their way down. Firemen and rescue personnel were able to go up and reach some who were disabled from the explosion. But the people on the first ten floors…"

Zhao trailed off.

"You can see for yourself."

Now came the million-dollar question. Maybe they already knew the answer. Troy had been out of the loop for more than half a day. He had been out of contact with his former team, with Missing Persons, with the outside world at all.

"Who did it?" he said.

"We have our suspicions."

"Tell me."

Zhao pointed down at the men in heavy gear and orange vests. "Not all of them are rescue workers. Some are forensic scientists, gathering evidence. There are traces of unusual chemical accelerants in the environment. This demonstrates that the bomb was not a mere fertilizer bomb that anyone with the will to do it could make. It was more sophisticated, which is why the explosion was so devastating. No rag-tag group could make this bomb on its own. The accelerants were made in a laboratory setting by people trained in their use."

"What are you saying?" Troy said.

From inside his goggles, Zhao was staring directly at Troy. Maybe this was the first time since they put these get-ups on that Troy had really looked at the man. He looked like something out of a post-apocalyptic film. Everyone around here looked like this.

Troy noticed now how the straps from the tight N95 mask were digging into his own face. It was an uncomfortable feeling. The goggles were doing something similar. People working here at the command center for hours on end must begin to enter a sort of agony.

"It wasn't Hong Kong protestors," Zhao said. "There had to be a state actor behind it, an advanced military."

Troy watched him, but said nothing. Tensions had been high between Taiwan and China for years, and had ramped up in recent months. Chinese fighter planes and bombers routinely violated Taiwanese airspace. But the idea that Taiwan would retaliate by doing this was nuts. The last thing Taiwan wanted was open warfare with China.

It was as if Zhao could read his mind. "Not Taiwan," he said.

Troy still said nothing.

"There is bank surveillance footage. I've seen it. We're not supposed to talk about it yet, but I will tell you. In the days leading up to the attack, two unknown Caucasian men in dark clothes were repeatedly spotted loitering close to the bank and loitering around other nearby locations. In one video, they placed something in a dumpster a few streets from here."

Troy shook his head. "That could mean anything. It could have been a sandwich."

"It was a large, flat box."

"They could be anybody. They could be bankers from New Zealand. They could be two guys from Sweden on holiday."

"We believe they are Americans," Zhao said. "We suspect they were the advance team for the attack."

What's this "we" thing?

"Of course we do," Troy said.

"More than that," Zhao said. "There were advanced metallic components from the bomb, and which were found in the wreckage, that suggest American technology."

Troy turned and looked at the bombed-out ruin again. There was a gaping hole in the building where the truck bomb had been placed. There was no evidence to suggest a truck had ever been there. It was immolated, utterly consumed.

What remained of it, if anything, was buried under layers of super-heated rubble. A vicious red and orange glow showed beneath the cracks and crevices. It would be weeks before the workers managed to put those fires out, or they burned out by themselves. What metallic components could they have possibly found under there?

There wasn't much to hope for from Zhao Fu, Troy realized. He worked for Chinese intelligence, and whatever storyline they concocted was apparently what he planned to believe.

Couldn't this man think for himself? They had decided to pin the attack on the United States under the flimsiest of pretenses, and Zhao was buying it.

For a split second, Troy had no trouble seeing how false flag conspiracy theories got started. There was a bombing. We took a picture of a couple of white guys nearby. We found a suspicious piece of metal in the wreckage. Ergo, the United States was behind it.

When the story didn't add up, when it was so transparently contrived from the start, cynicism took hold. Crackpots came up with a competing story because the official story was so phony. Then the competing story gained traction. Let this sort of thing play out a few times, and suddenly you had countless people believing utterly ridiculous ideas. It happened because the government was obviously lying in the first place.

Just tell the truth, dammit. Is that so hard? Can someone, anyone, please tell the truth?

Troy could just as easily believe the Chinese government was behind this, and killed hundreds of their own people, as an excuse to start a war over Taiwan.

"Zhao…"

Zhao's eyes flashed something like anger, or a warning.

Troy held up his hands, palms outward, as if to say DON'T SHOOT.

"Mr. Zhao. Look."

"That's why the city is closed," Zhao said. "No one can leave until we find these men."

Troy shook his head. "I don't believe a word of this."

Zhao shrugged. "Don't," he said. "It doesn't matter if you believe it. You're just an observer here."

Troy sighed. "Mr. Zhao, I think we need to…"

"Let's go back to the car," Zhao said. "Nobody cares what you think."

CHAPTER ELEVEN

January 21
12:45 pm Hong Kong Time
Lantau Island
Hong Kong Special Administrative Region
China

"My name does have meaning," Zhao said. "You were correct about that."

It was the next day. They were riding in Zhao's black electric vehicle, driving west out of the city. Troy knew from previous stops here that Hong Kong was made up of three areas. Hong Kong Island was the most heavily urbanized, thought to be the one of the most densely occupied areas on Earth, and what most foreigners thought of when they thought "Hong Kong."

Across the harbor from Hong Kong Island was Kowloon, which was also very urban and easily reachable by subway and ferry from the skyscrapers of downtown. Indeed, Hong Kong Island and Kowloon were very much the same city.

Outside of those two, and largely surrounding them, was the vast region called the New Territories. While most of the population of Hong Kong lived on Hong Kong Island and in Kowloon, more than 85% of the area's landmass was in the New Territories. The New Territories, and specifically, Lantau Island, was where they were headed.

"Do tell," Troy said.

He didn't know what to make of this change of heart in Zhao. Maybe his superiors had told him to play nice with the American. Or maybe he had come to his senses on his own. It was hard to say. For his own part, Troy didn't really care.

He was staying in some bland, generic, 10-story western-style hotel in the glittering Tsim Sha Tsui neighborhood of Kowloon. The hotel was called the Jade Emperor. It was perfect in the sense they gave him a room with a comfortable king-sized bed. It was all he needed.

Troy had fallen asleep the instant his head the pillow last night, and slept without waking for 12 hours straight. He had missed the continental breakfast the hotel served from 6am to 9am. They did have coffee in the lobby, so as he and Zhao drove out of his town, Troy was sipping lukewarm coffee from a travel cup.

The hotel was three blocks from the Hong Kong Avenue of Stars, which was based on the Hollywood Walk of Fame. Hong Kong had been the Hollywood of China for about as long as Los Angeles had been the Hollywood of America. They had their own movie stars, who got their own squares on the sidewalk.

Troy figured if this assignment didn't pan out, and it certainly looked like it was going that way, maybe he would take Davidoff at his word and treat this trip as a mini-holiday. For one tourist activity, he could go check out Jackie Chan and Bruce Lee and whoever else had a star embedded in the cement.

The horror of last night was fading. The bombing was a terrible thing, but it had already happened, and there was nothing Troy could do about it.

"Do you want to hear this or not?" Zhao said.

Troy took a sip of his coffee. "Of course I want to hear it. I'm the one who asked, remember?"

"Because we don't have to talk about it," Zhao said. "We don't have to talk about anything."

"No," Troy said. "I want to know."

If nothing else, it might break the ice between them the smallest amount, and maybe then Zhao would tell him why they were driving out to Lantau Island.

Zhao nodded. He seemed absurdly pleased to talk about this. Missing Persons knew a lot about a lot of things. He was a sharp cookie. It was good to keep that in mind.

"Okay," Zhao said. "Zhao is an ancient surname. A long time ago, it was the name of a man who led a rebellion against a powerful imperial dynasty. He had some early successes, lightning attacks, but over time the rebellion was crushed and he was killed. So the name can mean moving quickly or approaching quickly, which is what he was renowned for at first. But it can also mean attracting bad things."

Troy almost smiled. "As in attracting disaster?"

Zhao was serious. "Yes. Very much so."

"And then Fu?" Troy said.

"Fu means prosperity or good fortune," Zhao said. "So my name can mean good fortune approaching quickly, which is a very fine meaning. Or it can just mean the balance between good fortune and bad fortune. Which is okay as a meaning. Balance is good."

Troy nodded. "Balance is good."

"And your name?" Zhao said. "What does it mean?"

Troy shook his head. "Eh. Like I said, our names don't mean anything."

Zhao looked at him, a sidelong glance. Troy shrugged, and stared out the window. Already, the city had given way to steep green hillsides. In the distance was a tall, lush mountainside with some kind of watchtower at the high peak.

"Where are we going, Mr. Zhao?"

"We have been given a small assignment," Zhao said. "You are an observer, so they gave me something to do, and you something to observe. It is most unlikely to lead anywhere. I think my superiors would prefer if we do not go to the bombing site anymore."

"What is it?" Troy said.

Zhao gestured ahead with his chin. "There is a criminal gang, what you would call a Triad."

"One of the infamous Hong Kong Triads," Troy said.

"That's right," Zhao said. "*San ho hui*. In English, this is heaven, earth, and humanity. That's the great triad the gangs are named for. This Triad is known as the 14K. They operate here in Hong Kong, also in Taiwan, and other parts of the world. They bring heroin into Hong Kong from Thailand and Cambodia, and land small planes at a remote airstrip on Lantau Island."

"You know this for a fact?" Troy said.

"Yes."

"What do they do with the heroin after they bring it in?"

Zhao spoke as if he suddenly realized he was dealing with a young child. "They sell it to drug addicts on the streets of Hong Kong, of course. They also manufacture methamphetamine, what the drug users here call ice. It's possible they make it in labs hidden in the forests of Lantau. They also sell that. These drugs are strictly for domestic use."

"The local cops are aware of all this?"

Zhao nodded. "Of course they know."

"If that's the case, why don't you just stop them? Either you, meaning the Ministry of State Security or some other intelligence apparatus, or the Hong Kong police themselves?"

Zhao smiled. “You don’t understand China at all, do you? These things are very complicated.”

“Teach me,” Troy said. “We have time.”

Zhao nodded. “The Triads are protected, mostly by the local police. The police here are deeply compromised. We do not fully trust them. There are many holdovers still on the force from when the British ruled. But even if the police were perfect, the Triads are important organizations and cannot be eliminated. They are useful in many ways. For example, in the Hong Kong protests of a few years back, the 14K was used to break up the demonstrations in cases where perhaps it was better if the police did not do it. When a mob of what seems to be ordinary men beats protestors with sticks and clubs, then we say that the common people have had enough, and are rising up to put a stop to the educated elites and their western ideas.”

"Interesting," Troy said. "But they're bringing drugs in, which hurts people and undermines the health of the state."

Zhao shook his head. “It’s a small amount of drugs, and it is very controlled. There are perhaps 5,000 drug addicts in all of Hong Kong. Certainly less than 10,000. In a city this large, it is a tiny group. My organization knows who they are almost down to the person. Meanwhile, the 14K also smuggles heroin and ice into Honolulu, Los Angeles, San Francisco, Seattle, and Western European cities, in much larger amounts. So who is being undermined?”

Troy quietly marveled at what the man was telling him.

“So you let them operate because they weaken the United States?”

“There’s that,” Zhao said. “But that’s a small part. The 14K are closely aligned with the Great Ocean Triad in Taiwan. You see, both gangs were aligned with the Kuomintang, before Mao and the People’s Army ran the Kuomintang into the sea. The 14K came to Hong Kong, because the British ruled here. Great Ocean left the mainland, went to Taiwan with Chiang Kai-shek and his minions, and helped them control the island. Don’t you know? Taiwan is a dictatorship enforced by criminal gangs. Its recent flirtation with democracy is little more than a stage play, a farce to entertain the Americans.”

“And if the 14K is aligned with Great Ocean, that helps you how?”

Zhao’s smile was so broad, it nearly took up his entire head. “I believe the westerners wonder how we always know what is happening in Taiwan. They think they will black us out, but it never works. We have so many ears in Taiwan, it’s silly that anyone thinks of them as a foreign country. If the United States ceased to exist, China and Taiwan would be united a week later, and no one would fire a shot."

"The gangs are an arm of the government," Troy said, trying the idea out.

Zhao shook his head. "Not that simple. The gangs are a necessary evil. They are useful idiots."

"And we're going out here to visit them because…" Troy began.

Zhao shrugged. "Maybe some 14K people are out here. Maybe they are smuggling in drugs today. They have the ability to smuggle other things. We know they also bring in counterfeit money and consumer gadgets. Maybe they smuggled electronic components recently. Or maybe they know of someone who did. Who knows? Maybe we will even find evidence of a fertilizer stockpile out here. It would be a very lucky break for us. Not that I think any of that will happen. The Americans would not use a Triad to plant a bomb."

There was a gleam in Zhao's eyes as he pulled off the main road, onto a narrow strip of road that seemed to run straight up the side of a heavily-forested mountain.

He turned to Troy. "But it would be a great irony if they sent me here with you to keep us away from the real investigation, and we found the bombers ourselves."

"If they're so well connected, would anyone even arrest them?"

Zhao nodded. "For something like this, they would have to. My ministry would force the police to do their jobs. The bombers would be tried at the national level. Perhaps not the entire gang, not the leadership, but the individual culprits."

Of course, Troy thought. *The leaders will have plausible denial. They're protected, and not just by the local cops.*

Did Zhao even hear what he was saying? Apparently, you could order a building blown up in Hong Kong, killing hundreds of people. And as long as you didn't do it yourself and had the right connections, you could walk away from the whole thing.

"Should we be concerned?" Troy said. "We're going to visit the mafia, and I don't have a single weapon on me."

Zhao shook his head. "You don't require a weapon. There is no cause for worry. If I need to call for a backup from the police, it can arrive here in minutes by helicopter. There are police helicopters in the sky all the time. Anyone in trouble will surrender without a fight."

"Well, that's good," Troy said.

He supposed that when you lived in a police state, the actual police were always nearby and overhead, and could show up at a moment's notice. And since the gangs were in cahoots with the government, it didn't make much sense for gang members to fight an arrest. They would just get released anyway.

"As I indicated, this is a nothing assignment," Zhao said.

He looked at Troy. "But if we do meet someone, be careful what you say and how you act. The 14K don't like outsiders. You are as outsider as it gets."

Troy shook his head. It wasn't in his DNA to care what criminal gangs liked or disliked.

"I'll try to keep that in mind."

***

A few hundred meters up the steep hillside, the road turned to dirt and quickly became rutted and pitted. The dense green foliage was high on either side of the narrow roadway. Trees pressed in on either side, their branches scratching the sides of their car. The sleek electric car bounced slowly along, scraping bottom from time to time in the deep ruts.

"I'm not supposed to damage this vehicle," Zhao said.

Troy laughed. He thought back to times when he wasn't supposed to damage a vehicle.

"I think it's a little late for that," he said.

Just a bit further and there was a packed-dirt pull off. Zhao turned into it. From here, the mountain dropped away, with staggering views of the sea below them. In the far distance, the sun glinted off the water.

Troy gestured with his chin. "South China Sea."

Zhao nodded. "Yes." He powered down his window and turned off the car. There was no sound except for the wind.

"Don't slam your door," he said quietly. "Sound can travel far on these hillsides."

"Where are they?" Troy said, his voice matching the tone and volume of Zhao's.

Zhao gestured behind them. "Above us. A few hundred meters. If they're even here."

He pulled a pistol out from under his sport coat, checked it, then slipped it back inside.

"You're absolutely sure I don't need a gun?" Troy said.

Troy had already asked this question in another form just minutes ago. But some questions bear repeating.

Zhao shook his head. “I promise you. It’s not necessary. You’re just an observer. They won’t fight us. I am the government, and it’s pointless to fight the government in China. Nothing good can come of it. Besides, we’re just here to talk. Listen in, and pretend you understand what we’re saying.”

“Ever shoot anyone?” Troy said.

Zhao shook his head again. "Never. I was in the Navy before I joined law enforcement. I was elevated from a seaman to naval intelligence. I have never even discharged my weapon while on active duty, whether in the military, or with the Ministry. I hope I never do."

Troy nodded.

“Training grounds,” Zhao said. “Shooting ranges. I’m a good marksman.”

Troy nodded again. He and his Chinese counterpart had led parallel but very different lives.

“I get it. We’re not going to shoot.”

“So let’s go,” Zhao said.

Just beyond the pull-off, the road dwindled to a footpath between high grasses. Zhao led, Troy followed. They had gained some elevation, and it was colder up here than in the city. Before long, a wooden cabin appeared in the distance. It seemed to emerge from out of the grass, then it seemed to almost be floating on top of it.

In a few more moments, they were there.

It was an old clapboard shack, exposed on the hillside and beaten by the weather. It might have been here a hundred years. It might have been here since the dawn of history. The air grew heavy with an eerie stillness, as if time itself slowed down in this isolated place.

A scent wafted in the air, the smell of cigarette smoke.

“They’re here,” Zhao whispered.

There was a low porch. Zhao paused at the bottom of the three steps. He turned to Troy, his eyes filled with caution. There didn’t seem to be any sound inside the shack. They must have all gone silent at once. Either that, or they were mutes.

“Watch the perimeter for movement. Don’t speak. I will talk.”

Troy nodded. He scanned the area.

The mountain reached a sort of wide dirt plateau here, the trees cut back, the high grasses running along the edge of the woods. Set away from this cabin were three more just like it. It was hard to judge the distance.

Over by the other cabins was a white propeller-driven airplane. From here, Troy couldn't make out any markings or tell its make. It looked like a small cargo plane from 50 years ago. The airstrip Zhao had mentioned must be over there where the plane was.

Troy looked for video cameras or boom microphones, but he didn't see anything like that. He still wasn't convinced anyone was inside the cabin.

He scanned his body for signs of stress. He felt calm. His heart was beating normally. His senses weren't tingling. His thoughts hadn't gone blank in the way they so often did before combat. His body was telling him that nothing was happening here.

Suddenly, Zhao stepped onto the porch and quickly crossed it. He reached the door, grabbed the doorknob and found it unlocked. He opened it without hesitation.

Then he burst into the cabin. An instant later, he was shouting in a language Troy didn't understand.

Cantonese. It's got to be Cantonese.

From below the porch, Troy looked through the wide open door. Sure enough, there were a group of men sitting inside. It seemed that all of them were smoking. There was a sort of gray haze inside the cabin that leaked out through the top of the doorway.

Troy could see that a few of the men were shirtless, their upper bodies covered in dense tangles of tattoos. Gang tattoos, no doubt. It was odd that Troy hadn't heard or sensed them in there. It was as if the men had taken a vow of silence. More than just silence – total stillness.

Zhao stood in the center of the room, holding out his badge. He hadn't pulled his gun. He was still shouting, the men staring at him impassively.

When Zhao paused, one of the men said something. He was a heavyset man, slumped in a chair like a rebellious and resentful high school student, no shirt on, his head almost sideways, a smoke dangling from his lips.

Zhao stepped up to him. Troy thought Zhao might hit him.

Instead, Zhao pointed a finger in the man's face like a gun and shouted at him even more.

The man said nothing in response.

There was movement in the corner of Troy's eye. He turned in that direction. A slim man in a white shirt was running through the grass toward the buildings further away. Troy didn't see where he had come from. He must have been somewhere nearby.

He was booking it, making time towards that plane.

"Mr. Zhao," Troy said.

Zhao raised a peremptory hand, A STOP sign, without turning in Troy's direction.

A couple of men glanced out the doorway at Troy. Someone said something, and they all laughed.

Zhao shouted again.

Troy stepped to his right, out of the view of the doorway. Zhao seemed to have the situation well in hand in there. He had been right, of course. He knew his beat. The criminals weren't going to fight the all-knowing, all-seeing, all-powerful hand of the government. Not in China. They might make a few edgy jokes, but that was as far as resistance was going to go.

Instead of resisting, what they might do was make a run for it.

The man was really moving through the grass. He had places to be.

"Zhao!" Troy shouted. But Zhao didn't even turn around.

There was no sense waiting for Zhao. An instant later, Troy was running after the escapee. Troy's footsteps were muffled by the soft earth beneath him. With each step, Troy's heart pounded harder against his chest. Adrenaline coursed through his veins, sharpening his senses. His breathing came in sharp gasps at first, then evened out into an easy rhythm. He kicked on the jets, driving himself faster.

Zhao was an afterthought now. Up ahead, the man was going hard, but Troy was gaining. The man had started shouting breathlessly, his voice small against the vast expanse of the hillsides. Troy could see the outlines of the airstrip now, the plane waiting on the mown grass just off one end of the runway.

Several men came out of the shacks near the runway. Troy couldn't count them – he was moving too fast. Three, maybe, or four. Five.

The man who had run burst into one of those cabins. What did he think he was going to do, hide? That wouldn't work.

Three men came walking towards Troy, blocking his path. Two of the men were shirtless, their bodies heavily tattooed like the men in the first cabin. They were overweight and slovenly. They pitched cigarettes aside as they came.

Another man went to the airplane, opened the door by the cockpit, and yanked down a short staircase.

These guys really were making a run for it. They were going to fly away.

"Stop!" Troy shouted, running hard.

The three men in front of him pulled out weapons. They were sticks of a sort that extended out into longer switches. Troy slowed to a stop in the center of them. One of the men stepped up, the switch raised above his head.

Troy launched at him, left, right, left, like his old Golden Gloves boxing days. The man blocked the first left, then caught the right in his fleshy throat. The next left hit his face, shocking him, driving his head backwards. The switch came down with half the force it might have a second ago. It hit Troy in the shoulder.

It stung, though. Even a weak shot with that thing was a stinger.

Troy stepped in with another hard right hand, knocking the guy's head around sideways. The heavy man stumbled to his right and fell to the dirt.

The two other men came in with their switches, but Troy stepped between them and started running again. There was no time for a fight.

The slim man who had first run away came out of the shack, carrying heavy leather satchels in each hand. They pulled down his shoulders with their weight.

The engine aboard the plane roared to life. The propellers began to turn.

The door to the plane was still open.

The two men from the fight were running behind Troy, breathing heavily. He could hear them there, and he could feel them.

Troy was closing fast now.

The slim man in the white shirt dropped his bags.

The man was much smaller and much lighter than Troy. It was a mismatch, a pro linebacker bearing down on a high school running back.

The guy pulled a gun from his waistband.

He was about to raise it.

Troy hit him chest high, a bone-rattling collision. The two of them went flying together, crashing to the dirt. The plane was turning slowly, entering the top of the runway. The gun bounced across the ground. The man scrambled for it. Troy pushed him down.

The two heavy men were right behind him.

Troy felt, rather than saw the wing sliding over him. He dove to the ground, the propeller passing by inches from his back.

"Unh!" he shouted, an animal sound.

The plane was going to go. He was going to lose that plane. But the bags were still here.

A hard object struck across his back. It left another stinger. Troy rolled over, and one of the men with the switches was there. The man raised the switch again.

Troy placed his hands behind his head, braced himself, and launched his body forward, legs first. His feet drove into the man's stomach. The air whooshed out of the man like a leak from a hydraulic pump.

The plane bounced along the dirt runway, going very slow. At the far end was a cliff, and past that, nothing but water and sky.

The thin guy climbed to his feet and grabbed his bags again. He was a man late for a plane. He was going to try to board the plane while it taxied. Troy took three steps over, cutting off the man's escape. Troy's hands were free, and the man's arms were weighed down by the bags.

Troy measured him, then delivered a left uppercut and a right cross.

The slim man fell backwards, off his feet, and hit the back of his head on the ground. After that, he didn't move. His eyes were half open, like he was dead. But then Troy heard him gasping shallowly. His chest was rising and falling.

Troy turned to gauge what the others were doing.

One man with a switch was still up. Another climbed to his feet. The third approached.

Troy was breathing heavily.

The men stood around him in a rough triangle. They were ready to go again.

To Troy's left, and now well behind him, the plane was gaining speed as it made for the far end of the runway. It lifted off, the sun glinting off its wings.

Troy regarded the three men around him.

"*Hi hway shuo yingyu ma?*" Troy said.

It was one of his phrases. *"Do you guys speak English?"*

It was all he had. It was all he could muster.

Somewhere, a gunshot rang out.

BANG!

It echoed off the open hillsides. Everyone – Troy, the three men – stopped. They turned and looked back the way Troy and the slim man had run.

Zhao was walking across the plateau toward them. He was still pretty far away. His gun was raised in the air.

BANG!

He fired it again.

In the far distance, dark insects appeared in the sky. As the seconds passed, they were already growing larger and taking form. Helicopters. Zhao must have called in reinforcements.

Troy glanced at the plane, dwindling in the distance the other way.

Off we go into the wild blue yonder!

By now, the cops would have picked it up on radar. That thing was going nowhere. Any moment, some sort of fighter escort would appear and guide it back to the ground.

Troy walked over to the slim man's pistol and picked it up. He chambered a round. He walked back to the three men.

"Yingyu ma?" he said. He pointed the gun at the closest man's head. The man squeezed his eyes shut and shook his head.

"English," one of the shirtless men said. "Yes. I speak."

The man was thick-bodied, full-bellied, and had a huge tattoo of a dragon that wrapped around his entire torso.

"Who is that man?" Troy said, pointing at the thin man sleeping on the ground.

The heavy man smiled.

Troy pointed the gun at his forehead.

The man stared at Troy with hard eyes.

Troy shifted his aim. He pointed the gun at the man's feet and pulled the trigger.

BANG!

The man's entire body jerked. The bullet whined off into the distance.

"I swear to God, I'll put one in your skull. Who is that guy?"

Now, the man smiled. "Taiwanese."

"Great Ocean?" Troy said, using the name of the Taiwan Triad with whom these guys were supposedly allied.

The man shook his head.

"You wish you know. You wish I tell you."

The gun was pointed in the man's face again.

"You're gonna tell me," Troy said. "Or I'm gonna blow your brain out."

"ZDL," another man blurted. He was smaller, also heavy. But he was at least wearing a shirt. He was the one who had smacked Troy with the switch while Troy was on the ground.

Now Troy put the gun on him. "ZDL?"

"He ZDL! You no touch. You can't touch."

The big man shouted something at him. Troy imagined it was to shut up.

"Stark!" Zhao shouted. "Stark! Put that weapon down!"

Troy looked up. Zhao was maybe 30 meters away now. He was out of place in this rural area with these rundown shacks, overdressed in his sport coat, slacks and shoes. He looked like a man who thought he was going to a wedding at a country club, but he was really going to wrestle pigs in the mud.

Behind and above him, in the middle distance, three big choppers were starting to fill the sky.

Zhao pointed his own gun at Troy. "Stark. Drop it."

It was rude for Zhao to point the gun at him, but Troy let his own pistol drop to the ground. It was also rude for Zhao to call him by his last name.

The choppers were nearly here. They were troop carriers. It was okay. Everyone who was still on this hillside was busted.

Troy looked at Zhao. He raised his hands. Zhao's face was fierce, angry in a way that Troy hadn't seen before.

But Troy felt good. Now they were getting somewhere. He smiled, his hands still in the air.

"You're supposed to call me Mr. Stark."

CHAPTER TWELVE

7:45 am Central European Time (2:45 pm Hong Kong Time)
Headquarters of the European Rapid Response Investigation Unit (ERRIU)
aka El Grupo Especial
Outskirts of Madrid
Spain

"I gather it's been eventful here."

Miquel Castro-Ruiz sat in the conference room, across from Margaux Montgomery, Associate Director of Organizational Affairs at Interpol. People often referred to her as MM.

She had come in this morning on a flight from New York. She was on her way to Interpol headquarters in Lyon, but had stopped off here first, apparently to handle the question of El Grupo Especial herself. That was the reason for the early meeting.

She was an older woman, maybe early-60s. She was just off the overnight plane, but she didn't seem tired. She was known to be a no-nonsense type who rarely smiled in public. She was dressed sharply in a shimmering blue suit, but she had gray hair that she didn't color and all the wrinkles that came with age.

The woman's gray hair, elegantly styled, framed her face with a touch of wisdom acquired over the years. She seemed to wear her wrinkles proudly, like maps of countless experiences etched onto her skin. Her sharp gaze took Miquel in. She was not intimidated by him. She was not trying to intimidate him. There was an air of easy authority about her.

An old-school feminist, Miquel thought. *She doesn't care what she looks like. She doesn't care what people think of her. She is the one in charge.*

And on the heels of that, he thought:

I admire a woman such as this.

"I suppose I would agree with that assessment," he said.

The conference room still had its large video screen at the far end of the table, and its various data ports and other technology. At least they hadn't pulled that stuff out yet. The former staff had removed their personal and work-related belongings from the offices, but the desks and other furniture were still in place.

It was a building waiting for something to happen, a shell of its recent self. It was, in a sense, a ghost town like out of the old American wild west, a place where things used to happen, but which was mostly empty and forlorn now. If tumbleweeds rolled down the hallways, it wouldn't be a surprise.

Outside the closed door was a phalanx of men. Miquel wasn't sure who they were, other than they were traveling with MM. There were eight or nine of them, a few noticeably carrying firearms. It wouldn't surprise Miquel in the least if this meeting wrapped up and he was arrested right afterward.

He had basically come here this morning to surrender himself. What other option was there to run? It was a silly idea.

MM spoke. "There is some question that your self-styled…"

She made a gesture with her hands.

"Group," she said.

Miquel nodded. "We refer to it internally as El Grupo Especial. In English, you might say the Special Group."

MM shrugged. "Problematic, as you're probably already aware. The name seems to suggest special operations, or special forces, some sort of elite military squad, when your mandate has always been rapid investigations. The whole idea has lent itself to a certain amount of adventurism. That's what I'm hearing."

"I don't know," Miquel said. He shook his head. "Adventurism? No."

"You were a commando with the Spanish police, were you not?" MM said.

Miquel nodded. "I was at the Atocha train station. I was one of the first ones there after the bombing." In his mind's eye, he caught a sudden glimpse of the train platform, the severed torso of the office lady at his feet. The images would always be with him.

He looked up at MM again. "I have no love for terrorists or for violent criminals. I am who I am. And I built a team that could implement a vision I have in mind."

"Certain people are accusing your team of being violent criminals," MM said.

Miquel smiled and shook his head again.

“When the criminals accuse you of being a criminal, you know you’re on the right path.”

“The Albanian Ministry of Justice.”

Miquel nodded. “Right. Who are entangled with the mafias.”

MM shrugged. “They’re a partner of ours.”

“Yes. I know. And if we had shared our intentions with them before we went there, the missing women would have remained missing, and the Baruti gang would still be operating, still kidnapping women off the streets of London and other cities.”

“You can’t know that for a fact,” MM said.

“No,” Miquel said. “I can’t know it. But I know this. Mateos Baruti is dead. A group of trafficked women, imprisoned in the hold of a boat on its way to North Africa, were saved. And the men who kidnapped them are either dead or in jail. In fact, the daughter of the American ambassador to England was among those…”

MM half-smiled and raised a hand.

Miquel stopped.

"You're going to be who you are," MM said. "If that means you lose your group, if that means you go to prison…"

“Why would I go to prison?” Miquel said.

“Do I need to remind you that in a meeting in this very room, with Interpol Internal Affairs, you took complete responsibility for the actions of your agents, up to and including false arrest and murder?”

“I took responsibility,” Miquel said. “I take responsibility.”

“In that case, the Albanians want to give you a life sentence.”

MM picked her phone up off the table. She pressed a button, which automatically dialed a number. “Yes,” she said. “Can you come in now, please?”

She began to gather up the few things she had brought with her.

The door opened, and the men filed into the room. For the first time, perhaps, Miquel noticed that a few of them were quite large. Was MM traveling with a bodyguard now? Or were these men here to arrest Miquel, and ensure he went quietly?

“I’m sure you know that Hans Jute has petitioned to have your Grupo placed under his authority.”

Miquel nodded. “Yes.”

He felt his stomach sinking. There was no way he would ever report to Hans Jute. If that’s what she was going to do, hand him over to Hans Jute, then he supposed that this was all over now. They might as well arrest him and bring him to Albania. The tender mercies of

Albanian justice would probably be preferable to whatever Hans had in mind.

MM shook her head. "I've decided to decline that request. Maxim Davidoff told me last night that he had a meeting with one of your more controversial agents, Troy Stark, and that the meeting was productive. Maxim is open to continuing his oversight of your activities. Will that work for you?"

Miquel nearly laughed. Maxim Davidoff was the most hands-off boss he had ever had. Before the meeting two mornings ago, Davidoff had never even come here.

"Maxim Davidoff is a fine man," Miquel said. "And I think a very competent administrator. I'd be honored to…"

"Good," MM said. She stood. "Contact your previous employees and see which ones are willing to return here. As you know, many have already been reassigned. So you may have some rebuilding to do."

Miquel stood. "I'm not sure I understand."

MM looked at him directly in the eye. Her eyes were sharp and pale blue.

"We like what you're doing," she said. "But we also like to keep these things quiet. It's dangerous work, and we can't always…"

She trailed off.

"I think I get that part," Miquel said.

There was the question of Hans Jute, but now was not the time to ask it. If they were giving Miquel back El Grupo, they must have shut Hans down in some way, or offered him something. That officious pencil-pusher probably suffered a nuclear meltdown when he heard this news.

Miquel doubted he had seen the last of Hans, but it was a problem for the future, not now.

"There's nothing else to get," MM said. "These men here are agents Diaz, Smith and Teleroso. They're your bodyguards. We have intercepted communications about threats against your life by known mafia-affiliated individuals in both Albania and southern Italy. If you're making enemies like that, you must be doing a good job."

MM reached out and shook Miquel's hand.

"Good luck. If you need anything from me, you can contact my office in Lyon."

She was just about to leave with the rest of the men.

"But Maxim Davidoff is your direct line of communication, so…"

Miquel smiled and finished the thought for her. "…contact him first."

Now, she did smile. "That's right. Director Castro, it's been a pleasure."

A second later, and she was gone, leaving him with the three hulking bodyguards.

Miquel looked at the men. Everything was closed down here, but there might be some packaged food and coffee stored in the cafeteria.

"You guys had breakfast yet?"

CHAPTER THIRTEEN

3:30 pm Hong Kong Time (8:30 am Central European Time)
Hong Kong Police Headquarters
Wan Chai
City of Hong Kong
China

"You're going home," Zhao said.

Troy shook his head. He and Zhao were doing a funny tightrope walk now. Zhao had taken him out to that airstrip, and now he seemed upset that Troy had made the important bust.

"I just got here, Mr. Zhao. It's my first day on the job."

They were standing in an office with glass walls. There were of couple of desks and chairs in here, but outside of talking, it didn't look like it got used for much. Outside, in the larger open office, was a bullpen of probably 60 cops, each with his own small desk. The desks were situated in two long rows, extending back into the distance. Cigarette smoke hung in the air.

About a dozen members of the 14K were handcuffed and sitting slouched at nearby desks, being processed by the local Hong Kong cops. A couple of the 14K were still shirtless, their fat stomachs hanging out, the tattoos circling their fleshy bodies like a map of the criminal world. A few of them were handcuffed with one wrist bound to the chair where they were sitting, one hand free to smoke. The cops all seemed to smoke as they typed their reports.

The police teams had found drugs in those cabins on the mountainside. The tally hadn't come in yet, but they were talking about something like a million Hong Kong dollars in heroin, half a million in methamphetamine, and smaller amounts of designer drugs in pill form like ketamine and ecstasy. The leather satchels the man was carrying to the plane were holding 200,000 Euros in cash, plus smaller amounts of drugs. By all accounts, the thin man himself was a Taiwanese national, but he wasn't talking and they were waiting for an identity to come back.

All in all, it was a nice little bust. And Troy was still holding a small fact about it up his sleeve. He needed to act on it soon, he understood that. But for the moment, it was his and he wasn't sharing. The thin man might be ZDL, and whatever that was, the guy who told Troy this seemed to believe it made him untouchable.

ZDL. Maybe it was Taiwanese intelligence. Maybe it was a crime family. Troy had no idea, but he needed to find out. And he wasn't going to ask Zhao.

Zhao fairly sputtered at Troy. He was so angry that his English became less fluent and less understandable as a result.

"You are an observer here. That's all. You are not a cop. You have no job. You have no gun. You have no backup. You are not supposed to get involved."

He stopped talking for a moment and seemed to collect himself. His face was red.

"Maybe you are spy. Is that what it is? You are sent as spy?"

Troy shook his head again. "I'm a cop. You know that. In the end, that's what it comes down to. You're a cop, I'm a cop. What's the big deal? I came here because of the terrorist attack, but we went where the evidence took us, and we made a nice bust. Drugs off the street. Money seized. Gangsters locked up, at least for a little while."

"I discharged firearm," Zhao said.

Troy smiled. "I thought that part was good. I did, too."

Zhao pointed at Troy. "You understand NOTHING.. Don't you know? These arrests are worthless."

Troy stared at him.

"I told you," Zhao said. His breathing slowed down, his voice deepened, and his English fluency came back. He was on firmer ground here. He was going to give Troy a lecture.

"These men are protected. This gang is protected. These drugs are not important. A million Hong Kong dollars in street value. Equal to maybe 900,000 Yuan. Do you know how much that is in your US dollars?"

Come to think of it, Troy didn't know.

"No. How much is it?"

Zhao sighed.

"About a hundred and thirty thousand dollars. And the money in the bags… two hundred thousand Euros. On a global drug trafficking scale, we are discussing pennies. Small coins. How would you call it in English?"

"Spare change," Troy said.

Zhao nodded. "That's correct."

Troy shrugged. All right. It wasn't exactly record-breaking. They probably weren't going to be photographed in front of the seized drugs for the newspapers. But it was still something.

"They didn't even stop the airplane," Zhao said. "It left Chinese airspace, headed in the direction of Thailand."

Now Troy sighed. If this was real, then things were as bad as Zhao had indicated. The Chinese government worked hand in glove with the Hong Kong gangs. This was the kind of thing Troy should have known before he came. Why hadn't someone, Missing Persons or maybe Maxim Davidoff, told him this? They both seemed to think it was funny he was coming here. Now he had made a fool of himself, or worse.

"Okay," he said. "I see what you're saying. I get it."

"No, you don't," Zhao said. "If I make stupid arrests, I can lose my job. These men are protected, but I am not. Do you want to make me lose my job? I was already in trouble. That's why they gave you to me. Now this."

He shook his head again.

"We went there to interview. That was the entire task. It was what you would call an assignment to pretend to work."

"Make work," Troy said. "A make work assignment."

"Shut up," Zhao said. "Okay? Please. Just… just be quiet, and allow me to speak. The plan is this. I interview them, ask them what they saw, what they might know. You observe quietly. We do not look too closely at what they have in their shacks. We do not poke around very much. Perhaps they give us some small bit of information. Perhaps they give us nothing. Then we leave."

"I'm sorry," Troy said. "But I don't think you made that clear to me."

"I want you to go back home to wherever you came from," Zhao said. "It is not helpful for you to be here."

Troy nodded. "All right. I don't think that's your place to send me home, but if that's the way you want it, I'll go."

"That's what I want."

"I'll need somewhere private to call my superiors," Troy said. "There are no planes leaving the airport. I'll have to find some way out of here."

"The train is running to Guangzhou," Zhao said. "It's the only way out now. There is high security, but I'm certain they will let you on it. From Guangzhou, you can fly."

"Where can I call?"

"I'll let you have this office," Zhao said. "I will return in a little while. You can tell me your departure plans and timetable then. Afterwards, I will inform my superiors that you are leaving. They will not think of it as a loss. It's best for both organizations."

"All right," Troy said.

"I will leave you to make what calls you need," Zhao said.

Troy looked around at the glass walls. "You think it's safe to talk in here?"

Zhao didn't smile. He just shook his head. He went through the glass door and out into the wider office. He moved through the crowds of cops without interacting with them or their prisoners. If anything, Zhao's body language suggested he was sheepish around these other men.

The phrase "he hung his head" seemed to fit the situation.

He's ashamed. It was a bad bust he wasn't supposed to make.

"Oh man," Troy said.

The last thing he had wanted was to get Zhao in trouble. In his mind, he briefly played back what had happened. Zhao had gone into the shack and yelled at some men. Another man appeared from somewhere and made a run for it. Troy tried to get Zhao's attention, and when he couldn't, he gave chase to the man by himself. That was how it started. But yes, Zhao had told him the gang was protected and they were just there to ask questions.

Now Zhao had problems. That hurt, but it didn't mean Troy was going anywhere. This was his first day in town. It would be plain silly to think about leaving now.

He took out his smartphone. Jan Bakker's pirated and encrypted Chinese communications application *Fung Wah* was loaded on this phone. "The Magnificent Wind."

Even from here, there was a good chance Troy could use the app to call Jan directly. They didn't work together anymore, but that didn't matter. Troy considered Jan a friend. He didn't know if Jan would reciprocate that feeling, but he also didn't know if Jan thought about things like friends. Anyway, he was sure that if he could reach Jan, Jan would talk to him.

Troy pulled up the app and hit the green button with the word JAN.

There was a several second delay, then a beeping began. The tone was pleasant, and it went on for a little while. Troy was calling the other side of the world, so he was patient with it. For all he knew, the signal was bouncing off a dozen satellites and communications towers between here and Western Europe.

After a time, the beeping stopped.

"Hello?" a voice said.

"Jan?" Troy said. "Jan Bakker?"

"Agent Stark?"

"That's right. How are you? What time is it there?"

"Oh, it's a little past 8:30 in the morning. It's interesting you should call. I just spoke with Miquel. El Grupo Especial is being reinstated. He will have to rebuild the staff from scratch, but Interpol is giving him leeway to contact his former employees and offer them their jobs again."

"Somehow, that doesn't surprise me," Troy said. "Is he gonna offer me my old job?"

"I imagine he will, though he didn't say that."

Troy smiled. It almost didn't matter. He'd been through so many ups and downs in recent days, the most important thing to him was keeping his Madrid apartment. And seeing Dubois. Don't forget about that.

"Is he offering Dubois her job?"

"Almost certainly."

"He called you first, didn't he?" Troy said.

"I think so."

Troy's smile was broader than ever. He took a deep breath. He could just jettison this Hong Kong thing and go back. They didn't want him here anyway. The bombing was a terrible tragedy, but these people were never going to let Troy close to the action. It seemed like the Chinese authorities at some point were just going to decide who was behind the attack, and make that the reality, regardless of who actually did it.

Even so… Even so…

"You're in Hong Kong," Jan said.

"Yes," Troy said. "And I wonder if you can help me with something."

"If I can, I will," Jan said.

"Maybe this is nothing. But I was in on an arrest earlier today. A Taiwanese man was one of the people arrested. Someone told me the man was ZDL, or maybe CDL, and that meant we couldn't touch him. It sounded to me like ZDL. Do you think you could research and find out what this might mean?"

"I won't need to do any research," Jan said. "If the man is Taiwanese, and he really is part of ZDL, it's clear what that means."

"Okay," Troy said. "What does it mean?"

"ZDL is a sort of nickname using the Roman alphabet for *Zaodao Leiji*. It's Mandarin for *struck by lightning*. As a slang term, it can also mean *see you later*. You might call ZDL a Taiwanese terrorist organization, but that wouldn't be exactly accurate. They are fanatics, and accelerationists."

"Accelerationists?" Troy said. "Is that even a word?"

"They believe that war between Taiwan and the People's Republic of China is inevitable. So they want to bring it on as soon as possible. They especially want to make it happen while the United States is at or near the peak of its military power. There is a sense in Asia that the United States is waning. ZDL believes the time to fight the Chinese is now, and with American help, the Taiwanese will not only defeat China, but may be able to topple the Chinese regime."

"That sounds like a tall order," Troy said.

"At one time, it seemed possible, maybe even likely," Jan said. "You probably recall Taiwan was a military dictatorship for nearly 40 years, ruled tightly by the Kuomintang, who lost the Chinese Civil War to the communists. They retreated to Taiwan in 1949 after their defeat. For decades, most of the world still considered the Kuomintang the rightful leaders of China. It was only in 1991 that the UN voted to recognize what had been obvious for decades – the communists ruled China. ZDL members don't just want Taiwan to be independent of China. They want to take mainland China back and reverse the outcome of the Chinese Civil War."

"What are the chances of that happening?" Troy said.

"Effectively zero. There are 23 million people in Taiwan. There are over 1.4 billion people in mainland China. Taiwan is a small country with a dynamic economy. But it's really a fledgling democracy, bedeviled by corruption. Few other countries even recognize it as an independent entity. Meanwhile, China is a major world power and a high-tech police state. Including black market energy trading, global drug trafficking, and counterfeit goods, it may be the largest economy in the world. Its military is unrivaled except by the United States."

"So the Chinese would win any war between the two," Troy said.

"Yes," Jan said. "But it would be ugly, and the US might become involved. The Chinese would much prefer to take Taiwan intact. So they follow a dual strategy – terrifying threats of invasion, blockade, and bombardment, combined with a seemingly benign normalization of relations. The carrot and the stick. It's very effective. The sharp dividing lines that existed in the past are gradually being eroded. There are university exchange programs between Taiwan and China now, and worker exchange programs. There is tourism – hundreds of thousands of mainlanders visit Taiwan every year – and a tiny amount of direct trade and investment. They have language and culture in common. A small but growing population in Taiwan, especially among young people, is in favor of reunification with the mainland. In a sense, ZDL is in favor of this too, on their terms. But the sand is shifting under their feet. If China gets its way, Taiwan will simply be re-absorbed as a natural process. ZDL doesn't want that."

"Would the ZDL carry out provocations in an attempt to start a war?" Troy said.

Troy pictured that ruined bank building, its entire center blown out, hundreds dead and missing, the rescuers working amidst the rubble late into the night.

"Yes," Jan said. "That's about right for them, I'd say. Provoking a war is their dream. They also involve themselves in organized criminal activity, and some of them are closely aligned with Taiwanese politicians. In some cases, it's possible that Taiwanese politicians are members of ZDL themselves."

"Why would someone think that a ZDL member was untouchable to the Chinese police?"

"I doubt they would think such a thing," Jan said. "They were talking to you, weren't they?"

Troy nodded. "Yes." He could see where Jan was going with this. But his brain was a second behind. He couldn't quite articulate it.

"ZDL has powerful friends and sponsors in Washington DC and among other western governments. They probably meant YOU couldn't touch the man."

This was gold.

Maybe Zhao would want it. Maybe he would dismiss it out of hand. But it was a compelling lead, and the story added up.

A building gets blown up. A provocateur is still in the city two days later. He attempts to make a run for it when the cops show up.

And we still have the guy.

Troy looked through the glass at the various gangsters being processed. The slim man wasn't among them. Suddenly, Troy had a powerful urge to hang up the telephone.

"Thanks Jan. I'll be in touch. If Miquel calls, tell him I'll take the job, but he has to double my salary."

"Agent Stark," Jan said. "I don't think Miquel has that flexibility in his budget."

Jan had no sense of humor.

"I do think he wants you on board, though."

Troy smiled again.

"Tell him I'll have to think about it."

CHAPTER FOURTEEN

5:05 pm Hong Kong Time
Times Square Mall
Causeway Bay
City of Hong Kong
China

"They certainly enjoy a good mall here in Hong Kong," Troy said.

They were sitting at the edge of a Western-style fast food restaurant called Greenery, which itself was inside an endless indoor environment that was kind of like a mall, but also like the inside of an airport or a train station or an office complex.

It was like something out of a movie about the future, when no one would go outdoors anymore. The place was at least nine stories tall, and it went on for blocks, with stores and restaurants, movie theaters, supermarkets, and an entrance to the subway.

To Troy's right was a vast atrium. Escalators went up and down to each glass and concrete level of the mall, the escalators out in wide open space, carrying a handful of people through the sky to their favorite shopping experiences.

It was quiet, with some soft music playing in the deep background and the low hum of conversations. Tall men in green military uniforms and helmets were stationed on every floor, two at time, shotguns strapped across their chests.

Troy and Zhao were eating hamburgers and fries. Zhao had a soda. Troy had black coffee. The green in Greenery was apparently that you could order a desultory-looking salad, if you wanted one. Neither man did.

Zhao shrugged. "It's a crowded city. This place is normally packed with people. It gets very hot and humid outside at certain times of year, and it's not pleasant to be out there. In Hong Kong, malls are almost like public parks. They are essential spaces. When you go back to your hotel, you should go all the way to the bottom level. What you'll discover is that your hotel is actually inside Harbour City, one of the largest malls in the world."

“My hotel is in a mall?” Troy said.

“In a sense,” Zhao said. “It’s part of the mall, along with many other amenities. Or put another way, access to the mall is a feature of the hotel. There are several hotels, entertainment centers, health clubs, hundreds of stores and dozens of restaurants, as well as multiple subway stops inside that one mall. In fact, when we take our leave of each other, you can go downstairs here, pick up the subway inside this mall, and take it to your subway stop inside Harbour City. You can go from where we’re sitting now, to your hotel room miles away, without ever stepping outside.”

“You trying to get rid of me?” Troy said.

Zhao took a sip of soda through a long plastic straw.

“We both know the reality.”

They’d left the police headquarters and walked here through the narrow concrete canyons of the center city. The headquarters was ten minutes from here. Troy felt they were starting to get along, maybe even to understand each other a little bit. The hot-tempered Zhao seemed to have faded into the background. The calm and steady Zhao had returned, at least for the moment.

“What did you tell your superiors?” Troy said.

Zhao shook his head. “I didn’t tell them anything yet. I didn’t want to be premature. What did your people tell you?”

Troy shrugged. Then he lied through his teeth.

“They told me it will take a couple of days to get me authorization to leave the city. That’s okay. If you don’t want me around, if you don’t want me to observe, I won’t. I’ll go do touristy things instead.”

Zhao put the soda down and picked up his burger. He didn’t look at Troy.

“Maybe that would be best.”

Troy raised a hand. “But don’t dismiss me too soon. I have something that you might want. I didn’t care to talk about it at the police station. I’m willing to give it to you. And all I want in exchange for it is a partnership, like two cops, two colleagues, the kind of thing we’re supposed to have anyway. Only this time, I want it to be real.”

Zhao raised his eyebrows.

“You think you have something?”

"I know I have something," Troy said. "The question is, do you want it?"

“Where did you come upon this thing that you have?” Zhao said.

“On the mountainside earlier today,” Troy said. “Lantau Island.”

Zhao looked at Troy sharply. "If you discovered a piece of evidence during our trip to Lantau Island, you have the responsibility to surrender it to the proper Chinese authorities."

"You," Troy said. "Are you a proper Chinese authority?"

Zhao didn't answer. He just stared.

"Because as I indicated, I'll give it to you."

"Then tell me what it is," Zhao said.

Troy shook his head. "Do we have a partnership?"

"I can't know that until I know what the evidence is."

Troy shrugged. That was fair enough.

"You have to promise me. Give me your word. On your honor. Your self-respect." Troy found himself parroting the phrases Missing Persons had used during the whole "loss-of-face" part of their conversation. Maybe it would work. The "his name will mean something" ploy had sort of worked.

"If I have something worthwhile, then you have to cut me into the investigation."

"As an observer," Zhao said.

Troy raised his hands. "All right. That's why I'm here. To observe. But also to participate."

Zhao shook his head. "You have no power to make arrests. Your actions will lead to pointless incidents, like what happened today."

"I want in, Zhao," Troy said.

Zhao's eyes flashed… something.

"You called me Stark before," Troy said. "So you started that."

There was a moment when Zhao just chewed his burger thoughtfully. Then he nodded. "Okay. If it's good, I'll cut you in."

Troy looked around at the mall, his eyes going from floor to floor and store to store. The city was in lockdown, a bombed-out ruin was still on fire a few miles from here, no airplanes were leaving, and very few could land.

Even though the place was mostly empty, and despite the presence of the soldiers inside this gleaming terrarium, you'd have trouble guessing anything was amiss.

"The skinny guy, who made a run for it," Troy said. "The one I knocked out. The Taiwanese guy."

Zhao nodded. "Yes. Or so they claim. The one with the money in the suitcases. He tried to fly away, but the plane left him behind."

"That's right," Troy said. "He's definitely Taiwanese, because he's ZDL."

He watched Zhao to see what his face would do. It was carefully blank.

"How could you know something like that?" Zhao said quietly. "How do you even know what that is?"

"For one, I know things," Troy said. "So don't underestimate me. For two, I put a gun to a man's head and he told me. You should try it sometime. It's interesting the things people will tell you when they think you're about to shoot them."

"It was under duress," Zhao said.

Troy nodded. "Okay. But is it good?"

"People lie under torture."

"All right," Troy said. He bit his tongue. He didn't want to touch the Ministry of State Security and its long tradition of torture. History lessons could wait.

"I'll buy that," he said instead. "You can't believe what everyone says. But I didn't torture anyone. So please don't accuse me. You saw what I did. You know it wasn't torture."

Zhao's tongue did something funny inside his closed mouth. It looked, for a moment, like a fish was swimming around inside there.

"Why didn't you tell me before now?" he said.

"I didn't think you'd believe me."

"But now? Now you'll tell me?"

Troy shrugged. "I'm leaving anyway. We could wrap up this little relationship as soon as we finish our food. I can return to my hotel room, without ever going outside, and then go look at Bruce Lee's square or star or whatever it is tomorrow morning. Then I'm gone, and you never see me again. So you tell me. Is it good? A suspected ZDL member was in Hong Kong when a bank blew up, killing hundreds of people. You think the Americans did it? I doubt it. I can tell you the United States does not want World War Three, and definitely not over Taiwan. But ZDL? What do they want?"

Zhao stared into deep space for a moment, as though Troy wasn't there.

"They let the man go," he said finally. "They questioned him and released him. Supposedly, they didn't even have a positive identity yet. He gave his name as Lin Chen, and they accepted that. We can't trust the Hong Kong Police."

Troy wasn't sure how to respond to that piece of information. He eyed Zhao.

"What does it mean?"

"What does *what* mean?"

"His name," Troy said. "What does it mean?"

Zhao's eyes were hard. Still, he did not look at Troy directly. "What is it with you? Why do you care what people's names mean? It's a false name. It's so obvious. Lin is one of the most common surnames in Taiwan. In English, it means forest. Chen means large or vast. So it means vast forest. Clearly, it's not his name."

"He gave a fake name," Troy said. "And they let him go."

"I told you," Zhao said. "These people are protected by the local cops. It's a business arrangement."

"They released a guy from a Taiwan Triad, who gave them an obvious alias. It doesn't make a lot of sense. It smacks less of protection, and more of deep corruption."

Zhao shrugged, seemingly no longer willing to touch the question of corruption. Why would he want to ever touch it? The Taiwan Triads were tight with the Taiwanese government, and they were also in with the Hong Kong Triads, and they were both in with the Hong Kong Police, who allowed them to traffic hard drugs, and somehow the Chinese central government just winked at all of this, even though Taiwan and China were mortal enemies and constantly on the verge of war.

For an honest, crime-fighting FBI-type like Zhao, it had to be too much to accept.

"It's complicated," Zhao said finally. "You can't purge an entire police force."

Or an entire government.

Troy would allow that. "All right," he said.

"He has an ankle monitor on," Zhao said. "It's satellite based, global positioning system. They did that much."

"If we bring him back in," Troy said, "we can't take him to the cops."

Zhao shook his head. "No. We take him to my local office, and we hide him there."

"You're going to get in trouble," Troy said.

He could see this coming a mile away. Zhao had already overstepped. Now he was about to overstep again, and quite badly this time. Troy had done the same thing himself enough times to know.

"I'm already in trouble."

"Okay then," Troy said. "Can you get the location of the monitor?"

Zhao paused. For a long moment, his face was serious. Then the hint of a smile appeared.

"I do have a friend in the police department. She's in Information Technology."

Troy shook his head. He didn't know the nature of this friendship, and he didn't want to know. Maybe they were just work buddies, but maybe they were something else.

"Not good enough. I have a colleague in Europe who might be able to hack the system. You have to be sure. Is your friend both able and willing to give us the data? Can she keep quiet about it? Otherwise, we should try my friend instead."

Zhao nodded. "She'll do it. She owes me."

CHAPTER FIFTEEN

7:55 pm Hong Kong Time
Mong Kok neighborhood
Kowloon
City of Hong Kong
China

"This is it?" Troy said quietly.

They stood in a dark stairwell below an open door to the fifth floor. Zhao was above him on the landing between floors, but Troy could only see his outline, the dark suit a dark smudge against the surrounding darkness.

Very weak, almost nonexistent light came from the hallway above them, as if they were deep underwater and getting the last rays of sunlight before everything went completely dark. They had passed several figures huddled in rags on the stairway's lower levels. This was like a stairway to hell, only it went up instead of down. These were the slums of Hong Kong.

"This is the address he gave," Zhao whispered. "The signal confirms only that the ankle monitor is inside this building. Could be he cut it off."

"And went back to the mountainside," Troy said. "It was nicer there."

Zhao laughed, a barely audible sound.

"Why would he even be here?" Troy said.

The man was an international drug trafficker and a supposed member of a terrorist organization with ties to the Taiwanese government. He'd been busted with 200,000 Euros in a couple of leather bags while trying to jump on a small private plane out of town. There were nicer accommodations in Hong Kong that the man could well afford.

"It's a good place to hide," Zhao said. "Triads control everything here."

They had walked through the neighborhood to come to this dilapidated building. On the main boulevards of Mong Kok, bright neon signs with Chinese characters flickered and buzzed in competing colors, casting a trance-like glow over the crowds. Throngs of people moved quickly through the jammed streets, as if the city wasn't in lockdown, and they brushed against and bumped into each other, as if personal space was not a thing.

At some point, Troy and Zhao had turned and passed down an alleyway, one leading to another, and then another, a warren of intersecting walkways, some so narrow there was barely room to pass through. In the alleyways, the lights from the boulevards seemed to dim, unable to penetrate the shadows that clung to the walls and pavement.

The buildings above were tall and crowded together, with laundry lines hanging between them. Even here in the backstreets, in what seemed like no man's land, there were stores and hole-in-the-wall restaurants lit up by fluorescent lights, the neon signs outside advertising various wares and meals that Troy couldn't begin to understand. The pavement was rough and uneven, with patches of trash and slippery fetid puddles everywhere.

The air was thick with the strong smells of fried food and cigarette smoke, mixed here and there with the overpowering stench of garbage from overflowing dumpsters and sewage bubbling up from beneath the ground.

People had turned and watched impassively as Troy and Zhao, in their business casual suits, stepped over the dirty standing water, while Zhao scanned the crumbling buildings for the address. There couldn't be two more obvious cops in the world.

Troy wouldn't have been surprised if someone called ahead to Lin Chen, the infamous Vast Forest, to let him know they were coming.

The building, when they finally found it, was open to the alley. It had a green neon sign above the doorway. The sign was going bad. It blinked rapidly and made a sound like an old digital clock alarm with its battery dying.

Weh-weh-weh-weh-weh-weh...

Even now, as they entered the fifth-floor hallway, Troy could still hear it far below.

They stood in the bleak hallway and faced a solid green door.

Weak light from yet another neon sign outside filtered through a translucent window at the end of the hall. This sign was blue and red, flashing a sickly blinking glow through the window. The window appeared to be made of solid glass bricks. Some kid in short pants had probably gone out the original window by accident and ended up with a broken neck in the street. So they put these bricks in instead. The glass bricks gave the only light – the overheads in the hallway were all out.

Sounds echoed through the hallways, on this floor and others. The building was teeming with life. There were the exotic smells of cooking food. Laughter. Somebody shouting. Running, pounding feet. TV sets, four or five different shows competing from different apartments – the lights in the hall were out, but the power in the apartments was on.

Water dripped somewhere. Plunk, plunk, plunk. It never stopped, always dripping, finding its way downward and out, so that it could join the puddles in the alley.

Zhao positioned himself to the right of the door. Troy looked at him. Zhao nodded. Troy positioned himself to the far left of the door.

Zhao reached out and pounded on the door with the fleshy part of his palm.

BOOM-BOOM-BOOM.

The sound echoed down the hall. There didn't seem to be any sound from inside the apartment.

Zhao reached up and did it again.

Now, someone shuffled on the other side of the door. Instinctively, Troy took another half-step backwards and away. To his right, Zhao did the same.

A low, scratchy voice said something from the other side of the door. The inflection of the voice told Troy it was a question.

"Who is it?" probably, or something along those lines.

This is how it went before the madness started. Troy took a deep breath. He felt good. He felt nothing. He had no thoughts. Everything was focused on that door.

Zhao answered, his own voice deep and commanding, in Mandarin, or in Cantonese, or in some long-dead mysterious language of the ancients – Troy had no idea.

The voice on the other side of the door responded. It sounded harsh, maybe angry.

"Go away," Troy guessed.

Zhao spoke again. The sound of it went by in a blur, a cascading torrent of sounds. All Troy caught was "Lin Chen."

Now there was quiet. Zhao glanced across at Troy.

Here it comes.

BANG!

The sound of the gunshot was deafening in the confines of the hall. The shot ripped a hole through the door, the metal skin shredding as the bullet pushed its way out.

Troy was on the ground in an instant.

BANG! BANG! BANG! BANG! BANG!

Five more shots came, Troy counting them. Across the way, Zhao was on the floor, too, clawing inside his jacket for his gun. Troy had nothing, no weapon at all. This was the idea, foolish from the start. Troy was an observer here, and he was not going to need a weapon.

BOOOM!

The door came blasting open as the man kicked it from the inside.

Zhao had his gun out.

A shadow burst into the hallway. Troy guessed it was the thin man from earlier today, but it was hard to see. The shadow turned to its left, and leapt over Zhao, who lay on his back, gun trained on the wraith passing above him.

"Shoot him!" Troy screamed. "Shoot that guy!"

But then the wraith was gone.

"We need him," Zhao said.

"We don't need him that bad."

Troy was already on his feet. He kicked the open door out of his way and peered inside the apartment. It was one room – kitchen, bedroom, living room all together. An overhead fluorescent was on. Troy went in, passed through the tiny room, and checked the bathroom. A toilet, a sink, a narrow shower with a stained vinyl curtain. He shoved the curtain aside.

Nothing. No one here.

He went back out to the hall.

Zhao was at the entry to the stairwell, listening. Troy joined him.

"He's headed to the roof," Zhao said.

Zhao was breathing hard, nearly hyperventilating.

"The roof? Why would he…"

Troy stepped into the stairwell. Sure enough, the man's running footsteps were above them, going up. The guy was headed toward the roof. What could he have up there, a parachute?

A helicopter?

"Let's go," Troy said.

"I've never been shot at before," Zhao said.

"You've had a big day," Troy said. "You shot your gun. Now somebody shot back. Congratulations. You popped your…"

“People don’t shoot at you in this job,” Zhao said. “People don’t shoot at representatives of the people’s government.”

Troy shook his head. “The man’s a terrorist. Anyway, there’s a first time for everything.”

He gazed up into the gloom of the stairwell. That guy was making time. He was going to get up to the roof, and then whatever he had up there…

“Let’s go!” he said again. “Zhao! Let’s go!”

Now Troy was pounding up the stairs. He could hear Zhao’s footsteps just behind him. Good. Zhao was coming. No time to stop and ponder getting shot at, or questions of life and death. There would be time for that later. Now was the time for action.

They needed to move fast. Lin Chen had the jump on them. Troy climbed the steep stairs, dragging a bit at first, then catching that rhythm and starting to hit it. One landing, around the corner and more stairs.

Troy darted past two more huddled figures, heads hooded and facing down.

Do these people live here? In the stairwell?

Another landing, no idea where Lin was now. Did he stop on a different floor and go into another apartment? Why assume he was going to the roof?

Troy stopped and listened. All he could hear was his own heavy breathing, and Zhao’s breathing right behind him.

“The roof,” Zhao gasped, as if reading the question in Troy’s mind. “He had to go there. It’s the only way out now.”

The only way out?

Troy pushed on, going for the roof. He passed another hallway, then another, racing blind through near total darkness. Did he hear breathing above him? Maybe. Maybe.

He reached the top landing, eight floors, he thought, but he wasn't sure. There was a door here. It had one of those iron bars across it. If this were the United States, the bar would say: FIRE DOOR – DO NOT OPEN. This one was spray-painted a dark color, maybe black, as if it had once said something in Chinese characters that no longer applied.

“Push it,” Zhao said. “It’s all right.”

Troy pushed the door open slowly, ducking away from it in case more gunshots came. Nothing came. He shoved it all the way open and stepped over the threshold. The first thing he noticed was the city all around them. It was staggering, lit up in infinite colors against the darkness, impossibly vast, stretching away in every direction.

Far away, on the other side of the harbor, a towering skyscraper had been transformed into a giant digital billboard. It showed several Chinese characters descending in a line, 50 stories tall, lit in bright green against a black background. Then they faded into the darkness, and a message in English appeared.

HONG KONG STRONG.

Behind that, near the horizon, there appeared to be thick, dark smoke belching into the night.

"Is that the bombing site?" Troy said.

"Yes," Zhao said. "It's on fire again."

He touched Troy on the shoulder.

"Keep going."

Zhao turned to the left and Troy followed. Now here was something else new. There were people living up here.

The rooftop was covered in shanties, one-story makeshift structures constructed from scraps of corrugated metal, wood, and tarpaulins. They marched down the roof in a line on either side, one right next to the other, almost like an avenue. Black wires snaked on poles, crisscrossing above the little neighborhood. Colorful lights, like Christmas lights, were strung on some of the wires. There was a forest of metal antennas and a handful of tiny white and gray satellite dishes.

People sat on plastic chairs and overturned buckets outside their homes, smoking cigarettes and drinking from small glass bottles.

Zhao and Troy walked between them.

An old woman reached out and touched Zhao's jacket. He glanced down at her. She gestured to her left with her head, indicating a direction, but saying nothing. Troy could easily read the gesture.

He went that-a-way.

Zhao nodded and raised his left hand slightly.

Good enough.

No reason for the woman to say too much and get in trouble with the gangs.

Zhao's gun was in his right hand, pointed down.

For a second, Troy looked at the buildings surrounding this one. They were tightly packed together, separated only by narrow air shafts and alleyways. The rooftops were all covered in a chaotic patchwork of these haphazardly constructed shantytowns. There was a city up here, built on top of the city.

He moved slowly, a few feet behind Zhao, head on a swivel, looking on either side for the slim frame of Lin Chen. Then Zhao stopped.

He raised his gun. He held it in a two-hand grip, and his body dropped into a shooter's crouch.

A woman shrieked. People darted this way and that, crouching low, scurrying back inside their shelters. A glass bottle shattered.

"Careful…" Troy said. "Bullets will go right through the walls of these things."

Zhao shouted something.

Suddenly, just up ahead, on the right, a figure burst out from behind a dense tangle of plants that were climbing the wall of one of the shanties. Now he was running again.

Troy caught a glimpse of him – small, skinny, in a dark shirt and pants. White sneakers flashed on his feet. Lin Chen didn't shoot, and he could have. Whatever else he was, he didn't want innocent bystanders caught in the crossfire.

Now Zhao was running, and so was Troy. They were bigger, they were stronger, they were faster. They would catch him this time.

They closed the gap by half before Lin Chen reached the building's edge. A low brick wall marked the end. Lin never slowed. He hopped onto the wall, launched, and disappeared out into the darkness.

Zhao was uncertain. He slowed, then came to the wall and stopped. Troy was right behind him. The next building was lower and maybe three feet across an air passage. The shantytown began again right on the other side. Lin was over there, still moving.

Zhao leaped up onto the wall, hesitated for a second, then took the gap easily. Troy watched him touch down on the opposite roof. Troy jumped onto the wall and didn't hesitate at all. He bounced across the dark abyss, barely seeing it.

This was how it was. They were on a row of packed-together narrow buildings.

Up ahead, Lin was running between the rows of shanties. He reached the next gap and vaulted over it. Zhao and Troy gave chase, gaining again.

Another gap. Another long fall.

Troy's eyes were on Lin's narrow back. They jumped from roof to roof, dodging hanging wires and metal antennas, clotheslines, plastic furniture and God knew what all else. People scrambled to get out of their way. The residents were slowing Lin more. He crashed into them and banged off them, stumbling forward.

Zhao and Troy grew closer all the time.

They reached the end of the block, and Lin turned right. He crossed a long bridge made of three lashed together planks, hammered with spikes into the low walls on either side.

Troy stared at the bridge – it was almost impossible to believe. Eight stories above the ground, a long stretch of nothing surrounded by the abyss on either side. There was yet another shantytown across from here.

People probably crossed that bridge every day, multiple times a day.

Lin was out there. The boards bounced as he moved along them.

Zhao turned to Troy. He handed back his gun.

"Cover me. I'm going across. I'll be vulnerable out there. Don't let him shoot me."

Troy nodded. Now he had a gun. It was a small green semi-automatic. He didn't recognize the gun. It must be of Chinese manufacture.

He went to the low wall, and crouched along it. He drew a bead on Lin. As he was crossing, Lin reached into his pocket and came out with something. It was his own gun. He let it fall into the gap.

"He's destroying evidence!" Troy shouted.

He looked over the side. The gun dropped into the semi-darkness of the wide alley. There was nobody down there. It seemed like garbage was piled up, maybe to the first or second floor windows. It was an old, disused courtyard of some kind, and it had become a trash pile.

You'd need a construction excavator to find that gun in there.

Zhao was already crossing the planks.

On the other side, Lin jumped down, and saw Zhao was coming across. He ran again, into the next shantytown.

That was Troy's cue. Now he was up again, and he followed the other men onto the bridge.

Don't look down.

He zipped across, one foot in front of the other, moving quickly, his arms out to either side. He nearly caught up to Zhao before Zhao reached the other side.

They both jumped down, almost together, and were running again. This time, Lin turned and went into a stairwell. He slammed the door behind him.

Zhao yanked it open. Troy was a step behind.

Below them, Lin was pounding down the stairs now. Zhao plunged downward into the shadows, Troy practically on his back. Down and down they went, around and around, floor after floor, landing after landing.

Beyond Zhao, Troy could see Lin now, the top of his head.

"Go!" Troy screamed at Zhao. "Go!"

"I'm going! We got him!"

Too slow for Troy. Without thinking, he leapt over the banister to his left, passing Zhao and dropping through space. He landed on the stairs just steps above Lin.

Troy stumbled, lost his footing, and dove, toppling into Lin, driving him off his feet. The two men rolled in a ball down the stairs. They crashed into a man sitting huddled on the stairs below them, and then he was rolling with them too.

They came to a stop, but then Lin was up again and plunging down the stairs. He had barely paused at all. He must know that this time was for keeps.

Zhao leapt over Troy and the homeless man, stumbled, caught himself on the handrail, and then was taking the stairs two at a time.

An instant later, Troy was up and running again. He came to the last stairway, a long, steep drop to the street level. Below him, Lin passed through the open door and into the street. Troy saw him turn right, Zhao just steps behind him.

Troy blasted down, taking the stairs three at a time, his feet hammering with each drop. Then he was out in the street, right behind the other two. His breath came in rasps, almost like shouts. His blood was pounding in his ears.

The street was narrow and lined with food stalls. Just ahead, Lin tossed something into a cooking fire. Zhao didn't stop. He was bare steps behind Lin.

Troy ran to the stall. A man in a dirty sleeveless t-shirt was making something in a pan. It was a phone. Lin had thrown a cellphone into the man's frying meat. The man fished it out of the pan using a spatula.

"Give it! Give it here!" Troy shouted.

"Hot!" the man said. "So hot!"

"Give it."

The man held the spatula out, and Troy took the phone. It was in a protective rubber casing that had begun to melt. The burned rubber scalded Troy's hand.

"Ow!" Troy screamed, despite himself.

The Chinese man laughed.

Troy turned to the chase again. Up ahead, Zhao crashed into Lin, driving him into the stall of a greengrocer. Fruits and vegetables flew everywhere, like a fountain of produce. The stall collapsed and the two men landed on it, amid the remains of the food.

Zhao had Lin pinned. Troy walked slowly up behind them.

He put Zhao's pistol in his own pocket. He tossed the mobile phone from hand to hand, letting it cool off a little. The fact that Lin had tried to get rid of it suggested there was something on here he didn't want them to see.

On the ground, Zhao wrenched Lin's arms behind him and cuffed his wrists with steel manacles. He was saying something to Lin, under his breath.

"He didn't want to get caught a second time," Troy said from above them.

Zhao looked back, body still pressing Lin Chen to the ground. Troy noticed that Lin's pant leg was pulled up slightly. He was still wearing the ankle monitor.

"Do you have my gun?" Zhao said.

Troy shook his head. "I'm sorry. I lost it in all the excitement. But I do have his phone."

CHAPTER SIXTEEN

10:35 pm Hong Kong Time
Ministry of State Security
Cha Liu Au, Kowloon
City of Hong Kong
China

"He won't talk."

Troy and Zhao were inside a small room with a long wooden table and some wooden chairs. Troy was drinking a lukewarm coffee. It was awful, but it had been a long day, there were no Rock Stars anywhere in sight, and he was starting to wear down.

The furniture in this room was old and beaten by the years. They stood at a tall window, looking through the glass at Lin Chen. He was sitting slumped at a desk. He was chained to the chair he sat upon. There was no one in the room with him.

On Lin Chen's side, this glass was a mirror. According to Zhao, Lin couldn't see them in here – all he could see was himself. Even so, Troy had a hunch Lin knew what that mirror meant.

They were in a small, nondescript two-story building at the edge of a park somewhere on the outskirts of Kowloon. It was hard to fathom this as the Ministry of State Security headquarters in Hong Kong. The place shared a six-story concrete parking garage with the buildings around it. Hong Kong was a city of giant towers all squeezed together, everywhere you looked. Small buildings were rare. Somehow, a ministry that was crucial to the central government's police state was located in an undersized old building, which didn't even have its own parking lot.

Troy did notice that all the cars on the first two floors of the parking lot appeared to be Ministry cars, or the personal cars of the g-men types who worked at the Ministry.

He had carefully observed the situation here over the past couple of hours. Ministry personnel had questioned Lin, and gotten nowhere. They had shouted at him. They had given him nothing to eat or drink. They hadn't given him any cigarettes. He hadn't had a bathroom break.

At one point, an agent had splashed what looked like a glass of water in his face.

Nothing had amounted to torture so far, but of course they knew Troy was here.

Zhao had disappeared for a long while and had only recently returned.

"Does he know you have his phone?" Troy said.

Zhao nodded. "He knows. But he thinks we haven't broken the encryption yet. He thinks he has time. But he's incorrect. The information officers broke the encryption about 40 minutes ago. The phone is open."

"What's in it?" Troy said.

Zhao looked at him. "I'm sorry."

"Classified," Troy said.

Zhao turned and gazed through the glass. "Something like that."

"ZDL?"

Zhao was quiet for a long moment.

"He also doesn't know we're the Ministry for State Security. He might suspect, but no one has told him. I think he is hopeful that he's in the hands of the Hong Kong Police or will end up there. But he's wrong again. He has no friends here."

"Zhao."

Zhao said nothing.

"You can't do that, Mr. Zhao. We have a deal. You have to give me something."

"I need my gun back," Zhao said. "You have no idea the risks I've been taking."

"I've been taking risks too," Troy said. "I risked my life to help capture that guy."

Zhao sighed. He turned around.

"Officially, we are not even here."

"Who are we?" Troy said.

"The Ministry of State Security. When the British ceded Hong Kong back to us, the city was granted semi-autonomy. That was part of the agreement. It would have its own government, its own police force, its own intelligence service. We don't trust them anymore, so we've moved in."

"That's why this building is so rinky-dink," Troy said.

Zhao nodded. "It doesn't exist. It's an old Christian school."

"Ah."

"Yes," Zhao said. "I forced the Hong Kong Police to arrest this man, and several others, earlier today. That was an embarrassment for them, doubly so because the untoward actions of a visiting American caused the arrests to happen. But then the police let him go anyway. So I went and re-arrested him."

"Do the police know that?"

Zhao shook his head. "No. They don't know we have him. We have to keep that secret from them for now. But my superiors know what I did. It is a tricky issue. You cannot disrespect your partner agencies, no matter what you may think of them."

Troy gestured at Lin. "What is this guy? Just a Triad member?"

Zhao looked away. "He's what you suspected."

Troy nodded. So that was good. The man was ZDL. He was part of a terrorist organization. He was trying to spark a war between Taiwan and China. There was some chance that he was involved in the bombing.

"So we might be getting somewhere. That means you're off the hook. You did the right thing."

"It's not that simple," Zhao said. "Being right isn't always the most important thing. That seems difficult for you to understand. Anyway, I need my gun. If they find that I unholstered it, and then lost it… or that someone stole it…"

Troy shrugged. He didn't want to see Zhao get in trouble. That much was certain, if nothing else was. He reached into his pants pocket and came out with the gun. It was small. Troy could practically hide the whole thing inside his hand.

It was a somewhat ridiculous gun for the kind of work they were doing.

"Easy enough," Troy said. He held the gun out low, hopefully out of the sight of any prying eyes, and Zhao took it. Within a few seconds, he had tucked it away inside his jacket.

"Thank you."

"You can trust me, buddy," Troy said, and he meant it, as far as that went. Yes, he had lied at first about having the gun. Okay. But he gave it up as soon as he knew it would get Zhao in trouble. Troy figured Zhao must see the baseline sincerity here.

"I only wish that went both ways," Troy said now.

"You can trust me," Zhao said. "I told you what you asked."

"What did they get off the phone?"

“Information, mostly classified, as I indicated. Also, an address of a possible safe house. They’re looking at drone and satellite footage of it now. It seems there’s a group of men hiding there or were very recently. Maybe as many as ten individuals. We don't know who they are, but we believe they are Taiwan nationals and possible extremists."

“Here in Hong Kong?”

Zhao shrugged. “In a sense.”

Troy shook his head. “Mr. Zhao…”

Zhao sort of half-smiled. “It’s in Cheung Sha. It’s a house out on the beach. Yes, that’s still Hong Kong. A beautiful and desolate area. Not in the city.”

“Sounds nice,” Troy said. “You’re going to get a medal for this, maybe even a promotion. When are we going?”

“We don’t know anything yet. I’m serving my country, and medals for that are unnecessary. But we’re leaving in 20 minutes. I’m leading a 12-man team into the house.”

“Am I one of the 12?” Troy said.

“No.”

Troy flashed anger at Zhao. He was tired. Physically tired, yes. Mentally-tired, yes. Jet-lagged, yes. But most of all, he was tired of playing these games. Troy had proven himself valuable. He was sure of that. The leads they were following were ones that he had pulled together.

“Zhao…”

“Stark,” Zhao said. “My superiors will allow you to accompany and observe the strike team. But you must stay at least a hundred meters from the house at all times. I'm afraid I must insist on this. It's for your own personal safety and for the safeguarding of any classified information that may be discovered at the house."

Troy smiled. He raised his hands.

“See Mr. Zhao? All I ever want is to be included, to be allowed to do the job I was sent here to do. Is that really too much to ask?”

“You’re an observer, Mr. Stark,” Zhao said.

“Of course I am, Mr. Zhao. And I’m ready whenever you are.”

***

“Stay here,” Zhao said. “This is as far as you go.”

Zhao wore a black helmet with a light mounted in front, which was off at the moment. He also wore a black jumpsuit with a bulky ballistic vest over his upper body. He was carrying an electric prod instead of a gun.

Behind him, a group of three men waited, one with a small bat in evidence, two carrying short-barreled shotguns. Troy guessed the prod and the bat were to force compliance. If compliance failed, the shotguns would come into play.

The house was just down the beach from here, back in the dense woods at the foot of a heavily forested mountain. According to Zhao's scouts, an exterior light was on at the house, but there appeared to be no lights on inside. Two cars were parked in the driveway.

They were going to attack it in three groups of four – this one, Zhao's group, coming west along the beach, another coming east up the beach, and another coming in from behind the house.

Troy nodded. "Yes. It is. It's simple to understand."

"I mean it, Mr. Stark."

"I know."

Without another word, Zhao turned, and he and his men moved up the beach like dark ghosts.

It was a warm night with a gentle breeze. A fat moon rode high, illuminating the setting more than Zhao and his assault teams would probably prefer.

Cheung Sha Beach itself was long and wide, pale sand, a curving bowl that appeared to be miles long. The jungle came down off the mountains and right to the edge of the sand. The waves here were small, but crashed along the shoreline in explosions that were louder than Troy expected.

There was additional light on the horizon – Troy guessed from Hong Kong proper, or one of the many outlying settlements with groups of high-rises that peppered the New Territories. The shadow of the mountain cast an eerie shape on the sand, looming like a giant monster crouched in the darkness.

When the men were gone, Troy started counting backward from ten. He tried to count slowly.

"Ten," he said, his voice low, in case a man with a boom microphone was lurking under the nearby trees.

He waited a few beats.

"Nine."

He took a deep breath, exhaling it over several seconds.

"Eight."

He began to inhale again.

"Nah. That was plenty."

He moved up the beach, following the men. He wore the same outfit as them – dark helmet with light, and dark jumpsuit. He had no weapon, though, and he declined the heavy vest.

"No sense wearing it," he had told Zhao. "I'm not going to get shot. I'm not going to be anywhere near the action."

This idea seemed to please Zhao, or at least appease him. For that moment, anyway.

The guys were well ahead. Troy began to jog, the sand slowing his movement, making forward motion a chore.

He didn't know where the house was. He scanned the darkness back in the trees, looking to see where the teams had gone. He could hear his own breathing over the crashing of the breaking waves. That was not good.

He stopped. He had to be close. He moved along the tree line, gaining control of his breath. His heart thumped a tiny amount. This had been a long, busy day. Lots of running, lots of chasing, lots of tangling with the bad guys. It was just the way Troy liked it, with a bonus – no one had died. No one had even gotten hurt all that much.

"Fun and games," he whispered to himself. "Cops and robbers."

He was waiting. He knew that. He was waiting for shouting, doors being blown down, and then gunshots and screams. The sounds of the tumultuous entry.

He crept back into the woods, along a sandy path. Now he saw them, a gathering of spooks, first in a tight circle, then spreading out along the front wall of the house. A thick fog or mist was rolling down off the mountain. The house was hard to see from here, but it appeared to be a low, one-story bungalow, quite large, with a wide bay window facing outward toward the water.

Troy moved closer.

Suddenly, several helmet lamps came on all at once. They were very bright, LED, thousands of lumens. Troy was taken aback by the blistering brightness. It was like the harsh glare of a dozen suns. A man shouted. Two men moved to the door, wielding a battering ram. They swung it back, then delivered it at the door with immense force.

BOOM!

The door blasted inward on the first blow. The ram carriers fell back, and a wave of commandos burst through, brandishing weapons and shouting unintelligibly. Troy heard them moving through the house, shouting, securing each room. He could watch them moving from room to room through the windows, the lights reflecting on the glass. Gradually, the shouting died down.

There were no gunshots.

There wasn't even the sound of beatings.

There were no commands or threats being issued.

There was very little noise at all, just the low hum of conversations.

There was nothing going on in there.

As Troy watched, the two men who had swung the battering ram went into the house behind the others. One of them carried the ram by himself now, hanging from one hand.

Troy followed them. He came to the shattered door and hung back for a moment, not sure if he should reveal his presence. But he might as well. He was an international observer here. What good was he if he didn't observe what was going on?

He turned the corner and went in.

Zhao and several men were standing in a darkened living room. Their bright headlamps played over the room. There were five bodies on the floor, all lying in dark pools. The men had been bound hand and foot, gagged, and then shot in the head with a high-caliber weapon, execution-style.

There was a long, wide sofa against the wall. It looked like it might be white or yellow. It was hard to say in the play of shadow and the glare of the lamps. It had another body on it, bound and gagged, killed with a head shot, like the others.

Lights moved through other nearby rooms.

A man from one of the other rooms called out. Zhao answered him. Troy had no idea what they were saying. As he watched, Zhao took out a phone and made a call.

"All of them are dead?" Troy said.

Zhao looked at Troy. His eyes were sharp. He was not in a good mood.

Troy could see it. The ZDL lead had brought them nowhere. The chase through the rooftop slums of Mong Kok had brought them nowhere. All of it led to a dead end, and in fact, a pile of dead men. Now it was back to the drawing board.

Lin Chen, or whoever, was all they had.

They're going to torture him now. REALLY torture him.

Troy supposed that was true. He had caused Lin Chen to be arrested, twice as a matter of fact. He had also caused Lin Chen to be outed as ZDL. And Lin Chen's fate was completely in the hands of the

Ministry of State Security. He wasn't talking yet, but after this, they were going to make him talk. Troy wasn't sure how he felt about that.

It was one thing to be killed. It was quite another to wish you were dead.

"I told you to stay on the beach," Zhao said. "That was the agreement."

Troy shrugged. "I couldn't. My job is to observe, and you keep trying to shut me out."

Zhao shook his head. "You shouldn't have seen this."

Troy regarded the dead guys on the floor.

"I've seen worse," he said.

CHAPTER SEVENTEEN

January 22
1:05 am Hong Kong Time
Ministry of State Security
Cha Liu Au, Kowloon
City of Hong Kong
China

"You should go home now."

Zhao had just walked in. Troy had been sitting alone at a small table in a tiny, wood-paneled room for the past 40 minutes. He was done. At this point, he was like a piece of overcooked meat. The vital energy had drained from his body.

He still wasn't over the length of the flight or the time change. They'd been on the move all day. The culture shock here was wearing. Seeing the destroyed bank building, and the men digging helplessly in the ruins for survivors, was too much. Dealing with Zhao's reluctance to share information and the dictates of his "superiors," whoever they were, was the last straw.

They'd left him sitting here as though he was a prisoner undergoing interrogation. At one point, he began to wonder if the frosted glass door to this room was locked from the outside. He didn't bother to get up and test it. For one, because if they had him locked in here, there was nothing he could do anyway, and for two, he would get annoyed if that turned out to be the case.

Zhao stood over him.

"What's the deal?" Troy said.

"You look exhausted."

Troy nodded. "I am exhausted. But you don't look much better."

It was true. In the wan yellow light from overhead, Zhao looked almost sickly. He seemed wizened and hunched over like an old man, a far cry from the gung-ho, physically fit, patriotic type Troy had met last night. Zhao's face seemed pinched with worry.

"You're going home," Zhao said.

Troy leaned back in the old wooden chair. He noted that this was subtly different from saying, "You SHOULD go home."

“Can you give me a ride?”

Zhao shook his head. "I can't. I'm no longer your host. Two of our men are going to take you back to your hotel. They'll stand guard outside your room. Tomorrow morning, they'll be relieved, and two new agents will take you to the train station, where you're going to catch the bullet train to Guangzhou. From there, you'll go to the airport, and then back to the United States, or I suppose to Europe, if that's what you prefer. Our agents will escort you the entire way up until you board your plane. Your visit here is ending."

Troy stared at him. It was more of the same. Zhao, for all his good points, and he did have some, had been trying to get rid of Troy the entire time.

“What’s the matter, Zhao? You people have a bunch of dead guys on your hands, and that throws your whole pre-cooked *The Americans Did It* narrative into the dumpster? Is that it? So you have to get rid of me now because I saw that the whole story is a lie?"

“You people,” Zhao said. “Nice.”

Troy shook his head. “You know what I meant. Don’t play those games with me.”

“You can’t be trusted, Stark. People here don’t trust Americans to begin with, do you not understand that? Every time I request that you do something, you do something else instead. How difficult would it have been to stay on the beach, as I requested? In fact, I didn’t request it, I commanded it.”

Troy didn’t say a word.

“For your information, *The Americans Did It* narrative is alive and well. You’re going to find out anyway, I have no doubt of that. You’re a first-class snooper. So I’ll tell you the real reason why you’re leaving. We are expelling all nonessential, non-diplomatic American personnel from Hong Kong. Forensic teams have been going over the Cheung Sha house for the past hour. Here’s what they’ve found so far.”

“Do tell,” Troy said.

“Every man in that house was either known or suspected ZDL, a known or suspected CIA asset, or a Taiwanese intelligence agent. All of which points toward the United States as the sponsor.”

“I don’t believe that,” Troy said. “Not for one second. Why would American intelligence risk putting their own people on the ground here? ZDL, sure, of course. But the CIA? It’s crazy. The CIA knows you better than you know yourselves. They know everything here is wired, there are cameras everywhere, there are people watching on every street corner. They simply wouldn't do it. And send an entire hit squad in to kill those guys? The CIA couldn't do that if they wanted to."

Zhao leaned in and pointed at Troy. His index finger was inches from Troy's face.

"Wrong! Wrong again!"

The fact that Zhao was standing and Troy was sitting made it as if Zhao was looming over Troy, trying to intimidate him. Troy could picture Zhao using this technique on political prisoners in rooms just like this one, here in Hong Kong, in Beijing, everywhere in the country.

"Don't make me get up," Troy said. "Because I can tell you whatever you think you're doing, it isn't going to work on me."

Zhao pointed again, jabbing with his finger like it was a knife. "Shut up, Stark. It is the Americans. And we have the evidence now."

Troy's right hand curled into a fist. It did so almost by itself, as though it had a mind of its own. "Zhao, I will knock you into the middle of next week. I've been patient up until now."

'Don't even try it. Do you want to be under arrest? That can be arranged."

"You're brainwashed, Zhao. You're beyond redemption. Your superiors give you the party line, and you repeat it as though it's true, even though of course you haven't seen any of the evidence yourself. Because it's classified."

"Wrong yet again," Zhao said. "I have seen it."

Troy shook his head. "I don't really believe that."

"Don't believe it then. The house was full of plans to attack another building, a bigger, more important one. The Bank of China building in Central Hong Kong. The first attack was a diversion. It used a rudimentary bomb that didn't bring down the whole building. The next attack was to be more sophisticated. There were electronic incendiary devices stored in the beach house, not bombs, but the detonators that could trigger the bombs. The plan was to pose as maintenance personnel, infiltrate the building, and wire a series of explosives throughout the upper floors. At the appointed time, the explosives would go off one after the other in a chain, dropping each floor onto the one below. The weight and momentum of the ones above would drive all the floors below downward."

"It's a pancake effect," Troy said. "They use this technique to demolish old buildings all the time."

"They intended to do it in the mid-morning the day after tomorrow, when the building was full of employees. It was to coincide with the dedication of the Golden Dragon Peace Tower. Don't you see? While the country was celebrating the opening of the world's tallest building, the terrorists would take down another world-famous Chinese building. The hope was to murder many thousands, instead of hundreds, and humiliate the Chinese people during what should be a moment of pride."

"If that's the intent, why not take down the Peace Tower?"

"There's too much security around that event," Zhao said. "It would be impossible."

Troy thought about that for a moment.

"Were any of the bombs ever planted?" he said.

Zhao shook his head. "The Bank of China building is being searched thoroughly as we speak, but it seems the conspirators were killed before they could install the bombs."

"Were there bombs found at the house?"

"No," Zhao said.

That settled the question in Troy's mind.

"There were no bombs, Zhao. It's a fake. Those guys were patsies, and the whole thing was a diversion. Either it was a set-up by the government, or something else is going on here."

"There are bombs," Zhao said. "And we will find them."

Troy waved a hand in the air. It was a strange gesture, out of character for him. If anything, it belied the level of his exhaustion, and his frustration. "I fail to see how this means the American government, or any Americans at all, were in on it. Who is this CIA asset?"

"A man from Singapore intelligence, who has a history…"

Troy winced. "I'm sure Singapore intelligence is eager to get their little city-state annihilated by China. Would you please listen to yourself?"

"He's a rogue agent and has a history of cooperation with the CIA. We believe he has been on the American payroll since the early 2000s."

Troy shook his head. "Doesn't mean anything. You know that, I know that, and I'm sure even your superiors know that. A rogue agent? He's probably on ten different payrolls. He could be working for anyone."

"As I told you, there was a Taiwan intelligence officer in the same house with ZDL," Zhao said. "It shows you the dangerous game the Taiwanese are playing."

Troy had no answer for that. He had no idea if any of this was real or not.

"Okay," he said.

Zhao went on, but the tone of his voice softened. He was quieter.

"There may be a war now, after all. I'm very concerned. When this news is shared, there will be high-ranking people in the government, people in the Standing Committee of the National People's Congress, who will want to exact revenge on Taiwan. They will not care if the United States tries to protect Taiwan, or is drawn into the fighting. They might even welcome it."

Troy sighed heavily. He was suddenly even more tired than before. A weight seemed to settle onto his body.

The National People's Congress? It was a rubber-stamp for whatever the dictator and his ruling circle wanted to do. Zhao really was drinking the Kool-Aid here. He was drunk on it.

But since Zhao had changed his tone, Troy did the same. He addressed Zhao with the respect he was supposed to have used the entire time.

"Mr. Zhao, if the American government wanted this new attack to be carried out, as you seem to believe, then why are all the men in that house dead? And who do you suppose killed them?"

Zhao shook his head slowly. "I don't know."

Finally, a moment of clarity, and total honesty, from Zhao.

"All right, Mr. Zhao," Troy said. "I understand. It's been a pleasure meeting you, but I guess I am ready to go to my hotel now."

Zhao nodded. He was already moving towards the door. He paused and looked back for a couple of seconds before he went out.

"Mr. Stark, I wish you every success in your future work."

CHAPTER EIGHTEEN

2:45 am Hong Kong Time
The Jade Emperor Hotel
Tsim Sha Tsui, Kowloon
City of Hong Kong
China

"Amazing."

Troy stood at the window of his hotel room, drinking a bottle of beer, and staring out at the lights of Central Hong Kong, across the harbor from here on Hong Kong Island. The clustered skyscrapers over there gave a dazzling multi-colored light show, seemingly all of them flashing gigantic digital messages now.

Most of the messages were in Chinese characters, but a few were in English, dozens of stories high. HONG KONG STRONG was a common message. STAND WITH HONG KONG.

CHINA STRONG.

There were video streams of the rescue workers digging through rubble.

STAND WITH OUR HEROES.

Smoke was still rising from the destroyed bank building. Giant spotlights moved across the sky, illuminating the smoke itself.

The smoke was a nice touch. It made the attack ever present. Troy wouldn't be surprised if the Chinese government had installed a giant smoke machine at the site of the bombing as a public relations ploy. Maybe they had acquired a Godzilla-sized sheet of dry ice.

He smiled at the thought of it.

A knock came at the door. Troy turned slowly and looked at it. The last he saw, his two new minders were standing outside in the hall, at something like attention. They were serious young men in dark suits. They must work the night shift because they didn't seem the least bit tired.

They both spoke a little, but not very much English. They couldn't understand Troy at all, and he could barely understand them. It was hardly worth trying.

The whole situation was designed to make communication and negotiation next to impossible. He was getting sent out of here, and no amount of begging, horse trading, or cajoling was going to change that fact.

Anyway, he might as well see what they wanted. He went to the door and opened it.

A man stood there in a hotel bellhop's uniform. It was a black suit with a starched white shirt, black tie, and a red cummerbund. The man had a long rolling cart with him, three round metal food covers typically found in hotels like this one on top of a white tablecloth.

"You ordered room service, sir?"

Troy hadn't ordered anything. He looked at the man closely. He was not a tall man, and he was slight of frame. He was not Chinese, but closer to Middle Eastern or southern European in his appearance. He had a light growth of dark beard, what someone might refer to as a five o'clock shadow. He was very handsome.

It was Alex. The mysterious Alex, emissary from Missing Persons, who had disappeared right after Troy dropped through Aliz Willems's roof. It was a pleasure to see him in this context. It was more than a pleasure. It was a relief.

Troy nodded. "Yes. Yes, I did order room service. Please bring it in."

Troy opened the door wide as Alex trundled the cart through. Troy glanced at the two Ministry agents. They were tall like Zhao, but younger than him, and even more impassive. They looked like they hadn't smiled in their lives.

"Hi guys," Troy said. "Still with me?"

They looked at Troy with blank faces and said nothing.

Troy went inside the room and let the door close behind him.

"Don't lock it," Alex said. He brought the cart over to the small round table near the windows. "That's not normal."

Troy hadn't so much as touched the doorknob.

"How are you a bellhop here?" he said.

Alex was moving the platters from the cart to the table. He shook his head. "There's no time for that. Suffice to say it's a Canadian hotel. It's owned by a small Canadian airline called Canada East, which flies to Asia and wanted a place to park its passengers when they arrive in Hong Kong. The airline itself barely exists and is a front for something else. The best part of the set up is the rooms are swept for bugs on a regular basis. So we can talk. Good enough?"

Troy nodded. “Yeah.”

Alex took a breath. “We heard you got ousted.”

“That was quick. How did you manage that?”

Alex raised his hand. STOP. “No time. What have you seen?”

“About ten dead guys in a safe house on the beach at Cheung Sha. Supposedly one was Singapore intelligence, and a CIA asset. They say another was Taiwanese intelligence, and the rest were ZDL. As far as I saw, all bound and killed execution-style, with a pop to the head.”

Alex nodded. “Why did they let you see this?”

Troy shrugged. "They made a mistake. That's why they're getting rid of me. But it was my bust in the first place. Me and a Ministry of State Security guy named Zhao, who's been my minder. We caught a guy calling himself Lin Chen at a 14K airstrip early this afternoon. He's almost definitely ZDL. The Hong Kong cops let him go, so we went to Mong Kok and busted him again. Now, the State Security goons have him. I think they're gonna open him up like a tin can and eat him alive."

“Yeah,” Alex said. “Probably. That’s not your problem.”

He was taking the metal covers off of the plates and making a fuss over it. He clanged a couple of the covers together.

“What does it mean?” Troy said.

Alex shook his head. “No one knows. It doesn’t make sense. The Triads have no use for the ZDL. An apocalyptic war between China and Taiwan would be bad for business. War between China and the US would be even worse.”

“Maybe the Triads found out what these guys were up to, and put a stop to it,” Troy said.

Alex shrugged. “Maybe.”

“But they were letting Lin Chen leave the country on a private plane with a couple hundred grand in cash when we found him.”

“Maybe they didn’t know what he was,” Alex said.

Troy shook his head. “They’re the ones who told me.”

Alex took another breath.

Troy went on. “The plan, as explained to me, was to blow up the Bank of China building. It would be a much bigger disaster than the first one. They were going to wire the top floors with explosives on the inside, and pull it straight down like a controlled demolition, only with thousands of people inside. C4, maybe, or something like it. I doubt you could move enough dynamite without someone noticing. But I don't know. I didn't see any of this, it's just what Zhao told me. He said the detonators and the plans were at the house. The dead guys were going to pose as maintenance men."

"They think we were in on it," Alex said.

Troy nodded. "Yeah. So they claim. But in on what? Last I heard, no one had found any explosives, just detonators."

Alex began to wheel the cart to the door.

"Okay," he said. "I have to go before these clowns outside begin to think we're…"

"What am I supposed to do?" Troy said.

Alex stopped and looked at him. "Do about what?"

Troy raised his hands. "I'm getting kicked out of the country, Alex. Those guys aren't standing in the hallway for their health. Tomorrow I'm on the train to Guangzhou, with these two guys sitting in my lap."

Alex shrugged. "What do you think you're supposed to do? Escape."

He said the word as though it was so obvious, and so straightforward, it hadn't been worth mentioning.

Troy nodded. "Ah. Escape."

"That's right. You needed me to tell you that? Persons wants you in country, so escape if you can. We'll work out the diplomatic nightmare later."

"Why does he even want me here? If the ZDL guys are all dead, this thing is over."

"Nothing is ever over," Alex said. "You know that. We don't know who did the original attack, and the Chinese want to blame it on us. That's no good. It isn't going to stand. We also don't know if another attack is coming. Just because those guys are dead doesn't mean there aren't more of them."

He paused.

"Listen, your best bet to get away is at the train station tomorrow. It'll be crowded, a lot of people are trying to get out of the city, and you might be able to pull a fast one. If you manage to lose these guys, come to the taxicab stand on Level B2. I'll give you a ride."

"A ride to where?"

"A ride to wherever, Stark. Don't worry about that part now. One step at a time. But don't kill anybody, okay? We can't afford that."

He yanked the cart to the door. He gestured back at the table.

"The food is pretty good here."

"I wouldn't know," Troy said. "I missed the breakfast buffet this morning."

"You have sweet and sour pork. Chicken and broccoli with rice. A little dessert pastry thing, I'm not sure what that is. Also, I gave you a couple cans of Rock Star Zero in case you need a little pick-me-up."

Troy smiled. "I could use those."

Alex nodded. "I know. They're not easy to find over here, but I went the extra mile. You look like you've been run through the paper shredder."

"Thanks," Troy said. "Thanks for that."

Alex raised a hand. The door was already open. He wrestled the cart out into the hall. A second later, the door swung shut and he was gone.

Troy went over and sat at the table. The food did look pretty good. It was all nicely presented on white porcelain plates. Steam rose from it. The smells of chicken and pork went straight to his head. He felt like he might pass out. The last time he had eaten was in the late afternoon, at a food court in some mall. It seemed like a lifetime ago.

His mobile phone was on the table at his right elbow. Just before Troy could dig into the food, the phone began to buzz. It wasn't the music the phone played when Troy had a normal call. It was a distinctive sound, the sound of Jan Bakker's secret communication network.

A different kind of call was coming, brought by the magnificent wind.

Troy sighed, despite himself. He just wanted to eat, and then sleep. Maybe an escape route would present itself tomorrow, or maybe it wouldn't. Maybe he would just leave the country after all, and tell Missing Persons he couldn't get away.

He picked up the phone and opened the app.

"Hello?"

"Stark?" a voice said.

It was Jan. Of course it was. That was fine. That was good. It was Jan, after all, who had explained to him what the ZDL was. Jan was a consummate professional. He was, as people never tired of telling Troy, the best at what he did, maybe in all of Europe.

"Yes, hello. How are you?"

"I'm on my way," Jan said.

"On your way where?"

"To Hong Kong. I don't know if anyone has informed you yet, but you're being replaced. El Grupo has been reconvened, as I mentioned earlier. Everyone close to us who is thought to be in danger is under protection. Agent Dubois and I are being sent as your replacements. There is some concern about a second attack that might occur. Rumors are flying. Supposedly, there was a massacre at a beach house. The Chinese are willing to allow new Interpol observers, as long as they're not you. And as long as they're not Americans."

Troy let that piece of information sink in.

"Where are you now?" he said.

"I'm in Madrid, at the airport. Dubois should arrive from France in a little while. We're flying to Hong Kong together."

"When will you get here?" Troy said.

"If everything works out, in the evening your time. It's a long flight."

Tell me something I don't know.

"Where are you staying?" Troy said.

There was a pause while Jan dug out his itinerary. "Uh… it's a hotel called the Jade Emperor. It's in Kowloon."

"I know the place," Troy said.

"Will you still be in Hong Kong when we arrive?"

Missing Persons wanted him to stay here. Alex was already here. Jan and Dubois were on their way. There was a mystery unfolding. A horrible terror attack had taken place. A second attack seemed to have been thwarted. But by who?

Nothing is ever over.

That's what Alex said.

Whatever was going to happen next, at least Troy would have the right team in place to deal with it. He thought of the two men out in the hall. Their plan was to move him out of town and then move him out of the country, all with a minimum of fuss. With a little luck, their plan was going to go awry.

"Yes," he said. "I'll be here."

"Where will you be?" Jan said.

Troy loaded a fork up with chicken and rice.

"Don't worry," he said. "I'll find you."

CHAPTER NINETEEN

1:45 pm Hong Kong Time
Hong Kong West Kowloon Railway Station
City of Hong Kong
China

"We'll never get on a train here."

Troy had two new agents shadowing him. Sometime in the night, while he slept, the other ones had been replaced. Those guys were young, practically kids right out of school or after four years in the military.

These two were a bit older, maybe a touch savvier. One of them, Mr. Chang, spoke English very well. The other one didn't speak any English. In fact, he didn't speak much at all, not even to Mr. Chang. Despite the differences, these two were the same government-issue, nothing to see here, standard secret policemen as the others, with just a bit more experience.

Mr. Chang had worn wraparound sunglasses in the car on the way here. That was his nod toward an individual style. Troy didn't like Chang, so he didn't bother to ask him what the name meant.

In retrospect, Zhao had more personality than any of these guys. Zhao had stuck his neck all the way out, trying to get to the bottom of things. Troy couldn't picture Chang and his partner, or the two guys who spent the night in the hall, ever doing something like that.

"We already have reservations on the three o'clock express train," Chang said. "We'll have no trouble getting on board."

The place was a madhouse. It was a very modern station, with the same soaring glass and steel construction that seemed to be required for all new construction. The station must be ten stories high, almost all of it empty space. Far above their heads were glass skylights built into a sort of diagonally-oriented roof. There were wide pillars that bent at odd angles and didn't seem to serve any actual purpose. They reminded Troy of the pneumatic tubes in old buildings in New York City, which office workers once used to send messages from office to office and from floor to floor. Only these tubes were huge and thick.

Down here, on the ground floor, hundreds, possibly thousands of people stood like cattle crammed together to be loaded onto railway freight cars. The ticketing booths were mobbed with people. Some people were leaning in to the ticket booths windows, talking reasonably to the ticket clerks, explaining their case for leaving Hong Kong. A few people appeared to be shouting at the clerks instead. One man was jabbing a finger, much like Zhao had done at Troy.

Some people were crying. In fact, Troy noticed at least half a dozen women standing forlornly away from the ticket booths, each one alone in a vast crowd, weeping.

Tall men in military uniforms, black boots and helmets, stood in clusters near entrances and egresses, faces in permanent frowns, shotguns cradled to their chests. A scene like this, civilians packed into an enclosed space like sardines, was akin to dangling a piece of juicy, bloody meat in front of a terrorist. This was about as soft a target as you could have.

Announcements were being made every few minutes on the overhead public address system, but it was impossible to hear what they were saying. Troy couldn't even tell if they were broadcasting an English translation or not. The buzz of the crowd in the station was so loud, he couldn't hear a single distinct word coming from the speakers. All he knew was they were playing sounds.

Perhaps a hundred meters away, there was a booth with a sign above it that said INFORMATION, along with a translation in Chinese characters. There was nothing but people between here and there and not an inch of empty floor space. Troy couldn't imagine what kind of information all these people were hoping to glean from the people manning that booth.

Most likely, it was the information that their rationale for escaping Hong Kong was no more valid than anyone else's.

"How are we going to do that?" Troy said.

"It's simple," Chang said. "We are government agents. We will go to our track at the appointed time and get on the train. A conductor will find us our seats."

Troy sighed. Despite the circus atmosphere here and the crush of humanity, it probably would be that simple.

He was running out of time. Once they had him on that train, he was cooked. Travel was restricted. Even if he gave them the slip in Guangzhou, he could never make his way back here. It had to happen soon. He had to start looking for a way out.

He was loaded down by his garment bag and his overnight bag. Chang and his buddy had the advantage of not carrying anything. They probably planned to be back here before the end of their shift. Running away from them, through these crowds, while carrying these bags…

It wasn't going to work.

Level B2, the level Alex described as having the cab stand, was one floor above them. It was a sort of terrace level, half floor, half open air, which Troy could see from here. A food court was up there. Not far away, twin escalators ran up and down to that level.

"Mr. Chang, do you mind if I get a coffee and a bite to eat?"

He gestured upstairs.

Chang's face was blank.

Did they go to school to learn how to make that face?

"You should have eaten at the hotel," Chang said. "They offer a large hot breakfast buffet."

"I was running late," Troy said.

In fact, he had deliberately skipped the breakfast, in case needing food might give him an opening ploy.

"We noticed."

"What do you say?" Troy said. "I'll meet you guys back down here in twenty minutes."

Chang smiled at that. He did have a sense of humor, after all.

"We'll accompany you. We wouldn't want to lose you in this crowd."

"Oh, you don't have to worry," Troy said. "I'd find my way back to you. The last thing I need is to miss that train. I want to get out of this city before something else bad happens. The place is cursed."

Chang's eyes sharpened. His face seemed to harden. The blank, emotionless look from before was gone. It had been replaced by something else, something veering toward discomfort, maybe even anger. Troy was starting to push his buttons, just a little bit.

So he piled on.

"The whole country is cursed, as far as I'm concerned."

That got him.

"Let's go," Chang said. He gestured with one arm toward the escalators. "Stop your foolish talking."

"I'll lead the way," Troy said.

He threaded through the crowds, a bag on either shoulder, as the men followed right behind him. He found the escalator and stepped on carefully. They moved up through the open space, rising above the mass of people on the ground floor.

Troy scanned the new world they were entering. Getting food, or coffee, was a no go. The crowds were just as bad up here as down below. Troy didn't recognize most of the concessions. But there was a Starbucks with at least a hundred people online. Troy would be dipped in black tar before he waited an hour for burned, bitter coffee.

Coffee wasn't the point, anyway. He had two Rock Stars in his bag.

Chang tapped him on the shoulder. "Forget it, Mr. Stark. It's fruitless. They will have snacks and coffee on the train. You can eat then."

Troy's head swiveled back and forth, looking for something, anything. His mind raced ahead, bringing up rationales and excuses, and rejecting each one in turn.

I'm hypoglycemic. I need to eat NOW.

I'm diabetic. I need to eat NOW.

I have an anxiety disorder. These crowds are making me dizzy.

I have a blood disorder.

I'm anemic.

Maybe he should throw himself to the ground and foam at the mouth.

I'm a werewolf. I'm going through my transition.

There were bathrooms to his left. A steady stream of people were entering and exiting, both the men's and the ladies' rooms. Nothing good in that direction. There was no way he could shake these guys in the men's room. They'd just follow him in and wait around. Troy could hardly blend in with the crowd and slip away.

There was a door between the men's and the ladies' room. Troy stared at the sign. It was a picture, a little more than a line drawing, and less than a cartoon.

It showed a person holding a much smaller person on a table, easy enough to decipher in any language. It was a baby changing station.

"Chang, I need to use the men's room."

This had to happen fast. Pray that no one was in there.

Troy made a left, as though he was going for the bathroom, following the stream of men headed in that direction, being sucked there from all sides, the bathroom a black hole with a powerful force of gravity. Chang and his partner were right on Troy's heels.

The door to the changing station opened. It opened inward. Troy wasn't sure if that was good or bad. A young woman appeared, baby in her arms. The baby wore a light blue wool hat and was wrapped in a white or pale yellow hand-knitted blanket.

The woman came out, the crowd flowing around her but not pausing for a second.

Troy darted to the door, suddenly bulling through people.

"Stark!"

He caught the door before it closed, and he pushed inside. The agents were a step behind him. He could sense them there, looming behind him.

The details of the room hit him all at once, in a flash.

It smelled, for starters. It smelled like a baby, like dirty diapers. It was large, with a wet stone floor and white tile walls. The lights in here were bright. There was a toilet seat and a sink protruding from one wall. The mirror over the sink was a kind of unbreakable reflective metal.

The baby changing table was to the right. It could fold up into the wall, but was currently down. It seemed to be made of some hard plastic or fiberglass. To the left was a closet, the door left ajar by a careless janitor.

There was a bright yellow mop bucket in the closet, with a black wringer device attached at the top. There was a mop leaning by itself, the mop part turning brown with dirt and grime. There was a bright orange folding sign, the triangular kind a careful custodian would place on the floor outside after using the mop. It showed another cartoon, this one of a man slipping and falling backward.

There was a lot here.

Troy dropped his bags and turned.

Chang and the other man pushed in behind him, Chang first, the partner a half-step behind. The door was closing behind them.

"What are you doing?" Troy said. "Don't come in here! I'm using the bathroom!"

"This room is not for you," Chang said.

BAM.

Troy punched Chang with a hard right cross.

Chang's head turned to his right, just in time to catch a left from Troy. Then Troy's right returned, an uppercut low into Chang's mid-section.

Chang was caught utterly unprepared. People just didn't do this kind of thing here. Troy grabbed Chang's head on both sides. The partner was trying to slip to Chang's right and get out from behind him. He was reaching inside his jacket, maybe going for his gun.

The door fully closed.

Troy smashed Chang's head into his partner's face.

BANG!

He did it again, driving it like a hammer, like he was using a coconut to crack open another coconut

BAM!

Then he did it again.

"Sorry!" he shouted. "I'm sorry!"

Chang's eyes were totally blank now. It wasn't a put-on. It wasn't a practiced look. He was out on his feet. Troy shoved him aside. Chang took three lurching sideways steps, crashed into the wall, and fell to the floor in front of the toilet.

The partner was still up. His gun was out and in his hand. He was moving in the other direction, toward the changing table.

Troy grabbed the wrist of the man's gun hand and delivered a savage punch to the back of the man's head.

BAM!

"Sorry! I don't mean it!"

He punched him again.

BAM!

And again.

The man lost his gun. He sunk to all fours on the slippery floor.

BAM!

Troy punched him in the back of the head again. And again.

"Go down, you bastard. It's over!"

Troy reached up and engaged the lock on the door.

BAM!

He punched the guy again. His hand was starting to hurt. You couldn't endlessly punch a man would not go down.

What is wrong with this guy?

Troy stopped, stood tall, and kicked the man's arms out from under him. The man fell face-first onto the hard floor, the front of his suit probably soaked now.

Troy picked up the gun, a small, dark green semi-automatic that was just like Zhao's. This must be the standard issue sidearm.

Troy reached into the man's jacket pockets, looking for whatever else he could find. He came out with a small black flip-phone. That couldn't be his real phone. Troy dropped it onto the floor and stomped on it, smashing it to pieces.

He reached in again, and found a smart phone. He smashed that one-two.

He found a pair of steel handcuffs. Okay. They were getting somewhere.

Now he stood tall, the room spinning around him a little bit. The stench in here was unbelievable. There was blood all over the floor under the man's head. Getting someone else's head smashed into the vulnerable bones of the face would do that to you.

Troy's heart was pounding. He was breathing heavy and LOUD.

He was all in now. There was no turning back from this. This had an international incident written all over it.

This is what Alex told me to do.

Not 100% true, Troy realized. Alex had told him to escape. Escape could mean a lot of things. It could mean running through the crowds on the concourse. It could mean climbing out a window. It could mean jumping off a train platform and disappearing down the tunnel.

He told ME to escape.

Ah. True enough.

There was a sound behind him. Troy turned, and Chang was on his knees in front of the toilet bowl. He placed a hand on either side of the bowl and pushed himself slowly to a standing position. His knees were bent. His arms hung down.

"Chang," Troy said. "Wait a minute. Stop."

Chang turned around and reeled to his left. His eyes were wild, but no longer blank. They rolled and pivoted, looking for Troy.

Chang's hair was mussed. His dark suit was wet.

He reached inside his jacket pocket.

Troy pointed the partner's gun in Chang's face.

"Don't make me hurt you. I have a gun. Just stop."

Chang pulled his own gun, an identical green semi-automatic. Troy slapped it out of his hand. It clattered to the bathroom floor.

Chang's left hand came around and punched Troy in the face. Troy's head snapped back a bit. The man still had some zip in his punch. Give them credit. These guys were tough. What was the old saying? They could take a licking and keep on ticking.

"I suppose I deserve that," Troy said.

"You're under arrest," Chang said. "Cease all resistance."

Troy flipped the partner's gun over in his hand, raised it, and smacked the grip across Chang's skull. That did it. The lights finally went out.

Troy caught Chang and gently guided him to the floor. Troy laid him out on his back. Chang was making a sound, violent inhales and exhales, akin to rapid snoring.

Troy looked at the two men on the floor. They were knocked out in a baby changing room, right next to the public bathrooms, in a train station overflowing with people. This, right here, was a mess.

So make it even messier.

Troy rolled the mop bucket out of the closet. It was full of nasty brown water. He pulled the bright orange sign out, too. And the dirty mop.

"Okay," he said.

Behind him, someone tried the door and found it locked. Troy shouted something at the door, a series of unintelligible sounds.

He went through Chang's pockets, found one phone, and smashed it. Then he dragged both men into the closet. He handcuffed the partner's wrists around Chang's waist. He left the two of them slumped in there and forced the closet door shut on them.

Maybe they would sleep for a while.

What else? Troy put his own bags on the changing table, then spilled the dirty brown water all over the floor. He leaned the mop against the wall.

Anything else?

There was a sort of metal garbage chute hanging on the wall. This was a baby changing station, which meant that garbage bin…

Troy went to it, pushed it open, and pulled out a couple of bundled-up disposable diapers. The smell hit him like a wooden board between the eyes.

"Ah," he said. "Oh no."

He dumped the contents on the floor.

That was it. That was plenty. He grabbed his bags, hung them over either shoulder, and picked up the orange warning sign. He unlocked the door and went outside.

Another woman waited there, holding a baby.

Troy stood the orange sign on the floor outside the door and shook his head at her. He raised a hand to stop her.

"No go," he said, lapsing into pigeon English. "Very bad inside."

He had no idea if the woman would understand him or what she would do in response. The door was still closing. The woman looked around him, and made a pained face.

"Oh," she said.

Then Troy was walking away, moving at double speed. He didn't look back. He darted this way and that through the crowds. Above his head was a horizontal sign. There were a few large Chinese characters. There were also words in English.

Level B2 - Taxi Stand.

Up ahead, maybe 50 meters away, were a set of sliding glass doors. Through those doors was a sort of covered parking garage, or maybe a covered roadway. Troy fought the urge to run toward it. He was just a weary traveler, Mr. Normal, who had given up on getting out of town by train. There was no reason to run.

Three soldiers with their ever-present shotguns stood near the doors. Troy didn't even glance at them.

The doors slid open. There were numerous small steel poles standing vertically, about a meter high. Each one had a broad yellow stripe near the top. They were there to stop a car from crashing through the doors. The overhead ceilings out here were low.

Beyond the poles, parked at the curb, was a red sedan with a white roof. There was a white sign on the front door with dark Chinese characters. On the back of the car, the rear quarter panel was the word TAXI in white.

A man was leaning against the front of the car. He wore a dark suit, and a dark hat, like a chauffer. He was a smallish man with a Mediterranean complexion. If anyone wondered why a man who looked like this was driving a taxi in Hong Kong, no one seemed to be asking.

The man pressed a remote clicker that was in his hand. The clicker made a sound like a bird chirping, and at the rear of the car, the trunk popped open.

Troy went to the trunk, dropped his wet bags in, and slammed the door. Alex had already gotten in behind the wheel. Troy slid into the back seat like a man who was hiring a taxi.

No sooner was he inside than Alex had pulled away from the curb.

"How'd it go?" Alex said.

Troy shook his head. "I don't want to talk about it."

***

"Mr. Zhao."

Troy was standing between two sleek black electric vehicles when Zhao came out to the parking garage.

Zhao was dressed much as he had been when Troy met him – black suit, black leather shoes, pale blue dress shirt, hair perfect. His tie today was a sort of pale yellow with a dragon design in light red. He walked with his head down, eyes on the pavement, as if deep in thought.

He looked up when Troy spoke. His eyes went wide.

Instinctively, his hand went inside his jacket.

"What are you doing here, Mr. Stark?"

"Don't pull that gun, Mr. Zhao. That's not how you want this to go, and it's not how I want it to go. I have a gun, too."

Troy didn't bother to mention that he actually had two guns. Zhao was going to find out soon, if he didn't already know. Those two agents were going to turn up at some point, whether because someone found them or of their own volition. And when they did, Troy was going to be about as hot as August in hell.

Zhao's hand came out of the jacket. He moved it slowly. It was holding a cell phone. He held it up for Troy's inspection.

Troy nodded. "Good."

"Where are the agents who were escorting you?" Zhao said.

"They're okay," Troy said. "They're alive. Did they miss a check in?"

Zhao nodded. "Yes. And their phones are dead."

Troy didn't say anything.

"Are they injured?"

Troy shrugged. "They'll probably have headaches for a couple of days."

"This can't possibly work, Stark. If your country, or the spy agency you work for, put you up to this, you can congratulate them because they've doomed you. You're going to prison here in China, probably for a long time."

"I work for Interpol," Troy said. "It's not a spy agency."

Zhao looked away across the parking garage. "I've never seen an Interpol agent who operates like you."

"Doesn't mean anything," Troy said. "And it doesn't matter anyway. I'm the one making these decisions. No one put me up to it."

Now Zhao turned back to him. He still had his phone out.

"Even worse. There will be no one to intervene on your behalf. Listen, I'll give you 60 seconds to run away. Disappear in the same way you just appeared. Find your way out of the city, and out of the country, if you can."

"Mr. Zhao, something here doesn't add up. We're running out of time before the next attack. We have to do something."

"The next attack was thwarted," Zhao said. "The conspirators are dead."

"Who thwarted it?" Troy said.

Zhao shook his head. "I don't know. Neither do you. No one does."

"Someone knows," Troy said. "I don't believe for a minute the attack was thwarted. That attack was a decoy. The real attack is still on, in all likelihood, somewhere in Hong Kong. And in all likelihood, it's going to take place tomorrow during the Golden Dragon dedication."

Zhao said nothing.

"You think I'm disrespectful," Troy said. "You think I don't know what I'm talking about. You think I should leave the country. But the next attack is going to kill Chinese people, your countrymen and countrywomen, and I'm trying to save them. I'm risking my freedom, and maybe my life, to save them. Whoever is behind this is going to try again, only it's going to be worse this time."

Troy was saying these things and realizing the full truth of them only as he said them. They'd been following a trail, and then it went cold, and dead. It came to an end exactly where someone wanted it to. It was a diversion.

"I never said you don't know what you're talking about," Zhao said. "I never even thought that. I stuck my nose out because I believed you were right."

"I'm still right," Troy said. "The big one is coming. The clock is ticking down."

Zhao took a deep breath, and then sighed heavily.

"Mr. Zhao?"

Zhao nodded. "I know. I know it is."

"So what are we going to do?" Troy said. "Are we going to stop this attack, or are we going to let it go forward?"

"You're wanted now on suspicion of assault, kidnapping, and possible murder of two missing government agents."

Troy shook his head. "Assault. That's the whole thing. I promise you. I didn't kidnap or murder anyone. They will turn up very soon."

Zhao sighed again. "You're going to get me in a great deal of trouble."

Troy shook his head. "We're going to be heroes. And I will insist that you were not involved in my escape."

"They'll know that," Zhao said. "Security video will determine how you escaped, and if anyone helped you. But just standing here talking with you could get me put away in prison. Cooperating with you could be seen as treason."

"If the attack doesn't happen tomorrow, I'll leave town on my own. You won't have to know anything about it. In fact, I'd prefer if you don't."

Troy and Zhao stood facing each other for a long moment.

Troy had the new escape route already worked out in his head. Victoria Harbour was full of small sailboats. Troy was an expert sailor. He was going to steal a sailboat, load it with provisions, and take off for the Philippines. If he managed to slip past the Chinese coast guard, he was guessing five to seven days on the open sea should do it.

"For now, I need a place to hide," he said. "A place I can use as my command center."

Zhao grunted. He almost smiled. "You need resources for a command center. A team, intelligence gathering, something."

"My team from Interpol is on their way," Troy said. "They are in the air right now. If anyone can crack this, they can."

"Give me the guns you took," Zhao said. He held out his free hand.

"Guns?" Troy said. "What makes you think I have more than one?"

"You disabled two agents. Each man was issued a firearm. I know you well enough to know that you wouldn't take one and leave one. You took them both. You must surrender them to me. I have to be able to trust you. Also, I can't work with someone who has guns he stole from our own agents. There will be fallout at the end of this mission. That can't be part of it."

Troy nodded. He could see the truth in all of this. It was beginning to look like he wasn't going to be able to commandeer a gun in China and then hang on to it.

He slipped both guns out of his jacket, and passed them over to Zhao.

Zhao took them and put them away. They disappeared almost as quickly as they reached his hand. Maybe he had practiced magic tricks as a boy.

"I have a place that I keep secret," Zhao said. "It isn't monitored, as far as I know. It isn't the best accommodation in the city."

Jackpot. Alex had access to a safe house, but in all likelihood, the Chinese knew about it. Even if they didn't, it would have done no good to have Troy hiding away somewhere by himself. He needed to be close to the action. He needed to be with Zhao.

"Sold," Troy said.

CHAPTER TWENTY

6:45 pm Hong Kong Time
Happy Mansion, "The Beast"
King's Road, Quarry Bay
City of Hong Kong
China

"Tell me this isn't where you live," Troy said.

The tiny apartment was on the ninth floor of a tall, square building with a small courtyard in the center of it. There must be hundreds, if not thousands, of flats just like this one. Each one had a small terrace overlooking the courtyard. The outsides of the opposite terraces were painted red, green, yellow, white and blue, in thick, primary color painted you might slap on the side of a barn.

The colors were faded and peeling off. The building was old and badly dilapidated. Apparently, the official name was Happy Mansion, but it was clearly an unhappy place. Maybe that's why they also called it The Beast.

Zhao had dropped him off here hours ago, making exactly two comments before he left. "You can eat whatever you find," was one comment.

"Don't go on the terrace," was the second. The second comment came with an added bonus. "Someone might see you out there."

As the day grew long, the sunlight faded from the sky. Except for the glow of the city lights of Hong Kong, which came in at the top of the building, and the lights from neighboring apartments, the air shaft was dark. Troy could probably go out on the terrace if he wanted. But still, he didn't dare.

Now Zhao had returned. He hung his jacket on a peg by the door when he came in. The two men inside the apartment at the same time were two people too many. Zhao was carrying two brown paper bags, steam rising from the top of them.

"This isn't where I live," Zhao said. "Of course not."

Troy nodded. "Well, that's a relief."

The apartment was cramped, with barely enough space for a twin-sized metal-framed bed in one corner and a kitchenette along the opposite wall. The walls were a faded cream color, but the peeling paint revealed layers of previous colors. A small TV is mounted between the kitchen shelves and cabinets. There was barely enough space to walk between the bed and the kitchen. The floor was hard and cold, made of gray concrete with a few worn rugs covering some of the surface.

Next to the door to the terrace, there were two windows. They were covered with a heavy black curtain, blocking out most of the natural light. The apartment had a musty odor, probably from lack of ventilation. It was moist in here. There was also a hint of incense, as if Zhao was trying burn the smell and the humidity out of the place.

The walls were thin, allowing the noise from the neighboring apartments to seep in. Troy had spent much of the day on the bed, watching the TV across the room. The colors on the TV were blown out, and the images were indistinct. He couldn't understand a word that was being said, but he turned up the volume a bit to drown out the neighbors. The metal frame of the bed squeaked whenever he moved – it was stiff and uncomfortable, and the sheets felt damp.

Troy kept one eye on the apartment door the entire time, half-expecting a SWAT team to come storming in at any moment.

He was still lying in bed when Zhao stepped inside.

It was a coffin of a place, cramped and claustrophobic. In a weird way, Troy really was glad that Zhao didn't live here. There was no way a guy with his job should be living in a place like this.

"What do you use it for?"

Zhao sat at the small rectangular table along the wall of the kitchen. He began to take food containers out of the paper bags and place them on the table. He was less than two meters from Troy, at most.

Zhao shrugged. "I hide people here sometimes. Like I'm doing now."

"What do your neighbors think of that?"

"They know what I am," Zhao said. "They know to be careful. Also, I sleep here sometimes myself. It's convenient to my headquarters, to Causeway Bay, and to Central Hong Kong. My own flat is far out in of the developments of the New Territories, 45 minutes away by car. Sometimes, after a very long day, I don't want to drive. I just want somewhere to lay my head."

Troy said nothing to that. He had been in some rough places, but he didn't want to lay his head here. He had a reputation for being tough, he knew that. And he deserved it. There were few things tougher in life than being a Navy SEAL. But it bothered him to put his head on the pillows. He was a little concerned about what might crawl out from under them.

"When I am here," Zhao said, "I make sure I am a considerate neighbor."

He began to eat the food he brought straight from the cartons, using a pair of chopsticks.

"What's the word on the street?" Troy said.

He had been cooped up in here with no outside contact. It was like being in a prison cell. He had played the TV so he didn't have to listen to the neighbors, yes. But he had also played it because he figured if another disaster struck, they were bound to show the news of it on the tube.

Nothing like that had happened. They weren't even showing footage of the BCHB building.

"Say it again, but not in American slang."

"What is happening?" Troy said. "Are there updates about the situation?"

"Oh," Zhao said. "Well, the two men you attacked reappeared, as you said they would. One has a fractured skull and a concussion. One has broken facial bones and lost a permanent dental bridge."

Troy laced his fingers behind his head.

"I'm sorry."

"No, you aren't," Zhao said. "But at least you didn't kill them. When they are released from the hospital, they will be severely reprimanded, possibly even reassigned. There is a small chance they will lose their jobs. So while they're still alive, you didn't help their careers. We can say that."

"Why will they be reprimanded?"

Zhao looked at Troy. "They lost. Two armed men lost to one unarmed man. Two Chinese lost to an American. They weren't paying enough attention. They weren't skilled enough fighters. Their guns were taken from them. They were bound with their own handcuffs and left in a closet in a bathroom. It's a terrible humiliation. Behind their backs, they will be laughingstocks among the other agents, even though nothing funny has happened. They have lost face."

Ouch. There was that losing face thing again.

"I didn't see anything about it on TV," Troy said.

"Of course not," Zhao said. "But rest assured, they are looking for you. All the police and all the Ministry agents have your photograph. You're a wanted man. They know from surveillance footage in the train station that you acted alone. I doubt they suspect my involvement at all, because if they did, we'd both probably be under arrest by now."

"Okay," Troy said.

"Besides that, there's nothing going on. The Bank of China building has been searched by expert teams with explosive-sniffing dogs, and it's completely cleared. There are no bombs in that building. Data analysts have processed the past several weeks of security footage. The terrorists never seem to have gained access to the building at all."

"What about another building?" Troy said. "And another team of terrorists?"

Zhao shook his head. "There are thousands of tall buildings in Hong Kong. Which one? What if they decided to attack Shanghai or Beijing instead? There are thousands more buildings in those cities. You Americans have a saying – looking for a needle in a haystack. Finding another building that someone might attack, here in China, is like looking for one needle in a stack of identical needles."

"What do you want to do?" Troy said.

"Me?" Zhao said. "I'm going home."

He gestured at the bags and food cartons on the table.

"I brought you some food. It's good. The place is too small to sleep two. So I'll drive out to my place, and return in the very early morning. If you have some way to leave the city, as you suggested you do, I think it will be best if you go before sunrise. Suspicion hasn't fallen on me yet, but that doesn't mean it isn't going to."

"I thought you said no one knew about this place," Troy said.

Zhao offered a rueful smile. "If they decide they want to know everything about me, how long do you think it will take them to find out?"

Troy saw the truth in that.

"Mr. Zhao…"

"There's nothing we can do," Zhao said. "Everyone has moved on from the idea of a second bombing. There's no evidence of such a thing. There's a great deal left to investigate about the BCHB attack, and that's where my focus has to be. If something does happen tomorrow, there's no way we could have stopped it."

He was already shrugging into his sports jacket again.

"Mr. Zhao, my team hasn't even arrived yet."

"I don't know what help they can be," Zhao said. "They'll be jet-lagged and days behind the original disaster. If they're coming to replace you, they really will be tourists. I doubt the Ministry will even show them the bombing site. That's how all the trouble started in the first place."

"That's not how the trouble started," Troy said. "I didn't put Lin Chen on that mountaintop. I didn't kill all those guys at the beach house."

Zhao went to the door and opened it. He glanced both ways out in the hall. He turned back to face Troy for a moment.

"I leave all the lights on when I sleep here. When it's dark, the cockroaches come out."

And with that, he was gone.

CHAPTER TWENTY ONE

January 23
12:50 am Hong Kong Time
Happy Mansion, "The Beast"
King's Road, Quarry Bay
City of Hong Kong
China

The phone was ringing.

It caught Troy in a sort of fugue state.

He was trapped in this dismal, tiny apartment. All the lights were on. He was staring at the TV across the room, asleep with his eyes open. There was no way to investigate anything on his own. There was no way to know if another attack was coming. Zhao wanted him out of here in the morning.

If Troy was going to sail by himself to the Philippines, he'd better get some rest.

He glanced at the phone. It was there in the narrow, stiff bed with him, resting on his leg. It had launched the magnificent wind of Jan Bakker's *Fung Wah* application. This was the whole reason Troy hadn't ditched the phone by now. It was risky keeping it, but he needed to hear from his team.

"They must be here," Troy heard himself say.

His eyes rolled around the apartment, looking for the time. There was an old clock on the wall, lit up in blue and yellow, with a smiling clock face. The hour hand was just past 12, the minute hand near the 5. It was after midnight.

Troy pressed the button. "Hello?"

"Stark?"

"Don't say my name," Troy said.

"The app has end-to-end encryption," Jan said. "We are free to talk."

"That depends where you are."

"We're at the Jade Emperor Hotel. We just arrived a little while ago. The flight was delayed, and there was trouble landing and accessing the airport terminal. But we're here. Agent Dubois went to her room to freshen up, but she said she'll be back in a moment."

The hotel was a front. That's what Alex said. The rooms were swept for bugs.

"Okay," Troy said.

"We understand you're in trouble," Jan said.

"Who told you that?"

"The man who picked us up at the airport," Jan said. "Our escort. He said our activities will be restricted because our predecessor attacked two of their agents, and hospitalized them. So he just dropped us off here. Frankly, we were fine with that. It was a long trip."

Suddenly, Troy noticed his hands ached from punching Chang and his companion. It was his right hand that hurt the most, from trying to deliver knock-out blows to a couple of guys with hard heads. Probably, it wasn't just how hard their heads were. They also probably refused to go down because they understood the consequences of what Troy was doing far better than Troy did.

"Listen, Jan..."

"Where are you?" Jan said.

"I'd prefer not to say," Troy said.

Could he even describe where he was? He didn't know.

Did Jan sound just a bit hurt?

"We have end-to-end encryption," Jan said again.

"Never mind that," Troy said. "We have problems. I was in on a bust late last night. The guy from ZDL gave us the location of a safe house. It was on the beach at Cheung Sha, far out of town. The house was full of dead guys, most of them also ZDL. Maybe ten men. They were all bound and shot in the head, execution-style. Word is they were planning something big, another terror attack. They wanted to take out the Bank of China building. I need to talk to you and Dubois about this. I'm concerned that we're missing something. For example, why are they dead? And who killed them?"

"Here comes Dubois now," Jan said. "I'll put this on speaker."

"Hello Agent Stark," Dubois said, sounding cheerful. "I hear you've been doing the same circus tricks as usual. Beating people up, dropping out of sight. Have you killed anyone so far?"

Troy winced. Alex better be right about those bug sweeps.

"Listen. Please don't say my name."

"All right," Dubois said. "I was just teasing you. It's been a long day."

"I understand," Troy said.

"What can we help with?" Dubois said.

Troy explained it all again. The arrest of a ZDL member, and subsequent release and then re-arrest of that ZDL member. The dead men at the beach house. The suggestion that they were planning another attack, worse than the first one, but they had no explosives in their possession, and they didn't get anywhere near the target.

"I've seen this sort of thing before," Dubois said.

"Do tell."

"There are two likely scenarios. The first is the police are corrupt, or some of them are. They knew what was happening. When this Lin Chen was brought in, they realized right away that they had to stop the second attack. If they allowed it to happen, and they had a known ZDL member in their custody, who they let go… you can see how bad that looks."

"So they sent a death squad out to the beach house?" Troy said.

"It's not unheard of for police departments to have death squads," Jan said. "The Rio de Janeiro police had one for at least a decade."

"What's the other option?" Troy said.

"There were two teams," Dubois said. "Each one was assigned an attack. Both were expendable. If the first team failed, the second team would launch their attack. If the first team was successful, the second attack was canceled. After the cancellation, it was too risky to try to extract the second team from Hong Kong, so they just killed them instead."

Troy chewed on that for a bit. He still wasn't buying it.

"The second attack was designed to be much larger and deadlier than the first," he said. "It was also scheduled to coincide with this dedication of the new world's largest building, the Golden Dragon Peace Tower. A bunch of foreign dignitaries have been rounded up to attend this dog and pony show, including the American Mustard King Lloyd Garelli."

"They wanted to overshadow the event," Dubois said.

"That's the story I'm getting," Troy said.

"Well, the first bombing has already overshadowed it," Dubois said.

"Not exactly," Jan said. "I'm looking out my window, and the buildings across Victoria Harbour are all flashing Hong Kong Strong messages and things of that nature."

"I know," Troy said. "I've seen it."

"If the dedication is allowed to go forward, Hong Kong, and by extension China, will look stronger than ever. They will look resilient. Especially because the Peace Tower is being built by Golden Dragon Industries, of which the Chinese government is the major shareholder. They own 90% of it."

"What are they?" Troy said.

"High tech, of course," Jan said. "It's a sprawling conglomerate. The vast majority of it is transparent, like consumer electronics – smart phones, smart watches, smart homes. Some of it is less transparent, like defense research and spy satellites. A little bit appears to be impenetrable, very secret – we're talking about biotechnology, cloning, possibly the weaponization of bacteria and viruses."

"And Lloyd Garelli is going to the dedication of this thing?"

"Politics make for strange bedfellows. Golden Dragon denies being involved in the manufacturing of anything besides consumer gadgets. They also have a social responsibility division that plants trees in deforested areas of Central America, digs wells in parched African villages, and sweeps mines, particularly in Cambodia. These are a tiny percentage of their activities, but make for excellent public relations."

"Who make up the other 10% that own the company?"

"A handful of Chinese oligarchs," Jan said. "Billionaires with close ties to the Communist Party, and with American business interests."

"They have enemies," Troy said.

"I'd say very much so, yes."

It was a nagging thought that Troy couldn't seem to let go.

"What if the plan all along was to take down the Peace Tower?" he said.

"As a symbol," Jan said. "It might be worthwhile. Taking down the World Trade Center struck at the heart of American financial, military and cultural supremacy. The issues I see here are the building isn't even finished yet, and there will only be a relative handful of people at the dedication, maybe two hundred. As terror attacks go, this would be smaller than the BCHB attack."

"I imagine security for the event will be very tight," Dubois said.

Troy nodded. "I imagine it will. But somebody killed those guys at Cheung Sha Beach, and I'm guessing it was cops or security forces of some kind."

"The Peace Tower is in Central," Dubois said. "It's near the waterfront, crowded by, and rising above, many other tall buildings. That is a very busy, very congested area. There must be hundreds of thousands of people in that neighborhood in the early morning of a workday. If the building did come down, all the way down, like the World Trade Center…"

"Pancaked," Troy said.

"Right, or if it fell over sideways, it would be a disaster of epic proportions."

"Why would anyone take this idea seriously?" Troy said.

He thought of Mr. Zhao, who simply gave up and went home. Zhao seemed to think there was nothing more to be done here. But if they were going to convince local officials that there was a possible danger, they were going to need Zhao to do the convincing. Dubois and Jan had just gotten here, and Troy himself was practically an enemy of the state.

"I can model it on my laptop," Jan said. "I can plot a 3D map of Central, with the surrounding neighborhood, estimated number of workers in that neighborhood, estimated mass of the Peace Tower, and the amount of force a collapse would create. I can see it in my mind without even doing it. The sheer weight of the concrete and the increasing momentum would likely take down nearby buildings. I can make an animation of it, with expected destruction radii, depending on circumstances."

"Name the circumstances," Troy said.

"Explosives used, and amount deployed," Jan said. "Blast radius. Which direction the building falls, or whether it comes straight down. Whether it's a full or partial collapse. There are a lot of potential variables."

"How long would that take?"

"I don't know," Jan said. "A few hours."

"Are we dreaming here?" Troy said. "What if we're wrong? What if it's just a normal ceremony, and nothing happens?"

"I'm not sleepy," Jan said. "It won't hurt anyone if I model a potential catastrophe. I often make such models when I'm home."

"That's wholesome," Troy said. "Everyone should have a hobby."

***

In the early morning, in the deep darkness before dawn, Zhao came back in.

Troy was awake and waiting for him. The apartment was well lit. In fact, Troy had turned on every available light he could find. Roaches were not his favorite insect.

Jan had made the animated computer model, uploaded it to encrypted cloud storage that he had, and gave Troy access to it. The model demonstrated several scenarios, from best case to worst case. The absolute best case was that this whole idea was a hyper-vigilant, overzealous fantasy, and the dedication would proceed without any cause for alarm.

The scenarios went downhill from there. The worst cases had a Peace Tower collapse blasting the surrounding buildings to smithereens, and killing tens of thousands of people.

Troy was sitting on the bed fully-dressed when Zhao appeared.

"Are you ready?" Zhao said.

"I need to show you something," Troy said.

CHAPTER TWENTY TWO

7:30 am Hong Kong Time
The Golden Dragon Peace Tower
Central
City of Hong Kong
China

"Yes sir," Zhao Fu said into his phone. "I am the one who did this."

Zhao had come into Central Hong Kong to see the situation for himself. What choice did he have? Everything hung in the balance.

Several times, he had watched the computer animation that Stark had shared with him. At first, he wanted to be skeptical, and he was. He had come to the flat to get rid of Stark, not to consider another one of his half-formed theories. They weren't even theories – they didn't rise to that standard.

Hypotheses, maybe? More like guesses.

But this was different. As Zhao watched the scenarios play out, he became more convinced each pass. The worst-case scenarios were so bad that there was no way Zhao could avoid raising the alarm. The risks of inaction were too high.

The Hong Kong Police had bomb-sniffing dog teams. What harm could it do to have a few of them comb quickly through the building before the dedication event? They could do their work in the background while preparations were still being made.

But that wasn't the entire story, was it?

No. Zhao had stuck his neck all the way out again. Now, he was on the phone with Beijing, speaking to his boss's boss, a man named Kongbu. It wasn't going well.

"Where did you get the idea?" Kongbu said.

Zhao could barely hear the voice coming through his phone. He was standing in the grand lobby of the new skyscraper. The lobby was a vast expanse of gleaming white marble, stretching high into the sky with grand columns and a sweeping staircase in the center.

Of course, against the far wall there was a gleaming bank of high-speed elevators that went to the upper floors, but the thing you noticed when you came in from the street was the staircase. It was reminiscent of some gilded age that Zhao had never experienced – perhaps in Europe of the 1600s, or the United States in the days of slavery and plantation houses.

The walls were decorated with intricate patterns and elegant chandeliers hung from the ceiling in a line. Weak early morning sunlight came in from the street through the floor-to-ceiling windows.

Outside, the streets were busy. Many people marched dutifully by, on their way to their jobs despite whatever concern, or fear, or dread they might feel being trapped in Hong Kong. Stoicism was the Chinese way. They called it "eating bitterness," and it meant to persevere through hardship. That's what the people were doing this morning. A few paused and looked through the glass at the lobby of the Peace Tower.

Near where Zhao was standing, there was the gentle trickle of an indoor fountain. The water cascaded down a tall, intricate sculpture of a golden dragon reaching to the sky, with two regal lions sitting at its feet. The power of that fountain was astonishing. Zhao could barely take his eyes off it.

The dragon was wealth, strength, prosperity and power. It was the bountiful harvest. The water was the flow of wealth and money and all good things. The lions were strength as well, but also stability, and superiority. The word "auspicious" did not do this fountain justice. It could make you think that the building would stand for a thousand years and usher in an age of opulence and world domination.

People were crowding into the lobby now, their footsteps echoing softly against the polished floors, and their conversations creating a low hum. The dedication was set to begin in an hour. Dignitaries were already here. The American Secretary of State had come in with his security team a little while ago and embarked on a tour of the building.

"Zhao?" Kongbu said.

"I'm sorry, Director. There is a great deal of sound here."

"Where did this idea come from, Zhao? This idea that the Peace Tower might be bombed."

"It might not be true, sir. It probably isn't. But I received a computer model from agents of Interpol as to what might happen if it were true. The effects would be devastating, almost too terrible to contemplate."

"Is this the American agent?" Kongbu said.

"No, Director. These are his colleagues, the ones who were sent to replace him."

Zhao waited for the man to ask him how he got in touch with these replacement agents. It would force Zhao to lie and say he contacted them on his own initiative. So far, Kongbu hadn't forced Zhao to lie. Everything Zhao had said was the truth.

"Do you know where that American agent is, Zhao?"

Okay, now the lying would have to begin.

"No, sir."

"There is some concern that you became too close to him."

The walls were closing in. This was Kongbu warning him.

Zhao chose his words carefully. "No one has informed me of that, sir."

"I'm informing you now."

"Yes, sir."

"In the meantime, three dog teams are en route to the building. I understand they will arrive there shortly. Let's hope, for everyone's sake, that this idea of yours has no merit."

This idea of yours.

"Let's hope so, sir."

"Good," Kongbu said. "I will be monitoring developments closely."

He hung up, leaving Zhao standing in the lobby, holding a dead phone to his ear. He didn't want to put it away, for fear that would invite someone to come and talk to him. He wanted nearby people to think he was engaged in an important conversation. He needed the time to get his thoughts straight.

Zhao took a deep breath. He was all the way out on a knife's edge now.

The worst possible outcome would be if the dogs found a bomb in the building. But if they did, at least Zhao's actions would be proven sound. If there was no bomb, then Zhao called in a false alarm. He was under scrutiny anyway. He had lied to Kongbu about Stark.

It would take nothing, barely any investigation, for them to determine that Zhao was lying. There must be video footage of Stark and Zhao somewhere. Harboring a violent fugitive like Stark, after he hospitalized two agents of the Ministry of State Security, would be a crime. Zhao would certainly lose his job. He would almost certainly end up in prison.

At this point, when Stark tried to sneak out of the country, it would almost make sense if Zhao joined him.

A team of men and dogs appeared on the plaza outside the lobby. The men were the uniforms of commandos, with heavy explosive-proof vests, jackboots, and helmets. Zhao assumed that the fabric of their jumpsuits had steel mesh sewn into it. There were three dogs, two black Labradors, and a German shepherd. The men held leashes, but gave the dogs a meter of slack to lead them. They came in one by one, through the revolving glass doors of the lobby.

Zhao noticed that out on the plaza, two more police vans had pulled up. Now, there were three police vans out there in total. Three men and three dogs climbed out of the two arriving vans. Three dog teams, nine dogs.

It had to be done. They had to be called in. If Zhao had taken no action, and something had happened, he could never have lived with himself.

The first team was already in the lobby. They spread out, moving through the gathering crowds. The dogs walked along between people, stopping and becoming curious about individuals, or the bags they were carrying, and then moving on. The policemen followed along behind, as if the dogs were the masters and the police were the servants.

There was a white grand piano at one side of the room. A Labrador went to it and slowly worked its way around. Nothing there.

The Labrador moved to the white columns that soared upward to the ceiling.

I became curious about one of the columns. It sniffed the column, did a half-circle around it, pawed at it for a second or two, then sat down next to it.

It looked to the policeman at the other end of its leash. The cop came, reached into his pocket and gave the dog a treat. The dog ate the treat like any pet would.

Zhao knew the protocol. When the dog found explosive material, it sat down. Then the trainer gave the dog the treat a reward for doing a good job.

The cop was on the radio a second later. The radio was a large, hand-held rig nearly as long as the man's face. He was waving to one of the other team members. A second cop came with a second dog. They went to a different column.

The second dog barely hesitated before sitting down.

The second cop's eyes became very large.

Zhao could feel his own heart begin to beat inside his chest. He looked around the lobby. There were easily two hundred people milling around. There was no telling how many people had gone upstairs for tours.

Outside, on the streets, there were thousands of people. In the nearby buildings, tens of thousands, all arriving to start their day. No one suspected a thing, except these two dogs, these two cops, and Zhao himself. The panic hadn't started yet. But it would, any minute.

Zhao's breathing began to come very fast. It was louder than the sounds of the crowd.

The bombs are inside the columns.

And on the heels of that terrible thought:

We have to get these people out of here.

***

"It's amazing up here," Lloyd Garelli said. "Simply amazing."

Lloyd was on the roof platform of the Golden Dragon Peace Tower, receiving an orientation. From up here, Lloyd could see the entire cityscape below, laid out like a maze of streets and buildings, with the glittering harbor stretching west to the horizon. The unfinished skyscraper seemed to reach high into the sky, its metal beams and concrete pillars jutting out starkly against the pale blue.

The person giving him the orientation was a man from Mayor Xi's office. He was a young sharpie, thin and fit and handsome, but in a checkered suit that seemed too small for him.

Maybe that was the style nowadays. The kid's pants were halfway up his ankles. The sleeves on his jacket didn't quite come to his wrists. Otherwise, the suit fit like a glove. He was wearing a bright yellow bow tie. His shoes were some dark reddish color. The guy was incredible, in his way.

Lloyd tended to go for a more sober and conservative look, befitting his position as United States Secretary of State. But to each his own.

"There will be introductory remarks in the ground floor lobby," the young guy was saying. "The mayor will introduce you."

"Where is the mayor?" Lloyd said.

The problem on this trip was that the Chinese were not pleased to have him here. They had made that abundantly clear during his stay. The mayor was an exceptionally good-looking, exceptionally well-preserved woman in her 60s. She had met with Lloyd for a total of five minutes so far. It was quite a snub for the mayor of a city to give the Secretary of State the slip like this. It was really beginning to seem that she was avoiding him at all costs.

"She is en route now," the young guy said. "She has a large entourage around her, and as you can understand, she has been very busy because of the tragedy."

"I understand," Lloyd said.

"When the opening remarks are complete, we will come up here for more, briefer remarks, and a photo opportunity. Then we return to the lobby for the reception."

The man indicated a podium at the far end of the platform. Beyond it was a staggering, panoramic view of Victoria Harbour.

They were wide open to the elements up here. The thing about this building was that it wasn't even done yet. The top eight floors were just a skeleton frame. He wondered why they were doing a dedication now, and he couldn't seem to get a straight answer.

"It is an auspicious time," one of the mayor's representatives had said. That was the closest thing to a response Lloyd had gotten or seemed like he was going to get.

In any case, being out in the sky like this created 360-degree views of Hong Kong from the top of the tallest building in the world.

There was the harbor. There was Central Hong Kong. To the left, was Victoria Peak rising high above everything else. Just below it, and a bit closer, were the still-smoldering ruins of the BCHB building.

Lloyd and young guy were far from the only ones up here. Lloyd had four security personnel, two body men, and two guys who you might call advance men. The bodymen stuck to Lloyd like they were glued on. The other two weren't always around. Sometimes they would race out ahead and procure the next car or aircraft, check out the room before Lloyd entered it, and just in general get the lay of the land.

Then there was the Chinese contingent. A couple of them definitely worked with the Mayor. Others might be from the government or the Communist Party. Lloyd had lost track of who was who. He tended to do that.

His job, as he saw it, was to be charismatic, charming, welcoming, and in general to be bigger and better than everyone else. But in a way that made people happy, or maybe even honored, to be with him. He was six foot four, so the bigger part was mostly easy. In fact, so was the better part.

He came from A LOT of money. People thought it was just mustard, but it really wasn't. There were entire lines of Garelli food products, including ketchup, mayonnaise, olive oil, horseradish, you name it. On his mother's side, the family owned an oil pipeline that ran under the ground from Boston Harbor to Quebec. They also owned the ground that it ran under. There were vast timber forests.

There was so much money that Lloyd never, not once in his life, had bothered to try to count it. That just wasn't his problem. The money afforded him the best possible education from the time he was a boy, and as a practical matter, he had always been smarter than everyone else.

The State Department? It mostly ran itself. Being the biggest and the best. That was his job. The troubling thing was the Chinese didn't seem to agree. Lloyd had always felt that he could turn any bad situation around, but here in China, it seemed like they were trying to thwart and marginalize him everywhere he went.

It occurred to Lloyd that some kind of sound was coming from below them. Somewhere nearby, down in the streets, maybe even here in this building, alarms were going off.

"Are you comfortable giving remarks from this place?" the young guy said.

"Comfortable? In what way?"

The young guy shrugged and smiled. "It's quite high. Some are afraid of heights."

Who does he think he's speaking to?

"I'll be fine," Lloyd said. "Heights don't bother me."

One of his Lloyd's body men was touching his earpiece and speaking. He was only a few feet away, but he was speaking so low that Lloyd couldn't hear him. He frowned, showing he was worried about something.

He leaned in to Lloyd.

"Sir, we need to leave the building. There is a call to evacuate."

"Evacuate? Why?"

"Uh, there's some possibility that the building might explode."

***

"Fisher! What are we supposed to do, man?"

The scene in the marble lobby was controlled chaos. Out on the street, outside the glass doors and three-story windows, the chaos was out of control. People were running through the streets, falling, stepping over each other, getting back up again. The cops were trying to direct people, but it was impossible. Traffic was backed up. You could hear the horns blaring.

Suddenly, a car jumped the curb and sped along the sidewalk, knocking people aside like bowling pins. An instant later, a police car appeared, sirens blaring as it chased the first car down the sidewalk. Bloodied people were all over the place out there.

The evacuation was not going smoothly.

Fisher reached into the breast pocket of his jumpsuit and took out a Cohiba cigar that he was planning to smoke in celebration when this job was done. There was no telling what was going to happen next, so he might as well smoke it now.

He clipped the end off, took out a steel lighter, and lit up.

"Fisher!"

Fisher nodded. He held the smoke in his mouth for a long moment. God, that tasted good.

He was in command here, after all, or was supposed to be. He had a mixed-race, international team that he had never been completely sure about. On the face of it, this was an easy job. It was a simple demolition. The explosives were wired into the building. The very structure of the thing was the bomb.

All his team needed to do was follow along, a pretend security team from a private contractor. When the dignitaries went to the top floor, Fisher and his guys were to accompany them. The detonators were in a steel box on an iron catwalk above the roof. The heavy weapons were also up there. The BASE-jumping parachutes were packed and stashed on that catwalk. Every man on this team was an experienced jumper.

So that was it. The talkers would be standing at the podium, talking. Yak, yak, yak. Fisher and his guys would fade away, go upstairs, get the chutes on, plug the detonators in, set the timers. Twenty seconds, no more. The access point for the detonators was on the roof, but the explosives began six stories below the top.

By the time the first wave of detonations started, Fisher and his team would be jumping off the roof and steering for the harbor.

In the insanity to follow, the building would come down like a sledgehammer. There would be confusion, and smoke, and fire, and terror. The sheer weight of this building would hit the ground and blast outward. The buildings right around would collapse, setting off a daisy chain of disaster. Thousands would likely be dead.

Fisher and team would fly through the air, hit the water, ditch the chutes, and swim for the retrieval boat. Gone. Like they were never even here.

But everything had just fallen apart.

Now, Fisher had three guys standing around him, all dressed in the uniforms of armed security. They were a good-looking bunch – fit, hard – but at the moment, their eyes were wide and wondering. One of them was the other American on this gig, a black guy from Pittsburgh who called himself Dutch. Dutch was probably the only one Fisher fully trusted.

The other two were Han Chinese from Taiwan, mercenaries for sure, but also something closer to true believers. Fisher didn't love true believers. This was about making money. Missions and philosophies, and ideals… they tended to cloud people's vision. Revenge. Rightness and wrongness. History. Fisher didn't have a lot of time for these things.

Explosions. That was something Fisher did have time for. He'd be lying to himself if he claimed that money was the ONLY motivator here. This was going to be one whale of a bang. Fisher loved money, but he also had an appetite for destruction. The two of them together was a combination that was tough to beat.

"We could DD, man," Dutch said. "Nobody knows who we are. We haven't done anything."

Fisher took another drag on the cigar. He allowed that all of what Dutch had said was true. Except there was one glaring problem.

"Ain't nobody gonna pay us if we DD," Fisher said. "That what you want? To walk away from the biggest payday of your life?"

Dutch shrugged. "The jig is up, man."

"That's how you feel, man. I ain't gonna beg you to stay. Hate to see you go, though. I think we can make it."

"We go on that roof now, they're gonna spot us," Dutch said. "They're gonna have choppers up there. They're gonna watch us the whole way down. I don't see how we get away. They'll be waiting for us when we hit the water."

There was a pause between the two men. Fisher had respect for this guy. If this was his opinion, that's just the way it was. They could soldier on without him. Behind Dutch, people ran across the lobby. A small child was alone, toddling along, crying.

"Premeditated," Dutch said. "Capital offense. Mass murder. The Chinese government. If they get us, it won't be pretty. Think about it."

Fisher planted the cigar in his mouth and raised his hands.

"As I indicated..."

He let that sit there.

"I'm out," Dutch said.

Fisher nodded. "Good luck."

He and Dutch shook hands and bumped fists. Dutch turned and moved fast across the lobby. He was already pulling his uniform off before he hit the street. Then he was just gone, lost in the swarming crowds outside.

Fisher turned to the two remaining men.

"What about you guys?"

"We want to do it. That's what we came here for."

Fisher nodded. "Good men. What about your buddies over there?"

There were two other Taiwanese on the team who didn't speak English. They were standing several meters away, monitoring the situation here in the lobby, and out on the street. These two tended to speak for the other two. It wasn't an ideal set-up, but it had worked so far.

"They want to do it, too."

All right. He was down to five. That was okay. His mind raced out ahead. Dutch could be right. They could have the cops, or the army, or someone breathing down their throats. They might need to buy some space and time.

Fisher looked around the lobby, scanning for anything good.

That clown from the United States had just come out of one of the elevators, flanked by two bodyguards. The Secretary of State, Captain Mustard. He was taller than Fisher would have imagined. The men with him were also tall, in dark suits and white shirts, with earpieces. Maybe they were Secret Service. It didn't really matter what they were.

The three of them were standing around, looking not entirely certain about what they should do next. Everyone else was running for their lives. These three must be waiting for a special invitation to leave.

Fisher was glad they were still here. If things went sour, a high-profile hostage might be a ticket out.

With Dutch gone, they had an extra chute now. Fisher doubted Captain Mustard could jump, but you never knew. And even if he couldn't, they could always just toss him. The shock of watching the US Secretary of State falling from the world's tallest building would probably give some people pause.

"That guy," Fisher said, indicating the Mustard Man. "We need him."

Fisher pointed at his own men. He could never keep their names straight or even pronounce them correctly, so he had given the two of them simple American nicknames.

"Ace, get your guys. Turbo, come with me. We'll all meet at the elevators one minute from now."

There was a method to this madness. Ace was cool, the laid-back one. Fisher had never seen him get upset about anything. Sometimes he just leaned against a wall, smoking a cigarette. Meanwhile, Turbo was fast, a killer, and a martial artist. He was one of these guys who could fly through the air, kicking out lightbulbs that were dangling from the ceiling.

Fisher and Turbo walked toward the Secretary of State.

"Pop the big guy on the left," Fisher said.

Turbo nodded. "Got it."

Fisher had his gun out now, holding it low.

The Mustard Man watched him come. He frowned at the burning cigar.

"Sir," Fisher said. "I'm Agent Kent. Just give me a few seconds. We're gonna get you out of here."

All the air seemed to go out of Mustard. He slumped, as if there had been a metal rod inside of him that had just been removed. It was almost a cartoon-quality pantomime of the emotion called RELIEF.

"Oh, thank God. Our communications just went down. The rest of my men went to get the car, but..."

"There's a lot of panic right now," Fisher said. "There's congestion in the streets, as you probably are aware. The cell towers are fizzling – they can't handle the volume of calls. My boss just got a message to me. We've got an armored vehicle waiting around the side of the..."

BANG!

Turbo shot the first Secret Service guy, whatever he was, in the head.

The gunshot echoed through the towering lobby. The Secretary of State jumped. Even Fisher himself flinched a little bit. That one was sudden. Just like Turbo to do it like that – fast and unexpected. Somewhere behind them, a woman started screaming.

The second bodyguard stood frozen, eyes like saucers. One second, two seconds...

He reached for his gun.

Too late.

BANG!

Fisher shot him in the skull.

Both of the guards were on the gleaming polished floor now, halos of blood circling their heads as though they were saints.

Fisher grabbed the Secretary of State by the arm and began pulling him toward the bank of elevators, just 20 meters away. Turbo was already out ahead. To the left, the three other Taiwanese were moving in that direction.

The Mustard Man was hesitant to move, so Fisher pressed the muzzle of the gun against his temple. That freed the man up a little. You might say it lubricated his joints.

"Sir, I wonder if you would come with me, please?"

"My uh," the Secretary of State began. "They told me to stay with my bodyguards." He half-turned, as if he wanted to go back to them.

Fisher held him firmly and moved him along. He gave him a poke with the gun, right above the eyes. Up ahead, the team was converging at the elevators. A big, polished brass double door slid open. It looked like the elevators were still working. That was a blessing. It would be a long climb up the stairs to the top of this building.

"I wouldn't worry about those guys, sir. They're dead now."

CHAPTER TWENTY THREE

7:50 am Hong Kong Time
The streets of Central
Approaching the Golden Dragon Peace Tower
City of Hong Kong
China

"Oh, man. Look at all this."

Troy walked through the crowded streets. He was quick time walking, like in his old Basic Training days. He couldn't just hang around Zhao's flat anymore, being sidelined. So he left, taking his chances out in the larger world. If something was going to happen, he'd prefer to be in the middle of it.

If nothing happened, and no one from the Ministry of State Security or the Hong Kong Police recognized him, he would go down to the waterfront, steal a boat, and start to work his way out of the country.

He was using his phone as a map. The Peace Tower was so tall, it should be easy to find. But there were many tall buildings in Hong Kong, for the moment it was hidden. The biggest problem here was people were streaming in his direction. At first it was dozens of people, then hundreds. Now? He couldn't put a number on it.

Troy kept having to look up from his phone so he didn't crash into someone.

A call was coming through. Troy glanced at the screen. It was the Fung Wah app launching, bringing him news from Jan Bakker.

Troy hit the green button. "Jan! Talk to me."

Jan skipped past the niceties.

"Agent Stark. A crisis is unfolding. It appears our guess was right. The television news is instructing all civilians to evacuate the area around Central Hong Kong. Rumors are flying on chat boards. No one is saying exactly what's happening, but there are fears…"

Suddenly, an alarm started going off. It came from somewhere above the street. It was very loud, more like an air raid siren left over from the Cold War than a fire alarm. A loudspeaker announcement came on, a woman's voice, probably speaking Cantonese. It was somehow louder than the air raid siren. Troy couldn't understand a word of it.

All around him, people began to run. He wedged himself up against the wall of a building. He couldn't even tell if Jan was still on the phone or not.

"Jan? Jan! If you can hear me, I'm going to the building!"

He looked at the phone's screen. The call was dead.

Troy pushed off the wall into the surging crowd. He headed into the oncoming rush of them.

"Double time!" he shouted. "March!"

He plunged forward, doing the military double time now. Thirty inches a step, at 180 steps per minute. He fell into it as if it was the most natural thing in the world. He was moving. It was a fast pace, but sustainable, and one he could do all day.

People bumped into him, going the other way. He brushed them aside. He was running down the street, straight at people running toward him.

There was a cop ahead. He wore a white helmet with Chinese characters across it, and was blowing a whistle. It was loud, the shrieking sound of it cutting through everything. The announcements were still going on, the sirens were still screaming, but the whistle was somehow louder. The man swung his arms crazily, urging people onward.

Then he spotted Troy.

"You!" he said, pointing. "Wrong way! You no go here! Go back!"

Overzealous cop, he tried to grab Troy. Troy bulled past him.

"You! Stop!"

The streets were a sea of bodies, a chaotic mix of colors and shapes as people pushed and shoved, their faces contorted with fear and urgency. Each person seemed to blur into the next. Some were clutching belongings or dragging small children along. Others ran with wild abandon. Behind Troy, the cop's whistle started up again, but it was fading into the background.

The air was thick with the smell of sweat and sometimes body odor, mixed with the stench of garbage and exhaust fumes. Traffic was backing up, car horns blaring. As Troy passed, a man climbed out a car and abandoned it in the middle of the street. He just ran away from it, leaving it to block the traffic behind him. Other people got the message. Now, one person after another followed suit and ditched their cars.

A two-story red tram was stuck, people surrounding it. The driver tried to nose it forward, to no avail. The tram was like a great metal beast caught in the grasp of a frenzied mob. Windows lined its sides, some cracked and shattered. People pressed against its doors, trying to break in and get free from the crush of bodies.

The crowds surged, bodies pressed against each other, jostling and bumping in a panicked frenzy. Their eyes were wide like animals stampeding, being driven before some impending natural disaster. Troy's progress had slowed to a crawl.

He pushed through the people like he was swimming through an ocean of mud.

CHAPTER TWENTY FOUR

7:55 am Hong Kong Time
The Jade Emperor Hotel
Tsim Sha Tsui, Kowloon
City of Hong Kong
China

"I lost the call," Jan said. "I can't get it back."

Dubois and Jan were in Jan's hotel suite, monitoring the situation on TV and on a bank of three laptops positioned on the round dining table.

There was a bellhop in the room with them, bringing them breakfast. He was moving around and fussing behind them, looking for somewhere to place the trays. Dubois had barely looked at him when he came in. She had noted that he wasn't Chinese, but they were in a Canadian hotel, so she supposed that made sense.

"I guess I'll just put these on top of this dresser," the man said.

"Anywhere is fine," Dubois said.

On the TV, thousands of people were streaming away, not just from the Peace Tower, but from all of Central Hong Kong.

"Someone in authority has taken those computer models seriously," Dubois said. "They're clearing the entire area."

"Good for them," Jan said. "It's the correct thing to do."

He was hunched over the table, big shoulders rolled forward, scrolling through websites on one of the laptops. On the other two laptops, cell phone videos posted to Chinese social media were showing the chaos on the streets.

"If they even saw those models," Jan said.

Jan pulled up a page with a line graph. On the left side of the graph, the line hugged the bottom of the page. It did that nearly all the way across the screen, until it reached the right side, where it curved upward, like a rocket heading into outer space.

"This is local cell tower usage, tracked in very close to real time. It's a parabolic curve on the right, showing an exponential increase in cell phone calls in just the past few minutes. There are millions of people all trying to make calls at once. The whole system will probably go down in a few moments. It's not designed to handle this volume."

"The food is hot," the bellhop said. "It's quite good."

Dubois raised a hand. She was fascinated by the scenes of people racing through the clogged streets. Cars, trucks, buses, and trams were all being abandoned and left behind.

"Thank you," she said.

"I need to switch everything to satellite," Jan said. "At this rate, we may lose the internet."

There was a cell phone at Jan's left elbow. It came alive and began to play a song. Dubois couldn't put her finger on what it was. Something from a movie, something very familiar.

"It's not a cell phone call," Jan said. "It's the communications app I made. But I don't recognize the user."

His thick finger pressed a green button on the face of the phone. The application's default setting was to broadcast calls using the speaker phone option.

"Hello?"

"Mr. Bakker?" The sound was clear. Wherever this person was, it wasn't the frenzy of the Hong Kong streets.

"Yes."

"This is Zhao Fu of the Ministry of State Security."

Dubois and Bakker looked at each other. Last night, at Troy's urging, Jan had sent Zhao the application, with login credentials. Jan hadn't been happy about granting a Chinese secret agent access to his pirated Chinese communications app, but he had done it anyway.

"This will kill it, you know?" Jan had said at the time. "I wanted it for El Grupo use only. The Chinese will break it open, they'll block our access, they'll embed a virus or some tracking malware. This will be the end."

"We have to kill our darlings sometimes," Troy had said. "I need Zhao to communicate, and it has to be encrypted. He might not do it otherwise."

Jan had gone along with this idea. Dubois noted how, eventually, people tended to give Troy Stark what he wanted.

"Yes, Mr. Zhao," Jan said now. "How can I assist you?"

"I am on the fifth floor of the Golden Dragon Peace Tower," Zhao said. "I am with a canine bomb discovery team from the Hong Kong Police Department. We are finding high explosives inside the structure of the building, as though they were installed as part of the construction. The explosives are…"

Zhao trailed off.

"Mr. Zhao?"

"They seem to be everywhere."

Dubois turned around to see if the bellhop was in the room. This was highly sensitive information that Zhao was presenting.

The bellhop was still here. He was what she would consider a white man, but of southern European or North African descent. He was not tall but handsome enough that he could almost be a news weatherman or an actor in a telenovela. He looked familiar to her.

He was in the corner by the door, with a cell phone pressed to his ear.

"These explosives may go off at any moment," Zhao said. "The evacuations have begun. You and your team were correct. Thank you for your efforts."

Dubois turned and stared at the phone. Was this Zhao's goodbye call? Dubois had a bad moment where she pictured the call suddenly going dead, and outside their window, a massive explosion rocking the far side of Victoria Harbour.

"Mr. Zhao, Agent Stark is coming your way. He may be able to assist with…"

The app did a funny thing where it faded for a moment, nearly disappeared, then came back again, almost as strong as before.

"Why is he doing that?" Zhao said. "He shouldn't come here. Everyone must..."

Zhao's voice fizzled and died.

Instinctively, Dubois looked out the window. The Peace Tower was still there, far away, indistinct, one tall building among many. Nothing blew up.

"Good luck," Jan said.

He looked at Dubois. "I'm going to transfer everything to satellite. This may take some time. Most of the satellites available here will be of Chinese origin. We won't get access, and even if we do, we don't want them listening to us."

"All right," Dubois said. "I'm going to look at this breakfast."

Jan nodded. "All right."

Dubois turned and the bellhop was standing there.

"Agent Dubois, I need you to come with me," he said.

"How do you know my name?" Dubois said.

The man gestured at Jan with his head. "He called you that a little while ago."

"We're in the middle of something right now," Dubois said. "The city is in danger."

The bellhop nodded. "Yes, I understand."

He reached inside the jacket of his uniform and came out with a black matte pistol. He held it out to her in the palm of his hand.

"Take this and come with me, please."

Dubois reached and took the heavy gun.

"Jan?"

Jan barely glanced back at them.

"All connectivity has been lost," he said. "I'm trying to restore it."

"I'm going to go with this man," Dubois said.

Jan nodded, but didn't turn around at all this time. "Yes, okay."

They went out in the hallway. Dubois followed the man down the hall and into a narrow stairwell.

"What are we doing?" Dubois said. She wouldn't normally follow an unknown man into a stairwell, not on her own, but he had given her a gun. And he was very familiar to her. This entire episode was taking on the feeling of déjà vu.

"I need your help," the man said.

He led her up the stairs. It was a short climb, three flights which ended at a heavy door. The man opened the door with a key. No alarm went off.

They came out onto the roof of the hotel. The building, at 10 stories, was low compared to many of the surrounding buildings. The flat roof almost seemed to be in a valley, with modern steel and glass mountains all around it.

There was a white helicopter parked here. It was a small, two-pilot, four-passenger utility chopper, the kind used by police departments, militaries, and tourist attractions throughout the world. Dubois recognized the make right away. It was a Eurocopter *Ecureuil*, built in France. Her father had flown these. In English, the name meant "Squirrel." She couldn't imagine why they called it that.

The helicopter had the words "Canada East Airlines" stenciled across its body. There was a red maple leaf on the tail.

"What is this?" Dubois said.

The man walked directly toward the helicopter, and Dubois followed one step behind him. "Canada East owns the hotel. We have an express service to the airport for VIPs. It's a pretty quick hop. It'll save you half an hour, more in heavy traffic. Plus, you know, people just like to do it. It's a little adventure."

"And it's flown by a bellhop?" Dubois said.

Now, the man shrugged. He smiled. He opened the cockpit door for her. The configuration was a cockpit door on either side, and then passenger cabin doors behind that, which slid backwards to open. Inside the helicopter, the cockpit and the passenger cabin were open to each other. A passenger could tap the pilot on the shoulder.

Dubois climbed in and began to pull on her safety harness. The bellhop did the same.

They put their headphones on. Dubois had to navigate getting the fit right around the back of her head. Her hair was too tall to have the phones come straight down. The bellhop flipped a switch, sending power to the sound system.

"We're expected to wear a lot of hats around here," he said, his voice sounding tinny inside her ears. "I also check people in at the front desk, mostly late-night arrivals."

He was already running his flight checks. He went through them quickly, mechanically, as though he had done this a thousand times. Above their heads, the blades began to turn. The shadows of their passing created a sort of strobe effect in the cockpit.

She pulled the microphone down in front of her mouth.

"Where are we going?" she said.

"We're going to Central Hong Kong."

The chopper began to rise, pulling straight up among the high rises of Kowloon. It reached an altitude above the buildings, banked to the left, and turned toward the harbor.

In a few moments, they were out over the water. "That's where we're going," he said.

He pointed at the Golden Dragon Peace Tower, the tallest thing over there. Dubois hadn't considered how tall it really was. Nothing around it was anywhere close to its height. The top floors were unfinished, their skeletal structure reaching into the sky.

There was a literal Golden Dragon carved into the outside corner of the building. It had to be 80 stories tall. Light glinted off the dragon's skin. The skin seemed like the chain mail armor of a medieval knight.

"The detail on that dragon is astonishing," Dubois said. "The building is just..."

She couldn't seem to finish her thought.

“Yes,” the bellhop said. “It’s amazing. Let’s hope it stays that way.”

CHAPTER TWENTY FIVE

8:05 am Hong Kong Time
The Golden Dragon Peace Tower
Central
City of Hong Kong
China

Troy walked into the lobby of the building.

The streets outside were empty of people. There were a couple of wrecked cars and a few police vans parked on the front plaza. But everyone was gone, the swarms of people moving away from here like the shock wave from an explosion.

That was good. This place could become Ground Zero any second.

Why am I here?

Troy crossed the lobby, scanning for anyone or anything. It was very, very quiet in here. The ceilings towered high above him. A grand staircase went somewhere. Everything seemed to be gleaming white marble and polished brass.

There was a remarkable fountain with a dragon sculpture to his left. There were two lions at the bottom. Eye-catching, for sure. The water splashing down seemed to be the only sound. It was soothing. Troy supposed that was the point of it.

Nah. This is China. It probably has something to do with money or good fortune. Some damn thing.

There were a couple of dead guys sprawled on the floor near a bank of elevators. A woman was alive and on the floor next to them. This was something worth investigating.

Troy came closer. They were a couple of tall white guys. It appeared that head shots from close range had taken them out. There was a lot of blood pooled around their heads.

The woman looked up at Troy. Her eyes were puffy and red. Her cheeks were wet. She had just been kneeling here on her legs, crying.

She was wearing a uniform of some kind. Black jacket, black skirt, white shirt, sensible shoes for walking around a lot. She probably worked here and had something to do with the dedication event.

She was wearing a bronze name tag. It had Chinese characters etched into it, along with the name Peg.

"Hi Peg," Troy said. "Are you the only one here?"

She spoke a form of pigeon English. It was easy enough to understand. "Yes. My job. I cannot leave them here."

Troy wasn't sure if he agreed with that, but decided not to make an issue of it at the moment. "What happened?"

"These men shot and killed. US Secretary guard men. Dead. I saw it. So horrible."

"The US Secretary of State was with these men?" Troy said.

Peg nodded. "Yes. Too horrible."

Troy looked around at the empty lobby. "Who did this?"

"Don't know. Other men. Took US Secretary in elevator. Went to top level."

"How do you know that?"

She pointed at the bank of elevators. There was a digital readout along the top of each elevator. "I watched."

Troy crouched by the dead men. They wore dark suits. They each had earpieces in. They were definitely both shot in the head.

He reached inside one of their jackets. He came out with an ID. Travis Reid. State Department Security. All right. Died in the line of duty.

Troy tossed Travis's ID back onto his chest. God help him.

Both of these guys had guns in shoulder holsters. Troy reached inside their jackets and took them out. They were nice guns, Glocks with 15-round box magazines. He slid the mag out of one and checked it. It was full. He slid it back in and rammed it home.

Troy was armed now. That was always a good feeling.

He looked at the woman. "Peg, I'm gonna need to borrow these guns. I'm not stealing them. You understand?"

She nodded. "Yes."

"You should leave now," Troy said. "Your job here is done. There is nothing more you can do for them."

She nodded again.

"Now," Troy said. "You should leave now. Get as far away as you can."

The woman climbed to her feet. Still, she seemed hesitant. She gazed down at the dead men. Troy waved at her with both hands.

"Go! Far away!"

Peg started moving toward the revolving glass doors to the outside.

"Run!" he shouted at her.

Peg started running.

Troy grunted. People, man. Just doing their jobs until the last possible second. It was hard to find that kind of loyalty. He'd write Peg a letter of commendation, but he'd have no idea where to send it.

Nearby, an elevator dinged. It was an unexpected sound.

Troy looked at the bank of elevators. A round green button had lit up next to one of them. The door began to slide open. He moved to one knee and pointed a gun at it. He placed the other gun on the floor, right nearby.

Zhao Fu came walking out of the elevator, moving fast.

He looked like a man on a mission, and that mission was to get out of this building.

"Zhao."

Zhao stopped and looked at Troy. His eyes shifted to the bloodied dead men on the floor, remained there for about one second, then went right back to Troy. It was as if their presence was so strange that Zhao's mind couldn't absorb it. Or maybe he just didn't care.

"Stark, you shouldn't have come here," he said. "We need to evacuate. The whole place is wired to explode. There's no way to disarm the bombs. They're embedded in the structure itself. I've never seen anything like this. I've never heard of anything like it."

Troy shook his head. "We can't leave yet. Someone kidnapped the Secretary of State. I have to go get him if I can. They killed his bodyguards and took him upstairs. To the roof, maybe."

"Who did that?" Zhao said. "The bombers?"

Troy shook his head. "I don't know, man. I just got here myself."

They looked at each other for a few seconds.

Troy jumped to his feet.

"Ready?" he said. "Time is wasting."

They headed back to the elevators, moving quickly. To his credit, Zhao didn't resist the idea of going back upstairs.

"This is crazy," was all he said.

Troy nodded. "I know. You might have to discharge your firearm again."

CHAPTER TWENTY SIX

8:07 am Hong Kong Time
The skies over Victoria Harbour
City of Hong Kong
China

"It's beautiful here," Dubois said.

And it was. The sweep of water, with the curving skyline of Hong Kong Island, framed against the dark green hillsides and the pale blue sky. It was almost like a dream.

She sat in the passenger seat of the helicopter's cockpit as they approached the city center from across the harbor. The Peace Tower dominated the skyline.

It was quiet. The headsets were noise-canceling, reducing the loud chop from the rotors. In the background, there was the chatter of air traffic control. There was a cacophony of voices on there, most in what Dubois assumed was Cantonese, some in English.

"It looks better from the sky," the bellhop said. "Most things do."

"You're the guy from New York," Dubois said, finally getting it. "The helicopter pilot. The drone attacks. The Brooklyn Bridge. We stole a police helicopter."

The man shrugged. "I probably shouldn't say."

"You're friends with Troy Stark."

Then it hit her even further. This guy was always around. He turned up as a bartender at a human trafficking auction in Algiers. And Stark was always mysteriously dropping from the sky. When she was in the water after the boat exploded off the coast of Albania, Stark dropped out of a helicopter. When she was on board Istvan Gajdos's hijacked train racing through the Austrian Alps, Stark had landed on the roof.

There had been some talk about a helicopter taken at gunpoint from an Austrian government mountain rescue station. Stark was almost reprimanded for that, but he claimed he had no knowledge of any stolen helicopter.

"Am I friends with Stark?" the man said. "Really? I mean, I'd be friends with him, I guess. But Stark is kind of a hard nut to crack. I find him cold and distant."

Dubois nodded. "Hmmm. I hope he isn't."

The man gave her a sidelong glance. "You and him…"

Dubois shook her head. "No. We're just colleagues."

The man smiled and looked at his controls again. She sensed that this man could see through lies without much effort.

Outside the cockpit, the building was coming. The unfinished top floors stood like the remains of something long dead, poking out of the ground.

"What's your name?" Dubois said.

"You can call me Alex, if you like."

"Okay, Alex. Why are we going here? Everyone else is leaving."

"I received some news a little while ago that disturbed me," Alex said. "We might have to rescue someone."

Dubois glanced down at the gun in her small hand. She had almost forgotten it was there. She didn't know the model, she was not a weapons expert, but the gun had a heft to it. It was not a lady gun. It would put holes in things.

She stared out the cockpit, eyes taking in the whole scene. There were a lot of helicopters in the sky. The air was thick with them.

"There are all these other helicopters," she said. "Some of them must be rescue units."

"Airspace over the Peace Tower is restricted right now," Alex said. "No one can go in there like we can."

She saw the truth in what he was saying. A group of helicopters, the closest ones, appeared to be hovering at the edge of some radius around the danger zone. They were not over the building. Others were even further out. Many were far away.

"Why can we do it?" she said.

Alex sighed. "We do whatever we want, pretty much. Then we apologize."

"Or disappear afterwards," Dubois said.

Alex nodded. "Or disappear. Whatever the case may be."

The helicopter was jostled by air turbulence. A warm draft blew into the cabin from somewhere. The seal of the cabin was not perfect.

She guessed they were moving at close to more than a hundred kilometers per hour. Through the bubble windshield, just ahead and below them, the building approached. There was a platform serving as a roof of sorts, perched on top of the naked steel beams.

"It might get hot in a minute," Alex said. "Be ready."

Dubois glanced at him. He seemed completely calm, unflappable. She didn't know what he meant by that. How was she supposed to be ready? Ready with the gun? The cockpit doors were closed. There was no way to fire the gun.

"Who are we rescuing?"

Alex shrugged. "Someone kidnapped the American Secretary of State. They might have brought him to the roof. I don't really understand what's going on here. We're going to make a pass and check it out."

"Do you want me to get out?" Dubois said.

"I don't know yet. I'm not sure we can even land on that thing. The crosswinds up here are a lot to deal with."

He made some adjustments on the touchpad screen in front of him. The helicopter slowed. He steered it down and to the left. The building was ahead. They came in at it on an angle. The white platform on top of it stretched out in front of them. It was long and rectangular.

The scene was becoming clearer now. There was an even higher level than the platform. An iron staircase climbed to a sort of catwalk that ran above the left side of the platform. That thing was narrow and very high. People on there would be all the way out in space.

"What do you see?" Alex said.

Inside Dubois's headphones, the radio suddenly squawked. "Warning to unidentified helicopter. This is Hong Kong Tower. You have entered restricted airspace. Return to your original flight path immediately."

The air traffic controller was speaking in perfectly enunciated English.

"Here we go," Alex said.

Being inside this helicopter was like being inside a large soap bubble. Dubois looked down at the platform in front and below them, surrounded by the dizzying drop to the streets of the city below. They crossed over the top, and Alex put it in a hover.

"Unidentified helicopter, you DO NOT have permission to land. That is restricted airspace."

Alex hit the talk button on his radio. He glanced at Dubois and smiled. His smile looked sickly, more like a nervous grimace than anything else.

"Uh, Hong Kong Tower, this is an unidentified helicopter. We have mechanical trouble. Multiple warning lights. Request permission to make emergency landing on top of Golden Dragon Peace Tower."

"Permission DENIED. You are in restricted airspace. That is NOT a helipad. That is dangerous airspace."

Alex giggled like a child. Dubois laughed.

Alex flicked the talk switch off.

"We're not going to get anywhere with the control tower."

Dubois watched the roof platform. She could make out several men now. There were maybe half a dozen of them. Four were on the platform. Two were on the catwalk.

The chopper was lower now, coming in above them.

Most of the men wore black jumpsuits as though they were police commandos. There was a tall man in a suit. He was lying on the ground.

"They have guns," Dubois said. "The men in black have guns."

"I see that," Alex said.

The men on the catwalk had a pile of gear with them. There was a dramatic difference in size between the two men. The smaller one hoisted a heavy canister onto his shoulder.

Dubois pointed. "He's got a… he's got some kind of rocket!"

She felt a surge of adrenaline that was almost like being fired out of a cannon.

"Okay," Alex said. "Okay. We're leaving."

He pulled up on his controls. The helicopter began to bank away from the building.

Something launched from the tube the man had.

"Incoming!" Dubois said.

She watched the projectile come. There was no way to avoid it. It hit the metal frame of the chopper with a hard THUNK, then bounced back and fell away. Gray smoke rose from it.

Dubois was gasping for air.

"Must have been a dud," Alex said.

"Alex!" Dubois shouted.

A second later, another projectile was launched. It was coming straight for Dubois's side of the cockpit.

BOOM!

It hit the side of the helicopter and came crashing through the window. The hard plastic of the window shattered in fragments all over them.

The missile was a tear gas canister. It fell onto the floor at Dubois's feet. Smoke was rising from it. Dubois put her gun in two hands, turned, leaned out the missing window, and opened fire at the men on the catwalk.

BANG! BANG! BANG!

The two men hit the metal floor, ducking for cover.

Smoke was filling the cockpit.

"Get it out!" Alex shouted. "Get that thing out of here!"

Dubois picked up the canister and threw it back out the hole where the window had been.

The helicopter banked away from the building and out toward the water again. The cockpit was open to the elements. Wind shrieked in through the shattered window. Everything was much louder than just a moment ago.

"All right," Alex said. "That didn't work."

"What are we going to do?"

They were shouting at each other. Dubois didn't know if she was shouting to be heard, or because she was raging with adrenaline. Her whole body was shaking. She couldn't seem to control how her voice worked.

Alex breathed heavily. There were tiny shards of hard plastic all over him. It was on his lap, along his arms, on his shoulders. Dubois looked down at herself and saw that she was the same way.

It was hard to breathe in here, but with the canister gone and the wind whipping through, the smoke was starting to dissipate.

"We'll circle back around and try again," Alex said.

CHAPTER TWENTY SEVEN

8:10 am Hong Kong Time
The Golden Dragon Peace Tower
Central
City of Hong Kong
China

"Do you know this song?" Zhao said.

Troy and Zhao were riding in a gleaming white and gold elevator with black accents. The elevator could probably fit 20 people. Quiet Muzak was playing in the background. The elevator seemed soundproof, in the sense that it was hushed in here, and besides their voices, the Muzak was the only sound.

"I don't think so," Troy said. He watched the floors pass on the digital readout.

"An American made this song. Kenny G. The song is called Going Home. I love it. Everybody in China loves it. It's a beautiful song."

Troy winced. He shook his head. "I'm more of a Led Zeppelin guy, to be honest."

The sound seemed to be coming from everywhere at once. It wasn't overwhelming. It was almost like it was coming out of your own pores.

He gestured at the elevator speaker system, wherever it was.

"This, uh… This doesn't do it for me."

The numbers in the readout were rapidly approaching the top, a floor called SKYVIEW. Troy had a gun in each hand. He felt okay. His heart fluttered a bit. It was impossible to say what they might encounter at the SKYVIEW level.

"Where did you get those guns?" Zhao said.

"Would you stop with that already?" Troy said. "The whole time I'm here, you're trying to take my guns away. I got them off the dead guys downstairs. The bodyguards. They're American, not Chinese guns."

"They're Glocks," Zhao said. "They're not even American."

"In the sense that Americans owned them."

"But you're not licensed to carry a firearm in China," Zhao said. "Those men probably received temporary authorization because of their employment status."

"I'm gonna need these," Troy said. "You can complain about it later."

The elevator stopped.

Ding!

Troy hated that sound.

"Left and right," Troy said. "I'll go left. You go right. Space it out. Don't bunch up. Don't give them anything to hit."

The door slid open.

Troy had both guns up. He burst out of the elevator, turning hard to the left. He had a moment of disorientation. There was just a wide platform here, totally open to the sky. It was like being at the top of a mountain. The sense of enormity was almost overwhelming.

At the far end was a podium, as if someone was about to give a speech.

Three men stood on the platform. They wore black jumpsuits, like commandos. Asians. At their feet, a man in a business suit was sprawled on the ground.

There was some kind of iron staircase to Troy's left and behind him.

There was a white helicopter coming in hard. It came in sideways, a shooter at the side cockpit window.

Two men on the platform raised their guns at Troy.

BANG! BANG!

BANG! BANG! BANG!

Troy opened fire with both guns, the guns bucking in his hand. He shot one man in the head. The other was hit low in the throat. Both men fell.

The third was facing back toward the chopper.

The shooter in the window opened up and put several holes in the third guy. He did a little dance before he went to the floor.

"That was easy."

Troy was under the catwalk now. He looked across at the chopper. It hovered there, maybe ten feet above the platform. The shooter was small and dark, a woman wearing wraparound sunglasses. She had a large black Afro.

Dubois was the shooter.

To Troy's far right, Zhao was racing along the edge of the platform toward the man lying on the ground. He was out in the open, exposed.

On the far edge, beyond the podium, was a low concrete wall with an iron railing on it.

BANG! BANG! BANG!

Dubois was firing this way. Troy hit the deck. She was going to kill him with friendly fire.

DING!

A shot glanced off the catwalk above his head.

DUH-DUH-DUH-DUH-DUH-DUH.

The rip of a gun on full automatic came from the catwalk. Someone up there had a submachine gun. Bullets strafed the chopper, tearing into its shell.

The chopper pulled up and away, dwindling into the distance in seconds.

Troy looked above him, through the slats in the ironwork. There were two guys up there, fiddling with bags of gear. Troy had no shot at them. He'd have to run back to the bottom of the staircase and try to attack them by coming up the stairs.

No. That wouldn't work. The concrete wall across the way. That was better. It would give him cover and an angle on the men.

Troy took a deep breath, then let it out. There was nothing else to do.

He ran out onto the platform. He sprinted, reaching Zhao in seconds. Zhao was kneeling by the tall man in the suit.

Troy skidded to the ground next to them, tearing up his knees. He looked up the catwalk. The smaller man was shrugging into a vest, or a large harness. It was a parachute. He was putting on a parachute. Those crazy bastards were going to jump from here.

The bigger one already had his chute on. He was at some kind of electronic box, plugging in wires. Those guys were leaving. They weren't paying any attention to Troy and Zhao.

Troy looked down at the man on the ground. It was Lloyd Garelli. His eyes were open.

"Sir, are you hurt?" Troy said.

"I don't know," Garelli said.

"Can you get up?"

Garelli shook his head. "I don't know. I think I wet myself."

"Zhao, give me a hand with this guy."

Together, they yanked Garelli to his feet. They each got under one of Garelli's shoulders and ran him across the platform. The concrete wall was right there. It was maybe a meter high. Troy dove through the bars of the iron railing and landed behind the low wall. He grabbed Garelli by the upper body and dragged him in after. To their right, Zhao slipped through and took cover behind the wall.

Troy lay there, breathing hard, not moving.

Just then, gunshots rang out from the other side again. It was the ugly blat of that automatic weapon, further away now.

DUH-DUH-DUH-DUH-DUH.

DING!

A bullet whined off one of the iron bars. Concrete chips began to fly as bullets scraped the top of the wall.

Troy glanced behind him. The drop-off at the edge of the building was RIGHT THERE. Beyond it, the helicopter was coming back, flying low, coming in just above rooftop level.

Troy stuck his gun along the top of the wall and fired one-handed, not aiming at anything, just trying to suppress the guy with the submachine gun.

The wall was imploding, chunks of it flying into the air.

Then the shooting stopped.

Troy crawled along the wall, away from where he had fired, and poked his head up for a split second. Out on the catwalk, the smaller man ditched the machine gun. He fell from the catwalk and clattered on the platform two stories below.

Now, the two men ran along the catwalk to the far end of it.

The larger man reached it first. He barely slowed down. He simply leapt off, spread his arms and legs, and was gone. The smaller man was just a few steps behind. He didn't even hesitate or slow down at all. He just went off at a run.

Troy was breathing. He could hear it. His chest was pounding.

Something began to rumble beneath his feet.

"Oh no."

He turned. The chopper was nearly here.

The whole building was shaking.

There was the heavy THUMP of chopper blades against the wind. In a moment, it was over the building, and was dropping slowly.

"Zhao," Troy croaked. "Let's go!"

He stood and ran back to Zhao and Garelli.

The chopper was hovering, bare feet above the platform. The door to the passenger cabin slid open.

Zhao and Troy dragged Garelli back over the concrete wall and under the railing. They ran him across the platform, back the way they had just come seconds ago. This time, it was hard to stay upright. The platform undulated, cracks forming in the concrete, as though there was an earthquake.

"What the hell, man? What the hell?"

They shoved Garelli into the helicopter. Dubois was there at the open door, pulling him all the way in. Troy slid his guns on board. Then he shoved Zhao in.

"Go! You next!"

Troy felt the floor begin to drop away beneath him. He began to fall with it. It was happening. The building was collapsing.

"Oh, no."

Troy lurched downward. There was a sickening feeling, like a trapdoor had just opened under his feet. His arms shot upward.

Zhao caught him by the forearm.

"Gotcha!"

Troy gripped Zhao's forearm in turn.

But Troy was too heavy. He was pulling Zhao out of the helicopter. They were banking hard, and all the momentum was towards falling out. Zhao grabbed the doorway with his free hand. There was no way this was going to hold.

The ground dropped away. It was just gone.

Or the chopper was rising. It was impossible to say what was happening. Zhao held him, Troy trailing out behind. His legs were dangling. He screamed, an animal sound with no words in it. Dubois was there, hugging Zhao from behind, her feet planted against the wall of the passenger cabin, strong legs pushing them backwards.

It was no good. They were all going to fall, all three of them.

Troy swung his body and grabbed the helicopter's runner with his free hand. His legs were dangling. The ground was far below. There was nothing beneath him.

A sound was rising, a deafening roar.

Troy did a one-armed pull up, and swung a leg over one of the runners. Zhao was still gripping his forearm.

Troy needed that hand.

"Zhao! I'm up! Let me go!"

Then Zhao's hand was gone, and Troy crawled up into the chopper. He collapsed onto the floor. Above him, Dubois was strapping Lloyd Garelli into a seat.

"Aahhh," Troy said. "That was bad. I don't want to do that again."

Zhao had fallen away to his own corner. He leaned up against the low barrier between the passenger cabin and the cockpit.

The helicopter shuddered and whipsawed as it hit turbulence. Then it found some calm air, leveled out, and surged forward. Troy felt it gaining more altitude.

"Look!" Zhao shouted. He gestured out the door with his head. There were tears in his eyes. Troy got it. He understood. These were Zhao's people. What kind of wanton hatred could make someone want to do this to them?

Troy pushed himself to a sitting position and looked out at open space. The building had collapsed, falling in seconds. Far below them, a giant brown and gray dust cloud was rising. The force of the collapse was blowing the dust out in all directions.

"Oh my God."

In the chair above Troy, Garelli was silently weeping.

Dubois was already squeezing herself back into the cockpit.

Troy pushed himself to his feet. He looked around at everything. The chopper was a bit of a wreck. The window of the cockpit on Dubois's side was just gone. There were shards of plastic or safety glass everywhere. The wind was howling. The sound of the rotors was very loud. Inside the cockpit, the readout panels were shattered. Some sort of smoke rose from the dashboard. The whole place smelled like smoke, come to think of it.

Troy looked at the pilot. It was Alex. Of course it was.

"How is this thing still airborne?" Troy shouted at them.

"It's French made!" Dubois shouted.

Troy nearly laughed. "Great!"

The helicopter was circling far out over the harbor. The building was gone, a complete catastrophe. But there would be time to think about that later. They had done the best they could. To Troy's left, and far below them, he spotted two dark parachutes falling toward the water. They were about to hit it any second. Those guys thought they were getting away. It seemed clear now that they were the ones who had detonated the building.

Troy leaned into the cockpit and pointed down at them.

"Alex! We're not done here, buddy!"

Alex nodded. "I see them!"

"Let's clean this up," Troy said.

Alex banked again, and dropped the helicopter toward the water.

CHAPTER TWENTY EIGHT

8:17 am Hong Kong Time
Victoria Harbour
City of Hong Kong
China

"Turbo!" Fisher shouted. "Let's go!"

Fisher climbed onto the back platform of the boat, wedging himself along the side of the three big engines, and squeaking past them. He was still trailing his parachute. He shrugged out of the harness and tossed it in the water. The engines were on, and in neutral, the sound of them rumbling deeply under the water.

It had been one hell of a ride. That much was sure.

Turbo was 20 yards away, swimming like mad toward the boat. It figured that of all the other men who had gone on that roof, Turbo was the only one who survived. The guy had the moves. Give him that.

"Come on, man! We ain't got all day."

The boat was a tiny speedboat, painted dark green to blend with the water. It had stopped to pick them up, and that was a blessing, but Fisher didn't expect it to stay long. No one wanted to be associated with anything that had just happened.

Behind them, on the Hong Kong Island side, the building was just gone. Other buildings might be gone, too. It was hard to say. A brown and gray and white dust cloud was rising and spreading in every direction. The city was going to be fogged in with it. It was going to blanket the entire region in dust. A day or two from now, people in Taipei were going to be tasting that thing on their tongues.

Fisher turned away from it.

The boat bobbed in the harbor swells.

"Let's go!"

Turbo reached the boat, and Fisher yanked him up. Turbo was light as a feather. He had already ditched his chute in the water.

"Go!" Fisher shouted at the driver. "Hit it!"

The driver turned around in his seat. He was an Asian guy, maybe Han Chinese. Fisher didn't know. He hadn't hired the guy, and never met him before. They told him the boat driver would be there, and here he was.

"Where are the rest?" the driver said.

"Dead. They're all dead. So kindly get this thing moving."

The driver put the engines in gear and took off. A giant wake sprayed behind the boat. Fisher was nearly knocked off his feet by the sudden speed.

He looked in the direction of the destroyed building again. A sort of mushroom cloud was reaching thousands of feet in the air, much higher than any of the skyscrapers. It was amazing. It was so large that it seemed like an act of God.

Fisher caught a speck of something coming this way, and dropping down from thee sky. It was white and hard to see against the backdrop of the dust cloud.

He stared at it a long moment.

It began to coalesce into a shape he could make sense of.

"Helicopter," he said in a low voice. He was speaking to himself. There was no way the other two could hear him over the engines.

It was probably the chopper that harassed them on the roof. Fisher was pretty sure the shot that killed Ace came from the helicopter. They had torn that thing up, strafed it, punched holes in it, and it kept coming back for more.

This must be the same chopper.

Fisher caught a feeling that was rare for him. He would almost call it a sinking feeling.

He sighed, and a weight seemed to settle onto him.

"We got company!" he shouted.

***

The beat up chopper dropped hard, coming in right behind and above the boat.

Garelli was leaning forward against his safety harness, trying to talk to Alex. He had to shout to be heard above the heavy thump of the rotors.

"Sir! I, uh, authorize you to take us to the nearest safe helipad. Maybe a police or military installation. We don't… it's not our responsibility to uh…"

"I like your mustard, Lloyd!" Troy shouted. He was checking the magazines on his guns. At a guess, he had about ten rounds left. It should be enough.

"We'll get you home soon. Let's leave it at that, okay?"

Garelli nodded. "Yeah, uh… okay."

Troy leaned into the cockpit. There was a boat moving fast ahead and below them. It bounded over swells in the open water. But the helicopter was much faster, and closing in.

"That them?"

Alex nodded. "Yeah."

"Just get right in on top of them!"

"We might take fire!" Dubois shouted.

No doubt that was true. The wreckage of this chopper was evidence enough.

"Five seconds!" Troy shouted. "That's all I ask. Make a pass and see what they do. Then circle back and drop me in."

"Not a problem," Alex said. His face was calm. He knew the deal. He wasn't necessarily a gun fighter, or a fist fighter, but kamikaze runs in helicopters were right in his wheelhouse.

Troy was tired, but inside, he was on fire. There was no way on Earth these people were getting away from him. Not after what they had done. It was impossible to say what kind of damage was going on back there or how many had been killed.

There was some warning. The authorities had been evacuating people like crazy before the place came down. But it sure looked bad.

They zipped over the top of the boat, buzzing it close. There were three men aboard. The driver ducked. One man hit the deck.

One guy, the big man, fired at the helicopter. He was using a handgun. Maybe that was all he had left. Troy could hear the pops.

Dubois leaned out and fired back. BANG! BANG! BANG!

Garelli screamed.

They were moving too fast to hit anything.

"Shut up, already!" Troy shouted. "Sir? Shut up! We're trying to work here."

The chopper banked up and out, to the left, and circled far out where gunfire couldn't reach it. Then Alex dropped it in behind the boat again and started another run.

"Agent Dubois, nice shooting! Give me covering fire again, just like that. Doesn't matter if you hit anything. Just put their faces to the deck."

Dubois nodded. “Got it!”

"Okay, kids," Troy said. "This one's for all the marbles."

The door was open. Troy climbed slowly out onto the runners.

Zhao was right behind him.

“Zhao, what are you doing?”

“I’m coming!” Zhao shouted.

They were moving fast and low above the water. Just below them, the waves formed tiny whitecaps, beaten by the wind from the rotors.

Troy shook his head. “I don’t know if this is for you.”

Zhao stared at him. “It’s my country. It’s my people they tried to destroy.”

Troy shrugged. “Did you reload your weapon?”

Zhao nodded. “Yes.”

“Okay. Suit yourself.”

The chopper came in behind the boat. The big man on board took aim at Troy. Troy watched him. He was waiting until he could be sure to get a decent shot. The boat bounced and bucked on the water. Alex shielded Troy with the front of the chopper, coming in just a little bit sideways, tilting Troy out of the man’s line of sight.

Waiting… waiting…

Alex twisted the chopper back the other way. Now Troy was exposed.

Dubois opened fire from her window.

BANG! BANG! BANG! BANG!

She did not let up this time.

The driver of the boat turned hard left, very sharp, nearly capsizing it. He was trying to escape Dubois’s line of sight, but he knocked the big man off his feet.

The chopper cut left, coming back over the boat.

Dubois opened up again.

BANG! BANG! BANG!

They were right over the boat. Troy leaned out from the runner and dropped in. He hit hard, nearly lost his balance, but steadied himself. His guns were out.

“Freeze! Everybody FREEZE!”

He heard a THUMP as Zhao hit the boat right after him.

The two men in jumpsuits were both down. The big guy was on his back, hands raised. The smaller guy was on his stomach, hands underneath him.

Troy moved toward the driver, clambering over weather-beaten leather seats.

"Stop this boat!"

The driver was Asian. He half-turned, and there was a small pistol in his hand.

BANG!

Troy shot him in the head.

Blood sprayed. The man slumped over his controls. Immediately, the boat slowed, settling in the water and drifting to a stop. It took only a second or two.

The sudden deceleration knocked Troy forward and off his feet. He landed face down just behind the dead man. Then the boat bobbed and rocked in the swells.

Troy pushed himself up again.

He had dropped his guns, both of them. It wasn't clear where they were. They had to be at his feet here somewhere.

He turned, in case he needed to fight with his hands.

The big guy was sitting back on the floor. He was a white guy. This was the first time Troy had gotten a good look at him. The guy had a beard that was full and covered the bottom half of his face. His eyes watched Troy.

"American?" Troy said.

The guy made no sign.

Suddenly, the smaller man rolled over. He had a gun in his hand. He pointed it at Troy.

BANG!

The man's head snapped back. Then he lay where he was, eyes open and staring.

Troy glanced to his right and Zhao was there, in a two-handed shooter's crouch. Troy looked back at the guy on the floor of the boat. There was a neat red hole right in the middle of his forehead. A line of blood appeared there and began to run down his face.

"Well, Mr. Zhao. It looks like this time you really popped the old..."

"Don't you move!" Zhao screamed at the bearded guy. "Put your hands where I can see them!"

The guy slowly raised his big hands.

"I swear to God, if you move a muscle, I will blow your brains out."

It wasn't an empty threat. Zhao had just done it to the other one. Troy smiled. It had been a long, brutal morning, but it was finally over.

"Mr. Zhao," he said. "Now you're talking my language."

CHAPTER TWENTY NINE

2:15 pm Hong Kong Time
Ministry of State Security
Cha Liu Au, Kowloon
City of Hong Kong
China

"What is he?" Troy said.

Troy and Zhao were back inside the small observation room at the Ministry headquarters.

The room was a throwback to another time. There was a long wooden table and a few wooden chairs. The floor was made of wood and was warped and uneven. This might have once been an elementary school classroom, except there was no blackboard.

Dubois and Jan Bakker were at their hotel, compiling an incident report for Interpol. Alex was gone, evaporated. Secretary of State Lloyd Garelli had been taken by an American security team to an undisclosed location. He would probably be on a plane back to the States by tonight.

Troy was no longer a wanted man, but technically he was no longer assigned to the case, either. So he came here with Zhao, out of curiosity.

Zhao's superiors had stopped fighting Troy's presence. They probably weren't going to give him an award, but they weren't going to arrest him either.

Twelve people were known to have died, not counting the terrorists. Two of them were Garelli's bodyguards. Several dozen more were unaccounted for, but might still turn up. The world media already had a name for all this. They were calling it "The Hong Kong Miracle."

The physical damage to Central Hong Kong was incalculable right now, at least in the billions, more likely tens or hundreds of billions. The lost revenue from the offices that had been pulverized and the businesses destroyed would be staggering.

The cops, firemen, soldiers and paramedics had gotten people out before the building came down – that's what counted. Tens of thousands of people were evacuated at something close to a moment's notice.

Troy and Zhao stood at a tall window, looking through the glass at the large white man on the other side. He had a thick red beard. He wore the ragged remains of a black jumpsuit.

He was sitting at the wooden desk in there. One of his hands was cuffed to his chair. His ankles were attached with metal chains to thick bolts in the floor. He had one hand free to smoke a cigar and drink what appeared to be a can of Budweiser. He had chewed the end of the cigar to mulch. They wanted him to talk, so they were giving him things to help that along.

They had probably given up on trying to intimidate him for the time being. He ran about 6'2", maybe 220 pounds, and clearly had advanced combat training and experience. The guy had blown up a skyscraper during a gun battle, then jumped off the building as it started to fall. His eyes were sharp and narrow, like the eyes of an eagle or other bird of prey. He wouldn't be afraid of much.

There were two men in the room with him. The agents dressed in a style nearly identical to Zhao – black suits and white shirts, hair slicked back. These were the Chinese g-men. If their prisoner noticed the long mirror to his right, he gave no indication that he knew what it was, or cared.

There was a bright light shining in the man's face. Beads of sweat had appeared on the man's cheeks. The interrogation room was mostly dark otherwise.

"I don't know what he is," Zhao said. "He gives his name as Fisher, but nothing else. He says he's a mercenary hired to detonate the bombs."

"He looks like a merc," Troy said. Truth was, the guy could easily pass for a grizzled Navy SEAL or Delta Force operator.

"He claims he doesn't know how the bombs got there," Zhao said. "Listen."

Zhao flipped a switch at the base of the glass, and an overhead speaker came on.

"I told you already," the man was saying.

He had a deep, slow voice with a hint of a Southern drawl. He was clearly American. He seemed relaxed. All you could do was kill him, and he had probably given himself up for dead years ago.

Torture? Sure. Troy reflected that everyone could be broken. It was likely coming for this guy, but he might not realize that yet. It gave Troy a slightly uneasy feeling that when the guy finally did talk, he might say it was other Americans who hired him.

The man squashed that idea right away.

"I don't know who hired me," he said. "Businessmen, right? A government? I don't know. They looked like you two fellows, I can tell you that."

"But you don't know who they are," one of the agents said.

The man shrugged. "In my line of work, people contact you anonymously. They wire money to a numbered account. That's for starters. All it does is get the conversation rolling. You want to talk? Okay, we'll talk. I don't need to know who you are to work for you. I don't believe in your cause if you even have a cause. I don't care about you. You have money, I have skills."

"So you say the Americans were not involved, even though you are American?"

The man shook his head slowly.

"America had nothing to do with this. They trained me, sure. They taught me to be who I am. But that was a long time ago."

"It would be nice to believe you," the agent said.

Troy nearly laughed. "They're just gonna keep hammering that idea. It's ridiculous. The guy took the American Secretary of State hostage and killed his bodyguards. It's a bit of a stretch to say…"

"Ever notice in wartime," the man in the chair said, "that a lot of the equipment goes missing? Weapons, yeah, but pretty much everything. Billions of dollars worth of stuff goes missing, every time. Who steals that stuff? That's the people who hired me."

"And what did they tell you, these people?"

The man smirked.

"They told me war is good for business. And the best business move out there is war between China and the United States. Those are the big kids. It's going to happen eventually. It might as well happen now."

He lifted the can of beer and took a long, thoughtful sip from it.

"I agree with them, whoever they are. Think of the ordnance that would get expended. Every time you launch a missile, you have to replace it. Every bullet. Every bomb. Every airplane, every boat. Use one up, you gotta go and buy another."

"Where did you meet with them?" the agent said.

The man shook his head and smiled.

"In the air. At their castle in the sky. Out in the cold and dark of deep space. Listen. Who makes the bombs? Who runs those companies? Who are the CEOs? Who are the shareholders? Who signs the requisition orders? Who gives the green light to launch the attack? Who whips up the war fever on the TV set? You should go talk to those people. They're the ones who hired me. Don't matter which side you think they're on. They're all on the same side. So am I."

"You are in deep, deep trouble," the agent said. "Bad things are going to happen to you."

The man nodded, but didn't seem particularly concerned. "I know that. I'm a worker bee, low man on the totem pole. All that bad stuff runs downhill, doesn't it?"

"You did a terrible thing."

Now, the man shrugged. He took another sip from the beer.

Troy noticed now that there were three more beers on a plastic ring. Maybe if they got him drunk enough, he'd start to give them something.

"I'm just an instrument of your policies. You boys do terrible things every day."

The agents looked at each other and shook their heads. If they were the laughing types, which they were not, they might have laughed now.

"Check the owners of the building. They must have an insurance policy. See if it covers random acts of terrorism. Maybe the building was a money pit, and they just wanted to torch the place for the insurance payout. They could be the ones that hired me."

The two agents ignored that idea.

"Where is the rest of your team?" one of them said.

The man's smirk reappeared, and broadened into a smile.

"As far as I know, you guys killed them all."

Zhao flipped the switch off.

He sighed and looked at Troy. Zhao looked weary, but also happy. They had hung in there together despite their differences. Zhao had probably never really understood Troy, but he had stuck his neck out to protect him, and to help him, nevertheless.

"Well, Mr. Zhao. It's been a pleasure working with you."

"Thank you, Mr. Stark," Zhao said. "I feel the same. You are an exemplary agent. The best I've seen. We did a good thing together. Many lives were saved."

Troy grinned. "Many buildings were completely destroyed."

Zhao nearly laughed. "The lives are more important. They can never be replaced."

"Agreed, Mr. Zhao."

Troy hesitated for a moment, then brought up something he hadn't had a moment to think about until now. "You saved my life."

"You saved thousands of lives," Zhao said.

Troy shook his head. "Whatever went on, we did it together. I imagine you'll be in line for a promotion or some kind of commendation from your government. You took risks. You went above and beyond the call of duty."

Zhao shrugged. "It's hard to know what will happen. I was also insubordinate. I was secretive, and hid information from my superiors. I shielded a man who was wanted for assaulting our officers. This is itself a crime. It's a tricky situation. It's not a perfect performance. I am sure I will be called to many meetings. I suspect there are certain re-education classes in my future."

"Surely the results outweigh the crimes you committed," Troy said.

Zhao shook his head. "It doesn't matter. The results outweigh any accolades or punishments. I do my job the best I can."

"As do I," Troy said.

There was a long pause between them. Troy wasn't really a hugger, and he supposed Zhao wasn't either. So this was going to be it. An awkward goodbye. Maybe Zhao would give him a lift to the Jade Emperor Hotel, though it wasn't necessary. Troy could probably find a taxi going that way.

"You know," Zhao said. "When you first came, we talked about going to a bar and having drinks. Do you remember?"

"I remember," Troy said. "But we never did. There wasn't any time."

"Would you like to do that?" Zhao said.

Troy nodded. "Sure, Mr. Zhao. That sounds like a very nice idea."

"When do you think you would like to do that?"

"How about now?" Troy said. "Would now be a good time?"

Zhao smiled, a full-on, honest-to-God smile.

"Now would be a perfect time, Mr. Stark."

CHAPTER THIRTY

January 25
12:15 am Central European Time
Headquarters of the European Rapid Response Investigation Unit (ERRIU)
aka El Grupo Especial
Outskirts of Madrid
Spain

"Quite a welcome."

Jan, Dubois, and Troy had gotten in late, and after a long flight, had taken Jan's car directly from the airport to El Grupo headquarters. It was cold here in Madrid, and there was a fine crust of snow and ice along the sides of the roadways.

When they arrived, Miquel was there in a white shirt and red tie. His hair was slicked back as if he had just stepped out of the shower. He was wearing cologne, and his slacks were crisply pressed. His shoes were polished to a high shine.

In the conference room, he had spread out sandwiches and pastries from a deli. There were three bottles of champagne on ice. Where he got all this stuff in the middle of the night was anybody's guess. The food looked fresh, as if someone had just dropped it off a moment ago.

A few of the offices already had personal effects in them. Staff members were returning from wherever they had been assigned and were moving back in. People wanted to work for Miquel. That wasn't really any surprise.

Troy was tired, but felt good. When the cork popped, he accepted a flute of champagne from Miquel. It was gone in a moment, and then he accepted another one.

"Congratulations," Miquel said. "Congratulations to everyone."

"Congratulations to you," Jan said. "You've had your command re-instated. The organization is showing you the respect you deserve."

Miquel shook his head and smiled. "That is a small thing." He raised a glass again. "What you don't know is that during your flight back, the US Secretary of State was in contact with the General

Secretariat of Interpol. The State Department of the United States has commended you all directly, by name, and thanked you for saving the Secretary of State's life. They have also thanked your counterpart in China, an Agent..."

"Zhao," Troy said.

Miquel pointed at him. "Correct. Zhao."

"Zhao Fu," Troy said now.

"Yes," Miquel said, smiling broadly now.

Was it possible that Miquel had opened a bottle before they got here? He seemed like he was having a VERY good time.

"I think they're going to invite you for a state visit," Miquel said.

"That's so nice," Dubois said.

"This has nothing to do with El Grupo," Miquel said. "This was exceptional work on the part of individuals."

"Working as a team," Jan said.

Miquel raised a glass to that. So did everyone.

"Anyway, you brought us all together," Dubois said.

They all raised their glasses again. The first bottle was gone, and a few moments later, another cork popped. It was good to be the winners.

"Shall we eat?" Miquel said. "I believe the food is quite good."

Troy stood back for a moment and watched as the three others got paper plates and dug into the food. He watched Dubois in particular. Her hair was up in an Afro, as usual, tied with a bright yellow sash. She was wearing a form-hugging black body suit and combat boots. There was a bright yellow, shiny fake leather belt around her waist. She looked like the world's sexiest bumblebee. Should he tell her?

Troy smiled to himself. The drinks were already going to his head.

They hadn't had any time to talk, he and Dubois. During the operation, it wasn't appropriate. On the flight back, the plane was crowded with people finally allowed to leave Hong Kong. They sat three in a row, big Jan Bakker sandwiched between them.

That wasn't a good time to talk, either.

Troy frowned. There would never be a good time to talk.

Maybe that was okay. Maybe whatever happened between them, if anything, was part of the old El Grupo. A new El Grupo was starting, one where the overseers seemed like they were going to recognize the good work of the organization, and maybe even accept its methods. Troy and Dubois could probably just be colleagues in the new El Grupo.

That would be fine, he supposed.

The truth was, when he started catching feelings for her, his attitude toward the job had begun to change. He had felt nervous about her being involved in missions. He had become frightened for her welfare. The incident in the water (and he was coming to think of it that way, as "The Incident") had probably happened because he was so relieved to find her alive, and unharmed.

It was bad, especially bad if they planned to continue as partners. As a practical matter, you couldn't spend time worrying about your partner, not in a job like this. Everyone had to carry their own load, and everyone took the same risks.

If they were involved, the time would come when she would either have to stop working here, or he would.

Time passed, and another cork popped. Miquel and Jan were down at the other end of the conference table, talking closely about something.

Troy and Dubois stood a little way apart, chatting about this and that. Things of uncertain consequence. She needed to fly back to France in the morning and get some of her belongings. She was going to try to convince her mom to move here to Madrid, though she doubted it would work. They needed to talk more about security for family members.

Dubois moved closer, as though her feet weren't quite touching the ground. She had a flute of champagne between her fingers. The glass being held by her long, lovely fingers looked like a painting. Troy could see it, how he would do it, if he were an artist. With a little bit of abstraction, as though the hand were coming out of a fog or mist.

Troy had switched to beer. He'd found a few bottles in the company refrigerator, which seemed to solve the mystery of why Miquel was already in such a good mood when they first came in.

Dubois stepped closer still.

Troy could feel something coming off her in waves. A kind of warmth, maybe, or an emotion.

"What are we going to do, Agent Stark?" she said.

Troy smiled. "About what, Agent Dubois? About our need to tighten security measures for employees of El Grupo, and our families?"

Dubois smiled, too. Her smile could light up a room. It could light up the moon.

"No, Agent Stark. I'm sure we'll figure that out soon enough. I mean, what are WE going to do? You and I."

He wanted to grab her by the yellow patent leather belt and pull her even closer to him. He wanted to pull her all the way.

"I didn't know there was a you and I, Agent Dubois. Not long ago, I seemed to have been informed otherwise."

She stared directly into his eyes.

"That must have been a miscommunication, Agent Stark."

He nodded. "I guess it must have been."

There was a glint in her eyes now, something almost wicked.

"The real intention must have been lost in translation."

He glanced down the table at Jan and Miquel, the two of them still chowing down on food, and lost in serious, half-drunken conversation. They were probably plotting world domination, the return of the El Grupo empire. There was no stopping it this time.

Or maybe not. Maybe they were talking about the threat to El Grupo personnel. Or it could be the threat of another terrorist attack in China. Sure, they had saved a lot of lives in Hong Kong. But that didn't mean whoever was behind the attacks wasn't planning another one for tomorrow.

Troy turned his attention back to Dubois. There was nothing any of them could do tonight about all of the looming threats out there. Tonight was for celebrating.

"What time is your flight tomorrow?" he said.

"I don't know," Dubois said. "I haven't booked it yet."

"Hmmm," Troy said, as if pondering a difficult dilemma. "So what are you planning to do with the rest of your night?"

She shook her head, the smile positively beaming now. But the eyes gave the smile a different meaning. The eyes were like twin laser beams, about to slice Troy in half, right down the center of his body.

"I don't know that, either," she said.

She stepped even closer. If Jan and Miquel were to look up now, there was no way they could miss this. Troy flashed back to that moment in the dark water, at sea, the boat where the trafficked women had been held on fire against the black night.

He and Dubois kissed passionately, the helicopter with Alex inside hovering overhead, the wind from the rotors slapping the water all around them.

"Do you have any ideas for me?" Dubois said now.

CHAPTER THIRTY ONE

9:30 am Eastern European Time (8:30 am Central European Time)
A mega-yacht
West of Carpathos
The Aegean Sea

"Can you tell me who has taken me?"

Lucien Mebarak stood on the foredeck of a small fishing boat cutting through the pale green waters of the open sea. In the distance, to his left, was the rocky outcropping of a no-name island rising high out of the water. Lucien could fancy that he spotted a whitewashed mansion at the crest of the island's peak.

"Wait and see," said one of the gunmen. This man was tall with a spotty growth of dark beard. He wore a black beret and a formless black leather jacket that hung from his broad shoulders like it was hanging from a bargain store rack. Lucien took him to be the leader of the assassination squad.

Closer than the island, just ahead, was the stern of a giant white mega-yacht. It was a whale of a ship, more than a hundred meters long. The owner must be a hundred times wealthier than Lucien. A thousand times wealthier. A true sultan of the modern era.

Across the stern was the word *Cristina*, very large, etched in black calligraphy. Beneath that was the simple word *Monaco*. The bright early morning sun glinted off a hundred metal surfaces aboard the yacht.

Lucien felt sick to his stomach, perhaps from the movement of the small boat across the bounding swells, perhaps from the things he had witnessed this morning.

As they approached, the yacht became ever larger, the fishing boat diminishing in size all the while. Lucien was on the fishing boat with five men. One, an older man with long white hair pulled into a ponytail, was at the controls. The others were younger and carried submachine guns with cartoonishly long sound suppressors mounted at the muzzles.

The young men had appeared at Lucien's house just before dawn. They had murdered Lucien's entire contingent of bodyguards before

Lucien even woke up. Lucien had been pulled from bed, where he was asleep with two young lovelies, and dragged through a slaughterhouse. They had given him one minute to dress, then had dragged him down the long stairs past his infinity pool, and all the way to the waterfront, where this boat awaited.

His own motorboat had been punched full of holes with a hatchet or some other tool, and lay half-sunk near the shore.

Lucien wore white slacks and a blue collared shirt. He had sandals on his feet. He was without a jacket, and without socks. He was cold, even shivering, but he didn't suppose complaining about this would help him any.

"The girls?" he said now, considering their welfare for the first time.

"They're fine," the lead gunman said. "They were taken to Athens, where they will be released at a later time."

"Did they see…" Lucien began, and flashed to the memory of his men, bloodied corpses, strewn throughout the stark white rooms of his home. Those girls were young. While they were experienced in certain pleasures of the body, they were innocent in many other ways.

"Did they see it?"

The gunman was unmoved by the imagery in Lucien's mind. "Some things can't be helped. They saw what they saw. It may be good for them to know what they are playing with. They might think of a different path in life."

Lucien nodded, but didn't say anything. His girls were gone. His bodyguards were dead. His boat was sunk. All of these things were easily replaceable. Whoever had ordered this done was simply making a statement.

We will take everything from you.

At least they didn't burn his house down.

Then again, how could he know that? They might have torched it moments after he was taken away. They could kill him if they wanted. At this moment, he almost wished they would. It was humiliating to have his weaknesses exposed like this.

Lucien didn't fear death, not really. There was even some part of him that would welcome it when it finally came. There was an emptiness inside him that could never be filled. Maybe things were better on the other side. But these men weren't going to kill him. If that was their intent, they would have already done so.

Now, two men on the low deck of the yacht were tying the lines of the fishing boat. The fishing boat bobbed and heaved in the swells.

The yacht rose above their heads, looming like some monster from another world.

One of the gunmen grabbed Lucien by the shoulders, turned him around, and marched him across the narrow gap between boats. Lucien went limp, not physically, but in his mind. He was like a piece of meat. He was flanked by two men, shoulder to shoulder with them, as they climbed the outdoor stairs, deck after deck. Two men walked in front of him, and a man shadowed behind.

After a time, they reached a wide open deck. It was so large, there was a helipad with a small two-seat helicopter parked on it. They crossed this deck, and climbed one more short flight. They must be six stories above the water now. Lucien was breathing hard, his chest heaving a little bit.

He would not beg for his life. If it came to that, he would not do it.

They reached the top. There was a small pool up here with a bubbling hot tub.

Two men sat at a round table. The views from up here were astonishing. Wide open sea in every direction, as far as the eyes could see. Seagulls hung on the breeze above their heads.

It looked like the men had just finished breakfast. There were plates and trays in front of them with half-eaten fruits, breads, cheeses and eggs.

One of the men was old. He wore a light blue sweater and tan shorts. A gold watch dangled from his thin wrist. His legs, arms, and face were all deeply tanned. His hair was white, framing a bald head. The bald spot was deeply tanned. He wore dark glasses that made it impossible to see his eyes.

Lucien had never met him, but recognized him right away from newspaper accounts of his life. His name was Antonio Di Napoli DeLorenzo. He was a fugitive from justice in Italy and in several other countries. Conspiracy to commit dozens of murders. Bribery of judges and police and professional sports referees. Witness tampering. Identity theft on a massive scale. Industrial waste dumping in public waterways. Drug trafficking. Human trafficking. Extortion.

If it was a crime, DeLorenzo had probably organized it. He was thought to be among the most powerful men in Italy, if not Europe, if not the entire world. He was at the center of vast criminal networks stretching from this spot, to Africa, the Americas, Russia and the Far East.

The younger man with him was also deeply tanned. They must spend a lot of time on this boat, in the sun. He wore an open white shirt, displaying the dark hair on his chest. He gestured at a seat across the table from them.

Lucien sat down.

"You can call me Nico," the younger man said.

Lucien moved nothing except his eyes. The gunmen who brought him here had stepped back several meters, but he was aware of them hovering behind him. They wouldn't like unnecessary movements.

"Hello, Nico."

Nico indicated DeLorenzo with a nod of his head. "Do you know who this man is?"

Lucien didn't even look at the old man. "Yes."

Nico raised a hand as if to signal the command: "Don't say the name."

Lucien didn't say a word.

"How is your Italian?" Nico said.

"It could be better, in all honesty."

Nico shrugged. "No matter. I will translate for you."

DeLorenzo had a small white espresso cup in front of him. He reached onto the table to a round stainless steel container and poured a small amount of the black liquid into his cup. His hands were steady. Lucien thought the man might be 85 years old.

No one offered Lucien any food. No one offered him any coffee. There was no hospitality on display here. They had fetched Lucien like he was a thing to be retrieved. They probably had dogs somewhere that would get the table scraps before Lucien would.

DeLorenzo said something. It ran to a few sentences.

"You killed a man in recent days," Nico said. "He sometimes called himself the Bishop. Please don't embarrass yourself by denying this."

Lucien nodded. What was the point in denying it? They knew, or thought they did. With men like this, they would act on suspicions just the same as they would facts. On this ship, it didn't matter what was true and what wasn't. Antonio Di Napoli DeLorenzo created the reality he preferred.

"Yes. I did."

"Why?"

"I hired him to do a job for me," Lucien said. "He failed at the job. It was a complete failure. At the same time, he had gone to the trouble of discovering a great deal of information about me. A man who left a job undone, and also knew things he shouldn't know…"

Lucien paused.

"It was worrisome to leave him alive."

He waited while the younger man translated all of that to DeLorenzo. After a moment, DeLorenzo spoke again. He spoke with a shrug and a wave of his hand. Lucien got the idea without needing to know the words. DeLorenzo felt that Lucien's concerns were of little or no importance.

"You're an open book for anyone to read," Nico said. "Maybe you don't know this about yourself."

Lucien didn't answer. These people could probably find out anything they wanted. Things that were hidden from others were transparent to them.

"The Bishop was a friend," Nico went on. "A friend of our friends, but not a friend of ours. You're fortunate in that regard. He did work for us in the past, and his work was more than satisfactory. We are unhappy about his death."

"I apologize," Lucien said, hating the sound of that coming from his own mouth. "If I had known…"

Nico raised his hand again.

"The damage is done. We took repayment this morning."

Lucien nodded. There were dead men all over his house, including close and trusted employees. DeLorenzo had taken his pound of flesh.

"Yes. I see."

"What was the task you assigned him?"

Lucien looked at DeLorenzo, but couldn't see anything behind his dark glasses. His face betrayed nothing. He could be a blind man, a beggar in an alleyway. He sipped his espresso.

"I'm reluctant to share that."

"There are no secrets here," Nico said.

Lucien could see the truth in what the man said. They probably knew why he had hired the Bishop, and they just wanted to hear him say it.

"Okay. You're right. There's no sense keeping secrets. I hired him to kill a man, an American named Troy Stark. Stark is an Interpol agent, but also some kind of secret policeman for American intelligence. He was a military black operator at one time. Maybe he was an assassin, I'm not sure. He has hurt me in the past, and he's very hard to kill. I thought perhaps the Bishop could do this, but it didn't work. It didn't work at all. It only made matters worse."

Nico nodded, but didn't attempt to translate any of what Lucien had just said. DeLorenzo said nothing.

"This Troy Stark you speak of recently murdered a man, an Albanian named Mateos Baruti. Mateos was a friend of ours. A very good friend. You understand?"

Lucien nodded. "Uh-huh."

A *friend of our friends*, like the Bishop, could be murdered, and perhaps it would be forgotten in time. Things might move on from there. If *a friend of ours* was murdered… it was a whole different story. You couldn't kill a friend of ours without our permission. In most circumstances, you couldn't kill a friend of ours at all.

DeLorenzo's hand snaked out and picked up the stainless steel container again. He poured himself some more espresso, a small amount. He glanced at Nico and nodded.

"We will help you get Stark," Nico said.

NOW AVAILABLE!

ROGUE STRIKE
(A Troy Stark Thriller—Book #6)

"Thriller writing at its best. Thriller enthusiasts who relish the precise execution of an international thriller, but who seek the psychological depth and believability of a protagonist who simultaneously fields professional and personal life challenges, will find this a gripping story that's hard to put down."
--Midwest Book Review, Diane Donovan (regarding Any Means Necessary)

"One of the best thrillers I have read this year. The plot is intelligent and will keep you hooked from the beginning. The author did a superb job creating a set of characters who are fully developed and very much enjoyable. I can hardly wait for the sequel."
--Books and Movie Reviews, Roberto Mattos (re Any Means Necessary)

From #1 bestselling and USA Today bestselling author Jack Mars, author of the critically-acclaimed *Luke Stone* and *Agent Zero* series (with over 5,000 five-star reviews), comes an explosive new, action-packed thriller series that takes readers on a wild-ride across Europe, America, and the world.

After elite Navy Seal Troy Stark is forced into retirement for his dubious respect for authority, his work in stopping a major terrorist threat to New York is noticed. Invited to join a secretive new international terrorist-fighting organization, Troy must hunt down all threats to the U.S. that originate from overseas—and pre-empt them by any means possible.

In ROGUE STRIKE (Book #6), a group of terrorists have developed a biological weapon, and as they prepare to contaminate Europe's largest water supply, Troy is desperately needed to hunt them down and stop them. But in a never-ending trail of cat and mouse, Troy soon realizes all may not be what it seems…

An unputdownable action thriller with heart-pounding suspense and unforeseen twists, ROGUE STRIKE is the sixth novel in an exhilarating new series by a #1 bestselling author that will have you fall in love with a brand new action hero—and turn pages late into the night.

Future books in the series will soon be available.

Jack Mars

Jack Mars is the USA Today bestselling author of the LUKE STONE thriller series, which includes seven books. He is also the author of the new FORGING OF LUKE STONE prequel series, comprising six books; of the AGENT ZERO spy thriller series, comprising twelve books; of the TROY STARK thriller series, comprising seven books; of the SPY GAME thriller series, comprising nine books; and of the new JAKE MERCER thriller series, comprising five books (and counting).

Jack loves to hear from you, so please feel free to visit www.Jackmarsauthor.com to join the email list, receive a free book, receive free giveaways, connect on Facebook and Twitter, and stay in touch!

BOOKS BY JACK MARS

JAKE MERCER THRILLER SERIES
ABSOLUTE THREAT (Book #1)
ABSOLUTE DAMAGE (Book #2)
ABSOLUTE FORCE (Book #3)
ABSOLUTE PERIL (Book #4)
ABSOLUTE TREASON (Book #5)

THE SPY GAME
TARGET ONE (Book #1)
TARGET TWO (Book #2)
TARGET THREE (Book #3)
TARGET FOUR (Book #4)
TARGET FIVE (Book #5)
TARGET SIX (Book #6)
TARGET SEVEN (Book #7)
TARGET EIGHT (Book #8)

TROY STARK THRILLER SERIES
ROGUE FORCE (Book #1)
ROGUE COMMAND (Book #2)
ROGUE TARGET (Book #3)
ROGUE MISSION (Book #4)
ROGUE SHOT (Book #5)
ROGUE STRIKE (Book #6)
ROGUE ORDER (Book #7)

LUKE STONE THRILLER SERIES
ANY MEANS NECESSARY (Book #1)
OATH OF OFFICE (Book #2)
SITUATION ROOM (Book #3)
OPPOSE ANY FOE (Book #4)
PRESIDENT ELECT (Book #5)
OUR SACRED HONOR (Book #6)
HOUSE DIVIDED (Book #7)

FORGING OF LUKE STONE PREQUEL SERIES
PRIMARY TARGET (Book #1)

PRIMARY COMMAND (Book #2)
PRIMARY THREAT (Book #3)
PRIMARY GLORY (Book #4)
PRIMARY VALOR (Book #5)
PRIMARY DUTY (Book #6)

AN AGENT ZERO SPY THRILLER SERIES

AGENT ZERO (Book #1)
TARGET ZERO (Book #2)
HUNTING ZERO (Book #3)
TRAPPING ZERO (Book #4)
FILE ZERO (Book #5)
RECALL ZERO (Book #6)
ASSASSIN ZERO (Book #7)
DECOY ZERO (Book #8)
CHASING ZERO (Book #9)
VENGEANCE ZERO (Book #10)
ZERO ZERO (Book #11)
ABSOLUTE ZERO (Book #12)